THE
BABEL
TOWER

J.B. SIMMONS

THREE CORD
—— PRESS ——

Published by Three Cord Press
Cover by Konstantin Kiselyov
Translations by Babel

Printed in the United States of America

PART ONE

Come, let us build ourselves a city and a tower with its top in the heavens, and let us make a name for ourselves, lest we be dispersed over the face of the whole earth.
Genesis 11:4

1

Elizabeth Trammell breezed into Babel through the tall glass doors and the white marble lobby. The workers stopped what they were doing as she passed. It happened every day—this woman entering the company headquarters, face beaming. But that didn't make it less of an event. The sun rises daily, and it's special every time.

She stepped into a brushed steel elevator and pressed her thumb to the panel. Her eyes met the reflection in the mirror wall. She smiled, knowing she should be used to the attention by now. It was part of the job.

She frowned, squinted, made a fish-face. Straight white teeth. Cool blue eyes. Blonde hair in place, parallel to the lines of her face, and precise in length to her chin. She tilted her gaze down, confirming that her usual uniform was in order: no makeup or jewels, just dark skinny jeans, designer heels, and a white V-neck sweater. White meant it was Monday, with a long week ahead.

The elevator doors slid open to reveal Katarina Popova waiting in a black skirt suit, clutching a tablet in one hand and a coffee mug in the other. The young woman was stunning, with straight brown hair and dark eyes.

"Morning, Liz. Coffee?"

Liz took the mug and wiped away a drip that was running down the big rainbow block letters—BABEL.

Glass-walled offices lined the long hall toward Liz's office.

She eyed her staff as she passed. They were glued to their screens, staring at the latest company news and the sales data pouring in for Babel's devices. Katarina trailed close after Liz, giving the morning report.

"Forbes released its latest list," Katarina said.

"Oh?"

"They say you'll crack the hundred richest in the world after we go public next year. And the top five for women."

"Super," Liz said. "And the tabloids?"

A slight laugh escaped Katarina's lips. "The usual. You're a lonely tyrant bent on conquering the world. You're a pawn of a Russian spy and a security threat. You're a world-class narcissist who has cloned herself."

"If only it were so simple." Liz smiled, glad that Katarina was taking it lightly, for once. "How about the real news?"

Katarina summarized the rest of the papers. The company's miraculous little Babel devices were penetrating the world's most remote places. One article told how Babel had advanced peace in the Middle East. Another was about changed lives in Indonesia. Nothing new, Liz thought. It was what Babel had been doing since day one.

Liz stepped into her corner office and kicked off her high heels. The empty space was immense, with spectacular views of San Francisco. After a quick glance outside—and seeing nothing but fog—Liz perched on the edge of her desk.

She sipped her coffee and watched Katarina's lips. The words continued to come out in Russian, but they played in Liz's ears in English. Only the faintest echo of Katarina's natural voice could be heard past the quaint British accent.

Liz set her coffee mug down, its porcelain base clinging softly on the glass table.

"Are you listening?" Katarina asked.

"Sure, it's a full day." Liz slid off the desk, facing Katarina. "We leave soon to meet with marketing. What else?"

"And why are we meeting with marketing?"

Liz shrugged.

Katarina lifted an eyebrow. "How late were you up last night?"

Liz didn't answer. Katarina wouldn't understand. It wasn't just about the work anymore. Liz kept waking up in the middle of the night, unable to shake thoughts about her father and his designs—the blueprints smudged with sketches and the lines stabbing into the sky.

"What I was saying," Katarina continued, "is that marketing wants to tweak the rainbow logo. Then you're with software for a half hour. They'll demo new developments in … Is your Babel working?"

"It always does." Liz tapped her ear playfully, the device resting imperceptibly behind her lobe. "Marketing's always getting worked up over the details."

"The devil's in the details. We have only a few weeks before the official announcement."

"I know, but we've already hit our goals. It's just a matter of time now." Thinking about the next few weeks made Liz shudder. So much waiting, so much attention. She cared about the big picture. People like Katarina could handle the logistics. "When's my flight to Morocco?"

Katarina glanced at her tablet, then looked up again. She pushed her thick-rimmed glasses back to the bridge of her nose. "Three, this afternoon. You land in Marrakesh tomorrow. The King will be waiting."

"Now that's more interesting," Liz said. "I still need to

prepare for the trip. Why don't you sit in for me in the meetings today?"

"They're expecting you…"

"I know," Liz said, "but you can handle this."

"Well, there wouldn't be Babel without you, but…" Katarina grinned, "if you want me to sit in for you again, I'm happy to do it."

"That's what COOs are for."

"Oh, so now we have formal titles?"

Liz lifted a pen from her desk and ceremoniously lowered it to Katarina's left shoulder, then her right. "I hereby name you Chief Operations Officer of Babel and honorary Keeper of the Paperwork."

"It's *Operating* Officer. My first act will be to hire you another assistant."

Liz laughed. "I like it. You're loosening up."

"Thanks…I guess." Katarina pointed to the frosted-glass door behind her. "Your friends are here."

"Friends?"

"I knew you weren't listening…" Katarina crossed her arms. "You invited them to come last week. You said you needed independent voices—people who knew you before Babel took off."

"Right, I need to bounce an idea off them."

"Is this what you've been staying up late for?"

Liz sat back on her desk and grinned. "Don't look at me like that. You'll know soon enough. Does anything stay hidden from you around here?" Liz glanced at the clock above the door. It showed 8:28 in bright red digits. "Send them in."

Katarina nodded, then pointed down.

"What?" Liz asked.

4

"Shoes."

"Ah." Liz wriggled her bare toes. "COO rule number seventeen: never attend a meeting barefoot. But these are friends. Shoes can wait."

Katarina sighed and left to get Liz's friends.

Dylan Galant walked in first, followed by Rachel Conrad, Owen Strand, and Jax Wong.

They shared hellos, and Dylan stepped to the wall of glass. The clouds had parted, revealing slivers of the Bay. "You should have us up here more often," he said.

Liz eyed his silhouette against the city below. His red hair was like fire. "I know. Sorry. It's been crazy busy. How have you been?"

"Better than ever." Dylan glided past her, joining the other three sitting in front of Liz's desk. "We've had some breakthroughs in the lab. Great students this semester."

"Good to hear." Liz studied the familiar faces. They reminded her of home, of family. "Thanks for coming on short notice. I can't stop thinking about what to do next."

"Next?" Rachel asked.

Liz couldn't help but smile. "You still boycotting the news?"

"It's still all bad," Rachel said. "Murders, falling stocks, and cold winds off Lake Michigan. I have better things to do with my time. Like feed my baby."

"I can't wait to meet her," Liz said. "At least you got to use the company jet, right?"

"It beats flying coach."

"And it lets you be here." Liz leaned forward, hands on her knees. "Here's the point. Once Babel goes public, I'll have time to move on, do something new…something amazing."

"You could cure cancer," Dylan said.

Liz shook her head. "You know that's not me. Plenty of people are working on cures. This needs to be *new*."

"What do you have in mind?" Rachel asked.

"A million things, but...nothing that fits." Her father's designs flashed again in her mind. "I've been so wrapped up in this company that I've forgotten what makes me tick."

"So you brought us here us to help you remember?" Rachel let out a faint laugh, her brown hair swaying. "You could have just called."

"I know. But this is big, Rach. If you'd told me back in school that I could have unlimited resources, what would I have done?"

"Go to the moon?" Jax mused, leaning back in his chair and pointing to the ceiling high above. When he looked back at Liz, she noticed dark circles under his eyes. He'd never been a morning person.

"Okay...that's closer." Liz slid off the desk. She walked around it, her bare feet silent on the bamboo floors, and looked out over the city. She turned back to her friends, the Golden Gate Bridge framing her figure. "What else?"

"How about start a new country on an island?" Owen's typical, easy smile was on full display. He'd been Liz's lawyer from the beginning, and now he was Babel's general counsel. Way too young for the job, but whip smart and worked himself to the bone. And Liz trusted him.

"Go on," she said.

Owen adjusted his glasses. "You'll always be tied down in this country, and in any other one. So you could build an island, like the Chinese, but build it twelve miles from any country's shore. That way you can make it an independent nation, free from anyone else's sovereignty. Design your own flag. Make it self-sustaining, with schools and hospitals...all under the visionary President Trammell."

"Hmm...I'd prefer Queen Trammell." Liz returned to her spot on the desk and folded her legs underneath her. "An island nation sounds like something pirates or drug smugglers would do. I want people to join me, not to make them run away."

"Why leave the company?" Dylan asked. "Just because it goes public doesn't mean you have to find a new job. I mean, let someone else do all the work, but as long as you're with Babel, you could change the world with all that data."

Liz's expression tightened, her lips pressed into a thin white line. The four friends knew the look and tried to avoid it.

Liz spoke evenly: "Your words understood, *your secrets safe.*"

"Yeah, yeah, company motto and all that." Dylan waved the concern away. "But I say the data is worth more than your billions. It gives you access to so many conversations. Why not use it for good? You could stop terrorist attacks. Expose corrupt politicians. Connect long lost lovers. Imagine what your coders could do with algorithms running through every word spoken and heard on the planet."

Liz's head was shaking. "Babel is about overcoming limits, but we've made promises that have to be kept. Look, I appreciate the idea. I don't want to miss something brilliant, so keep thinking about it. But I want to *build* something. This isn't about opening Pandora's box or some one-off experience." She grinned at Jax. "As cool as the moon might be."

"So what's next?" Owen asked, always the practical one. "You want us to come up with a list of ideas?"

"Sure, that's a start." Liz reached down and picked up her earpiece and her high heels. "I'm off to Morocco later today, but let's talk again before I go. Katarina will slot you into my schedule."

The four friends followed Liz to the door, where Katarina greeted them with a professional smile. She scheduled time for each of them with Liz. She saved Dylan for last. She'd been listening to what he said about the data, about changing the world, and she'd been smiling. Anyone who wanted to use the data could be used.

2

Jax left the meeting with Liz and went to the vault at Babel headquarters. Liz had texted him to say she would come soon, before she flew to Morocco. So he waited, pacing before the computer and the code he'd written ten years ago. The code that started all this. A strip of tape was stuck to the top of the monitor, with the scribbled riddle: "What do we all have in common, but rarely share?"

Jax wrote it before he wrote the code. He'd never forget the answer. He liked to keep it there, as a reminder.

What do we all have in common, but rarely share?

Secrets.

It was a secret that he hated Dylan. It was a secret that he'd killed his first pet, a hamster, in a science experiment. "I woke up and he was dead," he'd lied to his mom. She believed it. The hamster was gone, but the secret lived on. Secrets were like that. The owners of secrets died, but not the secret itself. If Jax believed in heaven, he figured there would be a library there full of books composed of everyone's hidden words. The biggest library ever.

The things that only he knew were what made him who he was. No one could guess them. But everyone else had their own secrets, too. Some were dark. Some were illicit. Some were full of love.

Like his love for Liz. All his other secrets wrapped around it, like iron bands around a burning ember. The ember hadn't cooled since the day he'd cracked the Babel code. He had relived the memory so many times, from so many angles. This time he chose the view of an imagined fly on the wall of Liz's old bedroom in Chicago—the luckiest fly on the planet.

Here is what the fly saw: Elizabeth Trammell and Jackson Wong, two teenagers pressed close, not touching, but facing a computer screen full of living and breathing code that only one of them understood. He was the short pimpled boy who everyone called Jax. The other teen was his muse. She was perfect and celestial and always out of reach. Jax knew it, but it wouldn't stop him from trying. Every boy felt that way around Liz.

She turned to him. "You think it'll work this time?"

He nodded, soaking in her attention. "Give it a try."

"Any language?" she asked.

He handed her the headset and adjusted the speaker before her lips. "I vote for French."

"Too easy." Then her bright blue eyes concentrated. "*Eto komp'yuternyy kod budet izmenit' mir.*"

A smooth voice spoke through the headphones, in flawless English, with a hardly noticeable delay after her words.

"Sooo?" Jax asked.

She jumped to her feet, flinging the headset off. "It worked!"

"I told you." He stood, tilted his head up to her. "That was Russian, right?"

"*Da.* Does it translate anything, in any language?"

"Not yet, but it will. Every translator before this operated on a system of rules. It came out too literal. My code is different. It thinks for itself, understands what people *want* to say."

"How'd you do it?"

"My secret." He grinned and bowed his head like a performer receiving applause. He wasn't the only who had thought of using AI for translation, but he was the best at doing it. "So what should we call it?"

"*Le génie?*"

He hesitated. "Maybe something in English? More universal?"

"I got it: Babel."

"Like that old Bible story? Isn't that too obvious?"

She shook her head. "It's perfect. The myth is that God gave people a different language and they scattered. But it's more than that. When the people were connected, they were building a tower to the heavens. Nothing could stop them."

"Except God. Shouldn't we be worried?"

She laughed. "No. We can connect people again."

"So…it's our challenge to God. I like it."

Her eyes lit up. "This is just the beginning. We've got to improve the hardware. We can make the device small and easy to wear. So easy people won't even notice it. They'll never need to take it off. We'll patent it. Rachel can help, and Dylan, too. I'll handle implementation, marketing, sales…"

Dylan. The mention of his name made Jax wince. Liz didn't even notice. As she talked about plans to turn Babel into a product—*and a company…and a revolution!*—a little part of Jax withered inside. It was the little part that thought maybe, just this once, he and his invention would be enough to satisfy her. But like always, her ambitions towered over him.

"Hey," he interrupted. "Earlier, in Russian, what did you say?"

She smiled, nothing more than a friend's smile. "This

11

computer code will change the world."

"I know." His scrawny chest puffed up. "All in a day's work. But what did you say in Russian?"

"Just what I said: this computer code will change the world."

And it had, in only a few years.

Jax hadn't given up trying to crack Liz's code. It became his secret quest, and the only thing that got him out of bed in the morning. So many people had pieces of her now. Her face filled magazine covers and talk shows. Her company topped the news reports, along with her fortune. The entire world had stolen his place at her side, but he was the only one who could sit beside her in front of this computer screen.

They will never take this from me.

He read over the lines of code for the thousandth time. He laughed inside at how many hackers had disassembled a Babel device and tried to reverse-engineer it. Counting China, he figured a billion people had tried. And they'd all failed. None of them had the encryption key that Jax knew was hidden in Liz's DNA. Many called him a genius. Others called him selfish and petty and small, probably for cashing out from Babel.

He didn't care. The money gave him freedom, even if it couldn't buy what he wanted most. Whatever divine fortune had configured his brain to come up with this algorithm, it had also played the eternal joke on him: make the frog love the princess, but no kisses allowed. Life was no fairytale. That's why Jax had engineered the code to require Liz to sit beside him.

The door to the Babel vault opened.

"Stop drooling," said Liz's cheerful voice.

Jax turned and wiped at the corner of his mouth. "I missed it, that's all."

"The code, or our monthly session?"

"Is there a difference?"

She laughed and sat beside him. "One of these days someone is going to find us out, you know."

He breathed in deeply, letting her scent wash over him. "I don't think so," he said. "And what if they did? Even if they knew how I made the code evolve, they couldn't hack it without you."

"Thanks for the job security."

"Don't give me that look," Jax said. "Once Babel goes public, you can sell your shares and do whatever you want."

"You mean, as long as I come back so you can use my DNA?"

"Somebody has to make sure all this data doesn't end up in the hands of the dark side."

"You're such a nerd."

Jax smiled. "It takes two to tango."

She rolled up her sleeve and held out her arm to him, palm up. "Shall we dance?"

He took her arm in his hands. He let his fingers savor the touch for a moment longer than needed. Then he picked up the tweezers by the computer. He found the spot by the crease of her elbow, on the effervescent skin. He breathed in, then out, steadying himself, intoxicating himself with her closeness. He plucked three nearly invisible hairs.

She bent her arm back and forth. "Easy as ever."

Jax nodded. "Let's see which sequence it picks up this time." He placed the hairs under a scanner linked to the computer. He typed in a few instructions, and the code on the screen began to change.

"Amazing," Liz said. "How much data could you store like this?"

"Each hair can hold more than your computer. Every cell has six feet of DNA. It just has to be translated into the digital language."

"You ever going to tell me how you do it?"

He smiled. "Maybe in exchange for some sweet lovin'?"

Liz laughed and rolled her eyes. "The price is too steep."

"Hey, can't hurt to try. This secret is worth it."

3

Dylan and Katarina met at midnight, the door to the speakeasy bar unmarked. Members like Dylan knocked four times, and the bouncer welcomed them into the sparsely lit warehouse. They passed the bartender wearing an apron and grinding bitters with a mortar and pestle. The music thumped and kept each table isolated from the others, with its own dim light bulb dangling on a wire from the rafters high above.

The table where Dylan and Katarina sat overlooked the Bay. A waitress delivered their drinks in mason jars and guessed: *clandestine affair.* A sprig of rosemary floated in Dylan's drink, a lemon rind in Katarina's.

"Heard from your boss?" Dylan asked.

"She met with the King."

"Not bad. What did His Highness think?"

"He's already sold on Babel, but he wanted to test the newest language. It's what the Sahrawi people speak out in the desert."

"And?"

"He ordered ten million more Babels. All it took was one day riding along desert dunes with the great Liz Trammell, talking about silicon chips and languages." Katarina tapped the lemon rind with her crimson-red fingernail. It sank below the ice. "She's in Rwanda now."

"That's news. She texted me today, said she wanted to meet again tomorrow."

Katarina nodded. "She's back in the morning."

"Why Rwanda? Aren't they having some sort of crisis?"

"The UN is hosting an event there. And where the UN goes, we follow. They've ordered a few million units for Rwanda's tribal people." The lemon rind had fought its way back to the surface of Katarina's drink. She pushed it under again. "Liz wasn't planning to go, but you know how she loves synergies."

"Nothing like good press. Did she give a speech?"

"Same as usual. *With Babel*," Katarina recited, "*the world speaks the same language.*"

Dylan smiled. "Bored with the company pitch?"

Katarina continued in her advertiser's voice: "*Your words understood, your secrets safe.* A tiny, cheap device by your ear, and you can understand anyone, anywhere. But that's not all! The latest Babel-*plus* unit can scan the screen in front of you, detect the words, *and* read them aloud in your native language. Now the Internet has a universal language, and…It. Is. Babel."

Dylan was laughing. "You've got it down."

"Babel's projected stock price is the best measure of world progress."

"Which…is why you wanted to meet with me?"

"That's part of it." Katarina sipped her drink for the first time. "You know about Liz's plan after the IPO?"

He nodded, unsure whether he or Katarina knew more.

"Not everyone wants to step down from leading a company worth billions."

"Liz is not everyone," Dylan said.

Katarina smiled, darkly beautiful. "You must be wondering why I asked you to meet me."

"Not really. Most women ask for the same thing."

Katarina's smile widened as she met Dylan's eyes evenly. "Liz told me what you said, when you met with her."

"And?"

"You told her to stay with the company and use the Babel data."

"Yeah, I guess I said that." Dylan shrugged. "Seems like a waste to keep all that information locked up."

"Don't tell Liz I said this, but…I agree."

"So that's why you wanted to meet with me?" Dylan leaned forward, elbows crossed on the table, his fingers pressed into the cool condensation of his glass.

"I think we both know it's risky. The company is young. It still needs her."

"How so?" Dylan had figured Katarina would be fine with Liz leaving. It would probably mean a promotion for her.

"The company has sworn by the security of its data. If that fails, Babel fails."

"Babel's not going to fail." Dylan tapped his ear. "You've already captured the market. Does the UN buy from anyone else?"

"Competitors will come along."

"Unless they steal or reinvent your source code, you'll be fine. And you've only got, what, a trillion recorded conversations stored somewhere?"

"More or less."

"So what are you worried about?"

Katarina pulled the Babel out from her ear. She laid it beside her drink. The tiny chrome device curled like a miniature nautilus shell, with a small wire and an imperceptible microphone at its tip. Then she reached across the table. Dylan held still as her fingers grazed his ear and released his device.

She laid it beside hers. Two fish out of water.

"But isn't…" Dylan paused, eyeing the devices. "I thought the data was encrypted and secure in some hidden warehouse. And isn't it company policy to keep them in?"

Katarina smiled. "At all times."

"I guess every encryption has a code," Dylan said.

Katarina swept up the two devices in her hand and slid them into her pocket. She leaned forward. "Liz has access to the data." Her English was good, but her Russian accent was thick. "But she doesn't use it. It's only…to improve translations."

"That's what I thought," Dylan said. "It's a shame though. The company could do amazing things with the information. It could change the world."

"Liz's money…could also change it."

"Yeah," Dylan said, "if she uses it for something good, whatever it will be."

Katarina paused as if translating the language of her thoughts. "How much do you think she will spend?"

"Knowing her, whatever it takes."

Katarina pulled out a pen and scribbled something on her napkin. She slid the napkin to Dylan.

$5B. Cash out.

Dylan flipped the napkin over, covering the note. His second drink had arrived. He lifted his glass, swirled the amber liquid. That was enough money to buy a few countries, go to the moon a thousand times, keep millions of starving children alive. He met Katarina's eyes. "You really think she'll sell all her shares?"

"You know her better," Katarina said. "She's bored with being CEO. She wants a new project."

Dylan shook his head. He'd seen the list of the world's richest published last week. Liz's net worth had been estimated at $5 billion, most of it in Babel stock. He'd never thought she would cash out. But what Katarina said made some sense. Liz always had big ideas. He loved that about her. But this time it was about more than her. Her project, whatever it would be, could impact the whole world. "I'm supposed to be thinking about ideas for Liz," he said. "You have any suggestions?"

"We can both get what we want." Katarina's accented voice had dropped to a whisper.

"And what do I want?"

Katarina put her hand over Dylan's. Her eyes locked onto his. "You see how I look at you?"

He tried to pull his hand back.

She gripped it tighter, rubbing her fingers into his palm. "You want her to look at you like this."

Dylan shook his head. "We're friends. That's all."

Katarina released his hand and laughed. "You don't look at me the way you look at her. In Russia, we say a boy never loses his desire for the first girl who…captures his imagination." She paused, studying him.

He didn't answer, but his mind went to the memory. He'd been twelve, Liz eleven. She'd walked into the school cafeteria, the new girl, like she owned the place. All the boys had talked about her. *What's her name? Where'd she come from?* Dylan had been the first of his friends brave enough to approach her. She'd smiled up at him like a goddess descended from Olympia to his cafeteria, and he became her champion. As the years passed, he shrugged off his feelings. The guys would rib him. *When are you going to ask her out?* But Dylan never did. He lied to everyone, even himself, that it wasn't like that. Liz was like his little sister.

"So?" Katarina prodded.

"I was twelve when I met Liz."

"And?"

"I've moved on." *Mostly*, he thought. Liz had called him on Sunday. Said she had an important question. Said she needed him. He'd cancelled his Monday meetings, put everything aside for her, like always. And now she wanted to leave Babel and spend a fortune on a pet project? It didn't seem right. He lifted his drink but put it down. He couldn't keep dropping everything for her. "Alright," he said, "leaving Babel may not be her best idea."

"I have a better plan," Katarina said. "But this stays between us."

"It depends on what your plan is."

"Not good enough."

"I'm not signing up to kill anyone."

She grinned. "Between us."

"Fine, but I'm not doing anything I disagree with."

She clasped his hand again. "I...don't worry about that." She released him and reached for the napkin.

The first words she wrote made Dylan's eyes open wide.

Let her project proceed. Give the data to the world.

4

Rachel woke up in the middle of the night, sweating. She glanced around the unfamiliar room as her eyes adjusted. It smelled sterile, and soft metallic light oozed under the bottom of a heavy curtain. No sound had stirred her, no baby's cry. Then she remembered.

I'm in San Francisco. This is a hotel.

She regretted coming again, and so soon. It was hard being away from her little ones. They needed her so much at ages four and one—more than she felt like she could give. And it was always like this with Liz. She'd call Rachel out of the blue, expect her to drop everything and come at a moment's notice. Well, this was the last time. Rachel had gone to the first meeting, and she'd go again in the morning, but that was it. She couldn't keep this up. Her family needed her at home. No more impromptu trips to California. However close she and Liz had been back in school, they lived in different universes now.

But is that anger talking? Fatigue?

It couldn't be right, and Rachel knew it. A bubble of truth slipped through the pain: *love her and protect her.* That's what Liz's dad had said to Rachel the week before he committed suicide. Rachel hadn't understood it at the time. It made more sense after Mr. Trammell was gone.

This wasn't about her. It was about her friendship to Liz, because Liz needed her. If Rachel pulled away, what anchors

no mother, no siblings. Rachel
'hat Liz had. She couldn't just
was losing touch with reality,
her true self, and wondering
id her fortune into.

ιu flicked on the light. She
carpet, trying to let her mind relax.
. with Liz still haunted her. It was over a week
Monday after the meeting in Liz's office. Liz had
pressed her for ideas while they sipped lattes. She'd told Rachel
all the suggestions from Jax, Dylan, and Owen. They had
plenty of ideas for how to spend a billion dollars. Who didn't?
Rachel had shot them all down. The whole concept stank of
pride.

"The money doesn't have to dictate your life," she'd told
Liz.

"But I have it," Liz had answered, "so don't I have a
responsibility to use it for something?"

Rachel still felt frustrated. She hadn't responded well.
Everyone gave Liz their own visions of utopia. Rachel just
wanted to shake some sense into Liz, to make her understand
that she couldn't make heaven come to earth.

But Liz hadn't relented. She never did. "Rach, you've
known me since we were little girls. You knew my parents.
You knew me in Nebraska. Just give me an idea. Anything."

Rachel's reply was instinct, part anger, part joke: "Why not
build one of your dad's designs?"

Rachel had regretted the words the moment they slipped
out of her mouth.

Liz's expression had drawn back, a look Rachel knew well.
It was the focused Liz that nothing in the world could stop.

"You know…I've been waking up night, thinking about something like that. Deep down." Liz had stared at her intensely. "But you saying it means…yes, of course, that's it!"

Rachel kicked herself for not pushing back immediately. Many said it was Mr. Trammell's unbuilt tower that had driven him mad, like the design was haunted and doomed. But her coffee with Liz had ended, and her friend the CEO had flown to Africa. There were so many better things Liz could do with her time and her money, like find a husband and raise a family, for starters. Or put Rachel's kids through college.

Rachel shook her head. Being selfish wouldn't help anybody. She checked the clock. 5:05. The meeting with Liz was only a few hours away. She needed someone else on her side. Owen might be waking up soon. She grabbed her phone from the nightstand and called.

"Rachel?" Owen sounded tired.

"I'm sorry, I know it's late."

There was a pause. "It's early."

"Aren't you still doing morning workouts?"

"I had ten minutes until my alarm…" He groaned, or maybe it was a yawn.

"Well I'm glad I caught you," Rachel said. "Remember what I told you about my conversation with Liz?"

He was quiet a moment. "Something about a tower?"

"Exactly. I'm worried that she's going to try to build it."

"What's so bad about that?" Another yawn. "She's had crazier ideas."

"But she hasn't had billions of dollars to throw at them."

"Liz will be fine. Everything she touches turns to gold."

"Not this time." Rachel gazed out the hotel window, overlooking sickly yellow lights in a parking lot. "I'm going to warn her. She knows her dad killed himself over this tower. There are so many better things she could do."

"Liz wants advice, not some kind of warning."

"So you won't help me?"

"No, maybe, I mean…I just woke up. I'll think about it. Okay?"

"Good. We have a better chance of slowing this down if we join up. You know the company better than anyone."

"Has anyone ever slowed Liz down?"

"I'm telling you, this time it's different. She'll throw away her fortune chasing a dream that's doomed." Rachel crossed her arms, and she clutched her elbows the way she did when she felt a conviction. She'd never admit that she could be as stubborn as Liz. "Today might be our last chance. You know how she builds momentum with ideas like this."

"Yeah…nothing stands in her way."

"That's why I need your help."

"We'll see."

Rachel said goodbye and knew she couldn't go back to sleep. She showered, called home, and then knelt by the bed. She didn't know what else to do. In the quiet stillness of the hotel room, she prayed for wisdom. A thought drifted into her mind, landed with certainty: *God won't be steamrolled like the others.*

5

"I think I've got it." Liz sat perched on the edge of her desk wearing a yellow V-neck sweater. Yellow because it was Friday. "When I was in Rwanda this week, looking at those beautiful, innocent, hungry kids' faces, I saw despair. Do you know what they needed?"

"Food?" Owen said, half hidden behind his Babel mug.

Liz smiled faintly, but didn't laugh. "Of course, and I'll keep giving money for that, but their need is deeper. What they need is hope. Hope for humanity. It's what we all need, a symbol and a place of hope."

"So...the moon or Mars?" Jax asked.

"Neither," Liz said. "The needs are here, on earth. Just think, what do people always remember about a civilization?"

No one answered.

"Here's a hint: the Egyptian Pyramids, the Roman Coliseum, the Great Wall of China."

"You want to build a new world wonder?" Dylan asked.

Liz nodded to Rachel. "I've decided what to do. I'm going to use my dad's design to build the tallest tower the world has ever seen. A new Babel headquarters. A symbol of what our company means, and a secure place to store our data servers. A place of freedom and brilliance and hope."

"I wish I hadn't suggested it." The edge in Rachel's voice made the room grow quiet. "You already have a skyscraper."

"This building is nothing special," Liz said, noticing the

25

dark circles under her friend's eyes. "I want to build something spectacular. A symbol."

"This is one of the tallest buildings in San Francisco. You're on the top floor. You're in the corner office." Rachel stared down Liz like a big sister. "If this isn't enough for you, why do you think another column of steel would be? Just because of your dad?"

Liz hesitated. Rachel was probably just underslept and exhausted. Weren't new mothers always like that? Maybe Liz shouldn't have asked her to come again so soon. "It's not about me," Liz said.

"Rachel has a point," Dylan said, running a hand through his red hair. "It would cost a fortune. If you want to give the world hope, we can set up a new foundation. It could still be innovative. Like a seed fund or something." He paused, leaning forward. "Or how about a research institute to study the world's conversations? You have the data."

Liz shook her head. "I'm going to build a tower."

"Why?" Rachel asked.

Liz leveled her bright blue eyes on Rachel. "I already told you. It will bring together the best. It will be a beacon of hope and freedom. The possibilities are endless."

Rachel shrugged.

"You don't believe me...you want me to say it's for my dad?"

The room fell quiet. Rachel's voice came out soft: "It won't bring him back."

"It's what he would have wanted."

"You don't know that."

"Rachel, we saw him, hunched over his designs night after night. It was this masterpiece that dragged him down. You

26

know how much he wanted to build it."

"He went mad trying..." Emotion laced Rachel's voice.

"I won't let that happen to me." Liz glanced around the group. "I'm doing this for bigger reasons, and I have you to keep me sane, right?"

"We'll do more than that," Owen said, injecting a playful tone. "I'll handcuff myself to you, if that's what it takes."

Dylan laughed. "I'd share the honor."

Jax eyed the two other guys. "What can we do to help? That's why you called us here, isn't it?"

Liz nodded. "I can always count on you. We need to brainstorm."

"We're not architects," Owen replied.

"But her dad was," Rachel said.

"Yes." Liz met her friend's eyes calmly. "It'll be his design, only bigger. So my big question today is: where to build it? I have an idea, but what do you think?"

The group sat in an odd silence. Rachel was shaking her head, looking down.

"You probably want maximum exposure," Jax said. "The more people who see it, the better. And somewhere without earthquakes, I guess. Why not Manhattan or Chicago?"

"Boring," Dylan said. "Besides, if you want billions to see the tower, your best bet is China."

"That's insane," Owen said. "The Chinese government could just take it. We don't want to mess with that. It should be somewhere free from government interference."

Liz was glad she'd included the lawyer in this group. She hadn't known Owen as long as the others, but he was loyal. She watched his foot tap idly, each dip of the white leather moccasin revealing dark-skinned ankle under his skinny jeans.

No socks, lots of style. "Okay, so not China. Where would you build it?" she asked him.

Owen's foot stopped mid-tap. "Outside any country's sovereign territory, to have complete control. You could build it two hundred miles from the coast. Maybe south of Japan, in the Philippines Sea."

"Seriously?" Jax asked. "Asia? That's the best you can come up with?"

"It's a donut hole," Owen said. "Japan owns all the surrounding waters, plus the U.S. has military nearby, but one area in the middle cannot be claimed. It's the high seas, and we can build there."

"Works for me," Dylan added. "Half the world lives nearby—China, India, Japan, Indonesia."

"So...in the middle of the ocean?" Liz asked. "It's kind of deep, from what I hear."

"It can be done," Owen replied. "You just drill pylons into the ocean floor, like one of those deep sea oil rigs."

"And we'll add a desalination system," Dylan said. "That way we won't pull from other limited freshwater sources. The climate is warm there, too. The sides of the tower can grow enough food to feed everyone."

Liz smiled, imagining thousands of plants sprouting along its sides. She had envisioned something quite different—pure and simple, glass and steel. She turned to Rachel. "What do you think?"

Rachel breathed out heavily. "I think this is a very bad idea."

"Oh?" Liz said, her smile unwavering.

"I've been trying to figure out what to say, and...I don't know what to say, Liz, but my senses scream danger."

"Your senses?" Jax asked.

Rachel kept her eyes on Liz. "We all know what happened to your dad. And think about your company's name. You think it's just a coincidence? You're really going to build the Tower of Babel?"

Dylan let out a small laugh. "Oh, that's good."

"No, it's not," Rachel said. "Do you know what happened to that tower?"

"We're not here to talk about religion." Liz's brow had turned down, forming a severe angle across her face.

"What happened?" Rachel insisted.

"God knocks down the tower," Liz said. "No wonder, they were building with bricks."

Rachel shook her head. "God didn't knock down the tower. He made all the people speak different languages, scattering them."

Liz tapped the unit by her ear. "So what? We've solved that now."

"It's not that simple." Rachel looked to Owen, but he only shrugged. "What God cares about is pride, not languages or towers."

Liz stood, rocking on the balls of her bare feet, hand to her chin. "Look, I'm not denying it takes some pride to do this. I'm proud of what we've built at Babel, and I'll be proud of this tower. People have built plenty of impressive things that are still standing."

"It's *why* we build that matters. I'm worried about your reasons for doing this."

"You suggested it," Liz said.

"It was a joke. A bad joke."

"But you were right, Rach. The tower idea is perfect. We

just have to make sure we do it the right way." Liz paused. "I want a secure location. I've been thinking about somewhere in the midwest. It'll be visible for miles, much lower construction costs, and safely in the heart of the United States."

"Safely in the middle of nowhere," Owen said. "If you want obscurity, sure, stick it in Kansas."

"Nebraska," Jax said. "It would be better in Nebraska."

All eyes turned to him.

"Why?" Rachel asked, sounding alarmed.

"Two reasons," Jax answered. "The first is water. The midwest is not a bad idea if the goal is to build something huge and safe at a low cost, but the area is dry. We'd need some guaranteed source of water. And Nebraska sits on top of a huge underground aquifer."

"What's the second reason?" Rachel asked.

Jax looked up at her, then turned to Liz. "Because Liz was born there."

"I was born there too, but you don't see me trying to build a skyscraper in a cornfield." Rachel took a deep breath. "I care about you, Liz, so I'm going to be honest with you. I think the money has gone to your head. If you want to give it to the poor, I'll help. But building a tower is a waste, no matter where you build it."

"This is not going to be just a building. It's going to be a way to inspire, a place to gather the world's best to tackle the hardest problems. And our hometown could have front row seats."

Rachel crossed her arms, clutching her elbows. "You know this isn't about them. It's about *you*."

Liz shook her head. "They don't know what they're missing."

30

"You're not a savior."

The room was still. Then Liz spoke quietly, too quietly and too controlled. "I am sad you are opposed. But I know this is what I need to do. I'm sorry I won't have your support."

"So that's it?" Rachel asked.

Liz nodded. "Thank you for coming anyway." The implication was clear. Rachel was free to leave.

The tension fled from Rachel's face, replaced by sadness. "You know where I'll be."

No one spoke as Rachel stood and walked out. Liz's normally energetic body deflated like a balloon as she sat back on her desk.

"So...we're still with you," Jax said. "Want us to get started now, trying to find the right location?"

Liz studied her hands resting in her lap. "Yeah, that would be great. I need to try to get my dad's sketches. I thought Rachel would help with that..." She looked up, resolve in her eyes. "But Katarina can track them down. Owen, do some digging in Nebraska. Look for a place where we can buy 100,000 acres without breaking the bank and with some sort of government support. I want a break from regulations. Understood?"

"I'm on it," Owen said.

"How can I help?" Dylan asked.

"You're always good with big ideas. Think about what I might be missing. Something to get people excited." Liz gazed at the door where Rachel had exited. "I want this tower to withstand anything, from the government to God's fury."

Jax smiled. "Deep foundations. Lots of steel. We'll handle it."

"Good." Liz glanced down at her yellow sweater. It was

Friday, still early. "I want to announce it soon. Think we can finish before Babel goes public?"

"The whole tower?" Owen asked. "I guess it's possible, but we'll need a lot of cash. That could be hard before the IPO. It's hardly a year…"

"Right, and it's while I still control the company." Liz's eyes went to the door. "Some people might doubt us, but if we keep moving forward, the world will start to see. We're going to give people something to believe in."

6

Katarina felt right at home in the Babel company jet. Halfway over the Atlantic, suspended between Russia and America, she flew to the newest cradle of skyscrapers, Dubai. Liz's instructions had been simple: bring back my father's design, at any price.

That's Liz's problem, Katarina thought. The girl did not value her wealth. Americans were always flinging away their money. They had the freedom to use it, but without understanding how. Russians understood: money is power, and so money must be retained and multiplied at all costs. And where money was lacking, power must be used to acquire it. One could never last long without the other.

The jet landed in Dubai early in the morning. The summer sun was already so hot that it would have baked Katarina's pale skin if she exposed an inch of it. The black cloth covering her head to toe had some benefits. She walked to the white luxury car waiting on the runway and rode straight to the palace. It was amazing the doors that Babel could open.

Servants escorted her to an immense waiting room. She sat on an ornate chair and admired the art on the walls. It was more modern than she would have expected. A servant brought her an espresso. At 10 am sharp, the doors to an office opened. A man with a thin, oiled beard and a fashionable grey suit approached her.

"Ms. Popova?" His face wore a playful grin.

Katarina bowed low. "It is an honor to meet Your Royal Highness."

The prince's face registered understanding, which relieved Katarina. He was wearing his Babel. "Come, we will talk of your request."

She followed him through the tall, gilded doors into an office dripping in wealth. She took scrupulous mental notes. Thick, crimson curtains twenty feet high. White marble floors with golden veins. The desk and chairs had clawed feet standing on the marble, their polish reflecting the sun streaming through the windows. Much better than Liz's bare, modern office, Katarina thought. Power had to be projected properly to be wielded properly.

The prince motioned to two green velvet chairs by the window. A small glass table stood between them. Katarina sat and crossed her legs, tugging the black robe up to reveal her slender ankle. She needed whatever advantage she could get.

The prince sat across from her and clasped his hands in his lap. "You have made an interesting request."

"Ms. Trammell has grand ambitions."

"Just like her father. I never had the pleasure of meeting him, but many in my country were impressed by his designs."

"You still have them?"

"I agreed to meet with you, did I not?" He smiled. "It is only one large sheet of drafting paper, but I think it is what Ms. Trammell seeks."

"I would like to see it."

"You have an update for me?"

"She will be selling her shares. Maybe all of them by the time she's finished. She'll need the cash to fund the construction."

"And our plan remains the same?"

Katarina retrieved the paper from inside her black abaya cloak and laid it on the table between them. "Yes."

The prince took the sheet and reviewed it. His eyes met Katarina's. "You are an interesting woman."

"Our goals are not so different."

"Oh?"

"We both understand what it means to be second in command."

"My father is a good leader."

"I'm sure he is, but he stands between you and the position you were born to hold. For you, it is only a matter of time. For me, the company does not have such a succession plan." She paused. "So I am creating it."

The prince lifted a tiny espresso cup from the table. It looked like it was made of gold. He sipped it, eyes never leaving Katarina. "But still you would not have the majority of shares."

"Power takes many forms, Your Highness. Some are content to sit on the throne. Some to own the shares. I want access to the data."

"And the money?"

Katarina shrugged. "It will come."

"Your price is steep."

"I never claimed to be cheap."

The prince laughed, stood, and began to pace in front of the window. His figure cast a long morning shadow over Katarina and the room. He paused before Katarina and gazed down at her. "Stand."

It sounded like a test. She obeyed, rising and meeting his dark eyes.

"Let me be clear," he said. "You will be agreeing to serve my interests, *whatever I want.*"

Katarina put a playful tone in her answer. "The CEO bends over backwards to serve the shareholders."

"And I will own the majority of the shares. You understand my objectives?"

"To purify our words." She glanced down at the paper on the table. "It's written there. No more blasphemy. No more profanity, vulgarity, or heresy. We must know what people say to change what they say, right?"

The prince smiled. "You will unlock Babel's data for me. It is no small matter to change the language of the world." He stepped closer.

"Yes. The data will be yours." *And I will be the gatekeeper.* Everyone wanted the Babel data for some purpose. Dylan wanted it open to the world, but that would only destroy its power. The prince wanted to use it to change the world, but that was naive. Liz wanted it hidden, to feed her own company's profits. Katarina wanted it for power.

The prince took another step forward. His arm found the small of Katarina's back. His face drew close. She could smell his breath—coffee and cloves and cinnamon. "I own many rooms without cameras, without microphones," he whispered. "But you will be monitored wherever you go."

Katarina looked up into his eyes. "Except when I'm with you?"

The prince stepped back. "You must prove your loyalty. You have promises to keep."

Katarina nodded, her body tense, unaccustomed to being rebuffed. "I will keep them," she said. "And yours? The design?"

The prince stepped to the desk and pulled out a drawer. He held out a roll of blueprint paper. "This is the last design of Mr. Trammell. His daughter will be pleased."

"You're sure there are no copies?"

"Yes, as far as I know. It was the strict terms of the proposal that only hand-drawn entries would be accepted in the first round, and that no copies were permitted. We have not replicated this."

Katarina took the paper and unfurled it on the desk. She looked over the fine lines of the blueprint, the tower. She glimpsed a small handwritten note at the bottom: *This is the last of my vault. Behind the veil, the girl, and the hope—lost and gone forever.* She had no clue what it meant.

"Why did you reject the design?" she asked.

"It was my father's decision. He once said that our country would always be more than a single tower." The prince's royal finger traced the outlines of the tower's expansive base. "This design was too…open and free, even revolutionary. It would have dominated our land. It would have made our Grand Mosque an afterthought."

"So it was about your faith?"

"Something like that," the prince said. "It also would have cost five times as much as the other designs submitted. We could not justify it to our people." He paused. "You think this will be built?"

"With your help, yes. Very little stands in Ms. Trammell's way."

"It will be interesting to see." The prince rolled up the blueprint and handed it to Katarina. "She is the architect's daughter, after all."

7

Jax, Dylan, and Owen sat at a round corner booth with a faux black leather bench. Owen had taken the train to Palo Alto for the dinner, closer to Jax and Dylan. Jax had picked a vegan-friendly restaurant for Owen. Dylan was saying something about rowing, his strong hands mimicking strokes with his fork and knife, and Owen and Jax nodded along as if they cared. Morale hovered somewhere under the table.

After a while Dylan leaned forward and pushed his plate away. "Guys, I don't know about you, but I'm worried about Liz. That last meeting was weird, right? Rachel's her oldest friend."

"*Was* her friend…" Owen adjusted his glasses and looked to Jax. Dylan's gaze had also settled on the coder.

"What?" Jax held up his hands in innocence. "I had no idea she was going to tell Rachel to leave."

"Did you know about the tower?" Owen asked.

Jax shrugged. "Liz has mentioned it a couple times since her dad died, but she never talked about *building* it. You guys know she never talks much about her family."

"It's a bad sign," Dylan said. "She's been losing her grip ever since Babel took off. Maybe all the attention has gone to her head. She's not grounded like she used to be."

"Grounded?" Jax shook his head. "She was never grounded."

"I guess not, but she used to care about other things.

Seeing shows, going out for drinks, enjoying life." Dylan paused. "Remember how she used to laugh?"

"She still does." Jax grinned, but not in a friendly way. "Remember how you used to be funny?"

"You know what I mean…"

"I think it's the work," Owen said. "She's been working herself to the bone, first building the company, then traveling all the time, making pitches about Babel."

"Can you blame her?" Jax asked. "The company is changing the world, and it's worth billions."

"Why so defensive?" Owen studied Jax. "How big is your slice of the pie?"

"It's not about the money. Babel is my invention."

"You came up with the code, not the company." Dylan tapped the discrete unit by his ear. "It's Liz's masterwork, in case you forgot."

Jax downed a long drink. He wasn't going to rehash this debate, especially not with Dylan. The guy had been jealous ever since high school, when Jax came up with the code. Dylan, the class president and rowing captain, couldn't stand it when a short, pimply teen had suddenly stolen all of Liz's attention.

Owen leaned forward, elbows on the table, and fixed the other two with a relaxed gaze. "Look, we all love Liz. That's why she shared her idea with us. She's not crazy. She's just been working too hard."

Dylan was shaking his head. "It's more than that. You haven't known her as long as we have. She's never been the same since her dad died. Rachel's kind of right about that…"

"You find religion, too?" Jax scoffed.

Dylan smiled. "I believe in progress. Building a tower is

one kind of progress. But I have a better idea for her."

"Oh?" Jax asked.

"We're going to conquer death."

Jax laughed. "Now that's funny."

"I'm serious," Dylan said. "This isn't some holy grail anymore. We know the human genome. The genetics team at my lab has been doing amazing things with mice. Imagine what could happen if Liz brought together the best scientists from around the world, let them talk seamlessly with Babels, and set a huge prize for advances. She can even have them work in the tower if that floats her boat."

"I think we're getting ahead of ourselves." Owen rubbed his chin. The golden band of his watch glittered in the restaurant's light. "You seem to think she has the money to do all this, but I'm still not sure selling her stock will produce enough cash."

"She can cover it," Jax said.

"The tower could cost billions. And selling out has its own risks. We have to be careful about the securities laws. We're in the IPO process now." Owen paused as if worrying over the idea, always the lawyer. "Once the company goes public next year, it could fall into anyone's hands, along with the code and the data."

"Not true," Jax said. "I built the encryption. Not even the NSA can hack its way in."

"What if something changes?" Dylan asked.

"Like what?" Jax said.

"Well, with the IPO, couldn't any company buy a controlling stake in Babel?" Dylan asked. "Katarina told me about the risk."

"You talked to Katarina?" Owen's voice suddenly had an

edge to it. "What else did she say?"

Dylan leaned back in the booth, his face unreadable. "Nothing much. But she's close to Liz, you know? And she wants to make sure the company is protected."

"Liz has been giving her too much power," Owen said. "I don't like it."

"You're always worrying," Dylan said. "Katarina has been with the company for years. She's just doing her job. But you have to admit she's right about the risk with the IPO. Imagine all the data that could be lost. All those recorded conversations in the vault. All that stored human intelligence down the drain...just because Liz wants to build a tower?"

"The data can never be used," Jax said. "That's been Babel's promise from the start."

"Then why store it?"

"I've told you before," Jax said. "We need it for the algorithm."

"Okay, but remind me?"

"My code is constantly learning from real conversations. That's why the translations keep getting better. The more data we get, the better Babel translates. But to get more data, we rely on users' confidence that the data stays locked away. It all falls apart if the data isn't safe."

"And it's safe as long as you and Liz are around," Owen said, "doing whatever secret code update you do. That's why I keep suggesting some kind of security for her."

Dylan laughed. "She'll never accept that."

"I know...but she should understand the risk. This company has become too important for her to just cash out. If you guys care about her, you have to help me make sure she keeps her position."

"We'll see." Dylan swirled the remains of his drink. "Liz knows how to take care of herself, but I'll talk to her. She's going to like my conquering death idea."

"Good luck," Jax said. "I used to think the code would be enough to satisfy her. I was wrong. Then I thought the company's success, the fame and fortune would be enough. Wrong again. She's never been content for long."

"Think the tower will do it?" Owen asked.

"No," Jax and Dylan both said.

"So what will?" Owen asked.

Love, Jax thought but dared not say. "I'm not sure," he sighed. "But it's lonely for her at the top. That's why she wants us to help her."

Owen passed a serious look over Dylan and Jax. "So let's stay on the same page, okay?"

They both nodded.

"Good," Owen said. "Just so you know, I'm flying to Nebraska tomorrow to start buying land."

Dylan raised his drink. "Godspeed. A toast…to Liz and her tower."

8

A person, on average, meets over ten thousand people in a lifetime. Jacob Conrad was far from average. Only sixty people had ever met him, and most of them thought he was a simple young man. Handsome, sure, but he didn't talk much. His mother had long ago stopped trying to drag words out of him. When he was four, she'd threatened to drive him two hundred miles to a doctor—a real doctor—if he didn't say something. She'd gotten him all the way inside their red pickup truck before he'd spoken.

"I can talk, Mom."

That settled that. The following years had given his mother little reason to press the topic. Her boy did his chores, obeyed when asked, and learned his way around the farm. He was eight when he'd surprised her by coming back from the fields early with something to say.

"Pa's dead."

It was a tractor accident. The family had mourned for years. Jacob talked even less after that. But every night before his mother tucked him in, he'd kneel beside the bed and whisper his prayers. His voice never rose above a whisper, but his mother would listen in awe. She no longer worried about him being a simple boy. She worried about his beliefs, his unending fascination with theology, and his seeming lack of concern about himself and his future.

With his father gone, Jacob had grown into a man in a

hurry. He picked up everything he could from his grandfather. Jacob had no desire to expand their lands, but he worked them well. Whatever it took to be independent, off the grid. No one in the family lacked for anything. Except, his mother often thought, that Jacob needed a wife. Maybe someday somebody would unseal his lips and his lifetime of thoughts would burst like water from a dam.

But not yet. Jacob's mother was in no rush to give up her firstborn, so she greeted the rare visitor with some relief, because it was a man, not a woman.

The sixty-first person to meet Jacob Conrad was a very curious fellow, with dark jeans that hugged his legs tight and a pink shirt. The hue sure looked odd against his dark black skin. Not that Jacob's mother cared about the color of his skin, but most everyone around here—black or white—wore overalls, not pastels.

"You sure you don't want some tea or coffee?" she asked.

The man had a slim tablet laid out on their old wooden dining table, and his eyes seemed glued to the thing. "No thanks." He finally looked up through thick-rimmed glasses. "Maybe some water?"

"Sure, of course. We have a good well."

The man nodded. "How long did you say your son would be?"

"He usually comes back for a quick bite of lunch. Not always though. The first apples will be ripe soon. He might just pick one and eat it under the shade of the orchard. He loves it there. Not many folks have apple trees around here, you know?"

The man glanced down at his tablet, tapped it twice, then looked up again. "My next appointment is in an hour. Your son has been difficult to contact."

"I'm sure. He doesn't use a computer. Rarely uses a phone." She glanced down at the tablet. The top had the name "Owen Strand" engraved in sleek block letters. The screen showed a calendar jammed full of meetings and notes. "You could look for him in the orchard."

"Which way?"

"Won't you take a sandwich or something with you?"

He stood from the chair and patted the leather briefcase draped over his shoulder. "Thanks again, but I brought a lunch bar."

She didn't know much about lunch bars, but decided to let it be. They walked outside to a fancy black car. Dust already lay thick over its shiny frame. She told him the way to the orchard—just down one dirt road a mile, take the second left, and you can't miss the trees.

She was right. Owen didn't miss the trees. They were the only ones in sight in this flat universe of corn. As he stepped out of his car, he imagined Liz's tower invading the skyline. She would make these trees look like ants.

He didn't have to look long to find the farmer. He was sitting on a rock by a narrow creek that wove through the orchard.

"Jacob Conrad?" Owen asked, approaching.

The farmer stood and nodded. He wore faded blue overalls and a green hat with a yellow deer symbol on it. A half-eaten apple rested in his palm.

"Your mother said you'd be out here," Owen continued. "I have a proposal I'd like to discuss."

The man stared back at him like he was from another planet. Something in the farmer's eyes almost made him afraid.

It was like the man already knew what he was going to propose, and what his answer would be. It was like the farmer knew what the weather was going to be tomorrow, and the next ten years. His silence gave Owen the spooks.

After a few moments, the farmer finally looked away, up at the tree above. He took a few steps and pulled down an apple from a low branch. He held the apple out to Owen.

Owen took it. "Thanks." He motioned to the rock where the farmer had been sitting. "You want to sit while we talk?"

The farmer shook his head.

"Okay, I'll get to the point. We're interested in your land. I work for Elizabeth Trammell." Owen paused. "You know, the founder of Babel?"

No reaction from the farmer. Too bad. Just mentioning Liz's name had made the last two landowners' eyes open wide. They'd known they'd hit jackpot. This farmer seemed clueless.

"Let's make this simple," Owen said. "What do you think would be a fair price for the land?"

He didn't answer. Owen knew this type. Tough negotiator. Playing hardball. The marching orders were simple: acquire 100,000 acres, pay whatever it takes. This was an ideal region— flat and cheap and in the middle of nowhere, with plenty of underground water. The farmers around here had been falling like dominos; it was not the type of place where strangers normally showed up offering to pay cash at a premium. Owen had just a few more to convince, and the land would be ready. His research showed this farm was worth about one million. He might as well start there.

"How about one million dollars, cash?" he asked.

The farmer stared at him blankly.

"One million is more than this land is worth. We both

know that. You could buy yourself a bigger farm. Buy some new tractors. Take care of your family for a lifetime."

No response. Not even a blink.

Time to up my game. "I see you're not convinced, so I'll get straight to it. I'm authorized to pay 1.4 million for this land." Actually, there was no limit, but 1.4 million would set this guy for a long time.

Calm as a sunrise, the farmer lifted his apple, bit into it, and chewed slowly.

"Sir, can you tell me if you'll at least consider that?"

The man kept chewing.

"What do you think?"

The farmer swallowed, then he spoke calm and steady: "That's money."

Progress! Owen smiled at him. "A whole lot of money, right?"

Jacob glanced down at the apple in Owen's hand. "Not hungry?"

"I already ate." Owen held it out, then thought better. He needed to come to this guy's plane. He took a bite. It was crisp and juicy. "Pretty good," he said as he chewed. "What kind of apple?"

"My own variety," the farmer said, something like a smile curving up under his beard.

Owen had to admit the farmer had some charm with his dark brown eyes and high cheekbones. He looked like a movie star preparing for a role in an antebellum flick. "How'd you like to buy a lifetime of apples, of any variety in the world?" Owen asked.

"I eat what I grow. I don't sell."

"I can see that." Frustration crept into Owen's voice.

"Imagine how much you could grow on 1.4 million dollars' worth of land."

"More than I'd need."

"Exactly! You could sell the excess, earn a profit, buy yourself whatever you'd like. Or buy something for your mom. Maybe a new truck."

The farmer glanced past him, then settled his gaze on Owen. "I need to get back to work."

A warm breeze shuffled the leaves above them, allowing dappled light to shift over their contrasting figures. Jacob turned to go.

"Sir, please," Owen said, making the farmer pause. "I don't mean to keep you from your work, but you haven't answered my proposal."

"Don't need to."

"This is a once in a lifetime opportunity." Owen stepped forward as if to emphasize the point. "Your neighbors have made their deals, or are considering the price. You'll never get another chance to sell this high."

"Don't want another chance."

"Please, name a price."

"There's no price."

"But listen, Jake, can I call you Jake?"

The farmer didn't answer.

"What do you want me to tell my boss? You want to barter instead of sell? You want her to buy some other land, make an exchange? Please..." Owen was not above begging. "Tell me what you want?"

The farmer took a deep breath. "John told me he sold you his land. Said it was about a tower."

"That's right," Owen replied. "I told you my boss is

Elizabeth Trammell, founder of Babel. She's was born near here, and she loves the land."

"Babel?"

"Yeah, the software company."

The farmer shook his head.

"You haven't heard of it?"

The farmer stared at him, chewing calmly.

"Babel started about five years ago, and it's the hottest company in the world. Its rise was even faster than Google, Facebook. Seriously, this company is huge. It's changing the world."

"What's it sell?"

"We sell earpieces, but it's really about the software. A coder cracked the translation puzzle."

"What's that?"

"Well, using the algorithm he came up with, anyone can pop a Babel on their ear and understand any language, instantly. Pretty cool, right? And Elizabeth Trammell is the face of Babel. She's willing to pay a huge premium for this land."

The farmer bit into his apple again. He wiped away a drop of juice before it dripped into his beard. "Land's not for sale."

"So that's it? Land's not for sale?" Frustration swelled in Owen. He hated feeling powerless. "Everything's for sale, sir."

Jacob put his calloused hand on Owen's shoulder. "Back to work, sir. You take care." He tipped his green hat and walked off through the orchard, leaving Owen to return to his car and the civilized world.

9

Jax strolled through the open warehouse, watching the engineers code and the marketers market. His tech company had grown from four to forty-three employees in two years. This was success. His last company had made it only six months. But he'd written the Babel code. He knew he'd find the next big idea. He just needed time. He could always spot the little opportunities that others missed.

This one was fire hydrants. He and his team were turning every hydrant in the country into a spy, and he sold it first to the FBI, then to the CIA. Now FireSpy had contracts with five other U.S. agencies and two other nations. With face recognition software, they could know where everyone was, or at least the last fire hydrant they passed. In a year, maybe he'd sell the company for a few hundred million and move on to the next thing. Maybe robotic asteroid mining. Matter was overrated, but add a little code and you could change the world.

But today was about skyscrapers.

Because that's what Liz wanted.

Jax pulled three engineers into an impromptu meeting. Beck and Roger perched on stools across the ping-pong table. They ran FireSpy's innovation for sprinkler systems in buildings. Veruca leaned back on the exposed brick wall, her red curls almost matching the brick. She was FireSpy's steel expert, the one who installed undetectable cameras in metal, the final link for making hydrants spy.

Jax bounced a ping-pong ball and called the meeting to order. "Who wants a million dollar bonus?" he asked.

Postures straightened, eyes widened. "I'll take it," Beck said.

"We're going to build a tower. A really tall one."

"Nice," Veruca said. "Why?"

"It's for my friend, Liz Trammell. And for fun. I told you we'd push the envelope here." Jax bounced the ball up to the ceiling, then caught it. "We're going to help with construction, materials, and finding the best builders. The question is, how tall can we build it?"

"If Liz is funding it, we can build it out of the atmosphere," Roger said. "There's a company in Montreal that's working on a space elevator. Something to make launches easier. They want to tether it to a tower. Does that count?"

Jax had thought of that. "It can be the cherry on top, but the main goal is to make the tower the tallest in the world, by far." He laid down a copy of the design that Liz had given him. It was only a sketch, but it was stunning all the same. The group of them were quiet, studying it. Fine lines of metal arching up like someone had jabbed a pin up through the surface of the earth, only the surface had risen with it instead of breaking.

"Looks like steel," Veruca mused, looking up from the drawing. "Lots of it. We have a steel company in China. They're fusing metal in new ways. Really thick beams, 3D printed on the spot. If you build with that, go deep with the foundation, I bet you could go a mile high."

Beck was nodding. "It's all about the base. It would have

to be really wide. Where's the tower going to be?"

"Nebraska, middle of nowhere," Jax said. "The land's already bought."

Veruca laughed. "Random, but whatever. It'll cost a fortune to ship the materials. What's the budget?"

"No budget. Just think big." Jax looked to the two guys. "So Veruca leads on the steel, what do you want to tackle?"

Beck sipped kombucha from a styrofoam cup. "The problem isn't the materials," he said. "Think about our hydrants. That little hunk of red metal doesn't matter. What matters is the pipe underneath. Let's dig deep, like into the earth's core. We need a place with stable rock underground."

"That might be a problem in Nebraska. And there's another issue." Roger tilted his head back, speaking to the ceiling. He was dark and brooding and disagreed with everything. But Jax liked him. He kept FireSpy honest. "It's not the materials. It's not the foundation. It's the air." He lowered his gaze, leveling with the group. "You know which state has some of the worst tornados in the world?"

Jax listened, amused, as they talked on. Nothing like a million dollars to make three engineers tackle a problem.

He slid off his stool. "I've gotta handle some emails, but I like the ideas. Keep driving on your issues. Let's meet again after lunch."

The meeting broke off and Jax went to his office. He started doing his own research on the tower. He thought about what Liz wanted. She wanted to make everyone feel a sense of looking up, a tilting back of the head in wonder. Jax had always been short—five feet, two inches…three if he stretched—so if anyone could replicate that feeling, he could.

He scanned a few articles on Babel. More lies and slander

about Liz. They'd just started to pick up hints of the tower idea. Hard to hide it now that a Babel lawyer was buying huge swaths of land in Nebraska. One reporter claimed Liz was building a statue to spite a farmer in Nebraska who had spurned her advances. The press ridiculed her, and it made Jax furious. Sure, she could have given her fortune to fight cancer or something, but who were they to judge? Did they have a father who jumped off a building? Did they lose their mother at seventeen? Did they drop out of school to work all day and build a company from scratch that changed the world?

Media pricks.

They would always fire shots. They didn't have any stake in this. They just wanted to sell words, and right now no one played better in the news than Elizabeth Trammell. At least every takedown story showed Liz's face at the top. Her bright, smiling, blue-eyed face. They could hurl sticks and stones, but everyone who knew Liz loved Liz.

Love, Liz. Two words that haunted Jax.

He dug into more research. Towers and space elevators. Steel and foundations. He found some interesting information on the Eiffel Tower. Four hours later he was back at the table with his team.

Veruca reported on materials. "Add some advanced composites," she said, "and we can go ten miles into the sky, maybe more."

"Seriously?" Jax asked.

"Yep." Beck, the foundation guy, confirmed Veruca's estimate. He said they could dig deep for stability, and make it even stronger by spreading out the base. "You know the Burj Khalifa?" he asked.

Veruca and Roger shook their heads.

"I've been to the top," Jax said.

"Right, so it had a long run as the world's tallest building," Beck said. "Almost three thousand feet into the sky. It has a buttressed core, because the base is like a three-winged spear."

"Spear?" Veruca asked.

"Imagine a triangle, put a dot in the middle, then draw a line out to each corner. The base is like that. Each wing helps stabilize the skyscraper, and it deflects some wind."

Jax liked the idea of a deep foundation. Maybe they could put the Babel data servers down there, instead of hidden in the middle of a desert. It was one thing he'd never agreed on with Liz. They should keep the data close so they could keep an eye on it.

"Wind is still the biggest problem," Roger said. "If the tower goes up four miles, it will be facing regular gusts over a hundred miles per hour. The building will need large internal counterweights that shift weight to the building's center whenever the wind hits. Otherwise, it'll lean. Towers four miles high don't lean well."

Veruca nodded. "We'll also need steel shafts down the center of the building. Where else do we put the elevators?"

"You're missing something," Jax said. "The design by Liz's dad looks a little like the Eiffel Tower. Anyone know where its elevators are?"

"On the sides?" Beck asked.

Jax nodded. The Eiffel Tower was once the tallest structure in the world, and its engineering secret was a wide base. He remembered riding up an elevator along one of its curved edges. He remembered standing on the top, feeling tall. "Liz's building won't be used like others," he said. "She wants it to be a place where people could live, without needing to leave. That means high volume ground access isn't a big deal, and not every elevator has to rise from the ground floor. Imagine a wide, hollow base, sky lobbies, and a narrowing top."

"I like it," Veruca said. "All steel and glass."

"Really strong glass," Roger added.

Jax's gaze shifted to the ceiling, as if trying to envision the tower. "There's going to be a big construction team and builders, but they'll be stuck inside the box of what's been done before. You three keep pushing the margins, okay? Whoever has the best idea gets the million bucks."

"And what if we all have a good idea?" Roger asked.

Jax smiled. "You can split it."

"How long do we have?" Beck asked.

"Probably a few weeks." Jax glanced down at the calendar on his phone. "Liz wants to break ground this fall. So let's plan on September 15."

"We're on it," Roger said, holding out his lanky arms. "We can outdo Mt. Everest if we make the base just as wide."

"Great, just don't think small," Jax said. His life was a defiance of size. "Think about reaching the stars."

10

Owen waited for Liz at the airport in Lincoln, Nebraska. He stood beside the private jet runway, studying his reflection in the tinted glass of the black sedan. The thick-rimmed glasses and fresh new haircut did little to hide his fatigue. He straightened his pink polka dot tie.

The surrounding land was brown and flat. So flat it made him nervous. There was nowhere to hide. No trees, no dips, no knolls. No wonder Midwesterners came out honest and plain.

A jet appeared on the horizon and as it drew closer Owen recognized the colors of Babel. Only one plane had the bright stripes of a rainbow. The dose of radiance in this barren land made him smile.

He read through his briefing again. He'd already bought almost all the land they needed, and a couple weeks ago Liz had given him a new assignment: *get the governor's permission to build however we want*. The governor had been a tough opponent, sly and ambitious. He'd told Owen that he would agree to Liz's terms, but only with lots of publicity and tax revenues. He also demanded that Liz come herself to sign the deal. Owen thought it was pretty fair, and he hoped Liz would agree.

The Babel jet landed and rolled to a stop near Owen. The ladder opened to the ground.

The first person out surprised him: Katarina.

Liz had said nothing about her coming, but Babel's second-in-command had been joining Liz more and more lately. Today Katarina wore a black skirt suit, revealing supermodel pencil legs and a catwalk stride. She had style, but something about her gave Owen the chills. She always seemed a little too perfect for the job.

Liz followed after her, wearing her signature jeans and blue sweater for Tuesday. She smiled and waved. "Hey, Owen. Nice car."

"Welcome to Nebraska." Owen opened the car's back door. "The governor insisted we use his official limo."

Liz paused before getting in. "The governor's?"

"His driver, too. Be on your best behavior."

"Duly noted. I left my champagne at home, anyway." She eyed the limo. "Anything we need to cover before we get in?"

Owen shook his head. "The governor already stocked the bubbly, on ice, and my memo should give you the information you'll need. You got it?"

"I'll read it while we ride."

"Sounds good," Owen said. "One other thing. I've made no progress with the Conrad family. They won't budge. It's not about the money. I can't figure them out."

"Where cash fails, the state prevails. I'll raise it with the governor."

"Just make sure he signs the rest of the package first. Make them an afterthought."

"Sign first. Conrads next. Anything else?"

"Nope, we should go before we're late."

The three of them loaded into the black limo. Liz sat in the far back seat, reading Owen's report on her tablet. Katarina and Owen sat across from each other on the bench seat, like two competing advisors to the queen. Their eyes met awkwardly a few times. Owen skimmed the local paper that had been left inside—the front-page news was corn prices falling, and farmers looking for other work.

It was a short drive to the stately governor's mansion. The limo passed the white columns and black gate in the front and turned into a discrete driveway in the back. A group of men in suits approached.

Liz looked up from her tablet and met Owen's eyes. "Thanks for the report. Why does he want my support for campaign contribution limits?"

Owen glanced out the window, spotting the governor. "The last election was pretty close. He won by a few thousand votes. The tower could bring more people than that to the state. New voters, you know. But I think he's more worried about how you'll use your money."

Liz laughed. "That's easy—I'll use it on the tower. I've never given a dime to a politician."

"Don't tell him that," Owen said. "Better to let him think he might get something."

Liz agreed, and the three of them climbed out of the car. The governor and his entourage introduced themselves. They shook hands and exchanged formalities.

The governor motioned to the car. "Let's get going. We'll have plenty of time to talk on the drive."

Liz, Owen, and Katarina climbed back inside, followed by the governor, his chief of staff, and a security guard. The driver wheeled them out and within minutes they were cruising down a straight highway through an ocean of cornfields under a wide-open blue sky.

Liz followed Owen's script. She told the governor about how she had looked into alternatives. They'd considered Kansas, Oklahoma, and eastern Colorado, as all those states sat over the same aquifer. She told him about her hometown of Arthur, Nebraska, where she'd been born and lived until she was eight. "No traffic light. Lots of farms. Population of 145 when my family moved."

They'd been driving west almost an hour, well into the middle of nowhere but still three hours short of Arthur, when the governor's voice went from friendly politician to business. "Owen and I have been through the terms. My people wrote it all up, and last night I was ready to sign. But my gut was tied up in knots this morning. Lots of people are upset. Just today I got a letter from the elevator inspectors' association. They're beside themselves that they won't get to inspect your tower. What if I give you some special incentives to allow at least periodic inspections?"

Liz arched her eyebrows. "Elevator inspectors?"

"It's not just them. There's cops, firefighters, teachers. In Nebraska we try to give everyone an equal stake, fair dealing you know? Then you come in and want exceptions."

"You know how many jobs I'm bringing to your state?"

"Yeah, and that's great. You've got my support. But I can't just let you build unchecked. How about two days of inspections per year."

Liz shook her head. "No inspections."

"Owen says you're going to be building over a mile high. If something bad happens, if people get hurt, it's not just on you. People are going to blame me."

"No." Katarina spoke up for the first time.

The governor turned to her, his eyes lingering. "Katarina, right?"

She nodded. "If you let Liz's tower stay outside your control, you're shielded from blame for any specifics."

The governor didn't bat an eye at her Russian words. He wore a Babel like everyone else. "What kind of specifics?" he asked.

"Safety concerns, security issues, you name it."

The governor frowned. "Why should I be worried about security?"

"Just normal stuff," Liz answered quickly. "Nothing to worry about, but you know, people will come from all over the world. They won't vote in Nebraska, but they will bring lots of tourism money, and taxes."

"Tourists are still in my jurisdiction," the governor said. "I can't just create a new nation within Nebraska. This is still America."

Owen had an idea. He wished Katarina hadn't brought up security, but there was a workaround. "How about a waiver?" Owen asked. "You know how people have to sign a paper before they go rafting or skiing or whatever?"

"Yes." The governor paused. "But this is a building, not an adventure sport."

"It will be an experience," Owen said. "So we can do something similar. Anyone who comes to the tower will have to sign away certain rights."

The governor sat quietly for a moment. The corn stalks behind him blurred into a golden streak. "It might work, but...I read about how you might move the company's servers to the tower. So what about people who don't visit in person, but visit by Internet or whatever?"

"There's no risk," Liz answered. "It's just a few underground servers, and everything is encrypted. The real attention will be on the tower. That's the whole point. That's why I want to build in Nebraska, near where I grew up." Liz had fixed her bright smile on the governor, her voice sincere. "You care about your hometown, right?"

The governor's shoulders relaxed. "Sure do."

"So you understand why I want to honor the place?" Liz asked. "To help others see how great Nebraska is?"

"Yeah, I guess so."

"Trust me, I would never put my hometown, my tower, or my company at risk. Our goal is nothing but success. We are going to bring the world's best to Nebraska, and we want your support."

The governor was quiet a moment, studying Liz. Then he turned to his chief of staff. "Okay, Greg, the agreement?"

As the chief of staff retrieved a paper from his briefcase, Owen marveled at Liz's disarming charm. She'd done more with a single smile than he'd done in three days of negotiation. The governor pulled out his pen, scribbled a note about the waiver at the bottom of the agreement, signed it, then handed it to Liz.

She glanced at the new note, then at Owen. He nodded. She signed it without reading a word.

"Pleasure doing business with you," the governor said. "We've still got a while before we arrive. A toast?"

Liz smiled. "Yes. But there's one more thing."

"Fire away."

"Owen managed to buy the land I need, with only one holdout. It's a farm within sight of the tower. About one thousand acres, and the family is refusing to sell."

"Why does that not surprise me?"

"It's not about the money," Owen said. "I offered far more than the land's worth. They won't sell. They insist that they aren't moving anywhere."

The governor laughed. "That's a Nebraska farmer for you. I'm surprised you got everyone else to agree."

Money will do that, Owen thought. "I moved fast."

"So who's the family?" the governor asked.

"The Conrads," Liz said. "Heard of them?"

Her words wiped the smile off the governor's face. "Isaiah Conrad?"

"That's right," Owen said. "I talked to his grandson Jacob, who seems to be running things."

"Isaiah's still the figurehead," the governor replied. "He was a big player in my opponent's campaign. They're hard folks. Very traditional. You might as well leave them be."

"If they're already against you," Liz said, "can't you help us nudge them out?"

The governor shook his head. "I'm not going there. Think of all the farmers in Nebraska. Imagine what they'd think if I just ousted one from his land because you want to build a tower there."

At least the governor was being honest. Owen had already thought through this. His mind wandered as Liz began to debate the point with the governor. Finally, Liz turned to Owen. "You've studied the laws. Isn't there some way?"

Owen knew this debate was going nowhere, but he also knew Liz would never drop it on her own. He went with a tried and true tactic: delay. "Let me look into it more. There might be something else." He pointed to the champagne on ice in the corner. "In the meantime, time for that toast?"

The governor grabbed the bottle, and Liz gave in. Moments later they were sipping champagne and celebrating a victory. They rode on for a while and Owen noticed the small Conrad farmhouse ahead. He pointed it out for Liz, who studied it with a determined gaze.

They reached the proposed tower site a few minutes later.

The group exited the limo, stretching their legs by the empty plain where Liz planned to build. Owen felt a little tipsy, caught up in the bubbly banter of the others.

Liz came to his side. "Hey, nice work back there."

"Thanks," Owen said. "Just doing my job."

"And doing it very well." She smiled. "Hey, let's stop by that farm on the way back."

"The Conrads?" Owen shook his head, but what could he say? Liz was used to getting what she wanted. Sometimes she didn't even have to try, or she just put on a little charm like she did with the governor. But this farmer was different. "I'm telling you, they're not going to budge."

"We'll see…" Liz said, looking back toward the farmhouse. "I want to meet this Jacob Conrad."

11

Most people meet for the first time with a measure of curiosity and caution. A polite hello and how-do-you-do. A few times in a lifetime, it's different. Two people meet like electrons whirling through particle accelerators at critical velocity, colliding and exploding and leaving ashes in their wake.

Liz thought of her life as a particle accelerator. Some unseen force drove her with ceaseless compulsion to something bigger and better. She fully expected to collide with another electron someday. She did not expect to collide with a Midwestern farmer named Jacob, but the man was standing in her way.

Owen had given her the file on Mr. Conrad. It was short. He had no social media. The Internet didn't even know he existed. The only records came from local intelligence. Neighbors said he was a good man, a normal farmer type. Grew his crops. Fed his family and his chickens. Wore a beard. If anything was going to stop her from building her tower here, it was not this guy.

The governor had agreed on the pit stop, as long as it was brief and as long as he wasn't involved. Liz promised it would be quick. She was planning to turn on the full-force charm offensive. Owen had called the Conrad home from the limo, so they were expecting her.

Now, as she walked toward the farm and spotted the farmer outside, clearly having seen her coming, she started to wonder what this unusual person might be thinking. He stood strong yet relaxed, an arm reaching out easily to rest on a fencepost. He wore boots, jeans, and a tucked in white shirt. He looked almost Amish if not for the green trucker's hat. He somehow made the fencepost look like a slouch.

He didn't smile, didn't say anything, as she came closer. She let her natural energy show, with a bounce in her stride and a bright, confident smile.

"Jacob Conrad?" she asked.

He nodded.

"Liz Trammell. Thanks for agreeing to meet me on such short notice. I heard about your meeting with my lawyer."

He didn't react, though his eyes missed nothing.

"We can make this quick, let you get back to your farming, okay?"

He stared at her with an interminable grin. Up close he looked straight out of the Civil War in a dignified sort of way. Maybe like a general, like Stonewall Jackson. Except for the grin. There was something charming about it.

He surprised her by stepping closer, into her space. She suddenly felt his presence, like the sun slipping out of the clouds and basking over her. He smelled of sweat and dirt, but it wasn't bad. She didn't pull back. She wouldn't retreat. He reached up by her face, grazing her ear, then pulled something away and held it in front of her eyes. It was some flaxen, stringy thing.

"Corn silk," he said, his dark eyes amused.

She took the string out of his hand.

"Hard to see the silk in your hair. It takes to you."

She felt her face going red. "You know why I'm here, right?"

"The tassel is the male part of the corn," he said. "The ear, the part we eat, that's the female part."

"Mr. Conrad, I did not come here to learn about corn."

"Call me Jake."

Not the most promising start to a business negotiation she'd ever had, but she was the one with something to say, after all. So she launched ahead.

"Okay Jake, I'll get right to it. I've purchased all the land surrounding your farm, and I will be building the tallest skyscraper in the world within a mile of where we're standing." She gestured in the direction of the building site, which was currently only rolling hills of long grasses. "I realize this will be a big change, close to your doorstep. But I hope you understand it is not just you this is affecting. It's your neighbors. It's the whole state of Nebraska. Everyone is excited about this. The tower will bring new business, tourism, and jobs. It's going to be one of the greatest feats of humanity."

She paused, trying to gauge his response. She got nothing, but she pressed ahead to lay it all out on the table. She knew the normal negotiating tricks wouldn't work with this guy. Owen had already tried.

"I'm not just talking about how tall the building will be," she continued. "But also how we'll use it. We'll have top-notch research and collaboration to tackle the world's challenges. Jake, we could conquer death right over there. Can you imagine that? And we want this land right here to be part of it. Now I want to be fair. We'd like to make your dreams come true at the same time. We're all in this together. Tell me, what do you want? Is there any other place you've ever wanted to be?"

She had turned on the charm, built up the energy, and set it free. She waited for a response. And waited a little longer. She knew it was a lot to take in—the great feats that would happen where he currently plowed land.

Finally he answered. "There is no better place."

His voice was firm and steady. Not excited or energetic. As if she had not affected him at all. She tried again.

"Jake, we're talking about a princely sum for your land. We can make you and your family happy for the rest of your lives."

"Miss Trammell, with all due respect, money can't make a person happy."

"Please, call me Liz. I know I'm making my own dream come true here, and I realize it's going to affect you. You won't be isolated out here much longer. Thousands of people will be coming. Making noise."

"I don't mind visitors." He might has well have been talking about the chances of rain tomorrow.

"Well, I want to make this good for you, too. Think of it as an opportunity. You can get away from the disturbances here, and go wherever you want. It could even be a farm twice as big and only a hundred miles away. Give me some hint of what you'd like, to achieve your own dream. You might be surprised what I can make happen for you."

In the silence that followed, he looked at her with such calm intensity that she looked away. The green of the grass was so bright. She heard a bird chirp, and the slight rustle of the trees in the breeze.

"My dreams can't be bought."

She wasn't quite sure what to say to that. But at least he'd admitted he had dreams. "Jake, I can pull strings, hire people, get the best minds on an issue. What is it you care about? Is there a cause? Is it your family? What can I say or do to persuade you to consider partnering with me?"

She noticed the cadence of her speech slowing the longer she spoke with him. Her breathing became steadier, deeper. Her shoulders loosened and she stood taller, letting her arms fall by her sides. Her smile became more relaxed. Her overwhelming curiosity about this person in front of her, and what made him tick, was not a frustration. It was more...wonder. *Who is he? How does he live? What would it feel like to be so tied to a place that no amount of money makes you want to leave? To have no desire to live some other, better place?*

A long-dormant place inside her began to prick her consciousness: Is it possible to feel that way? No one she knew did. It was always about the next thing, the big achievements, the milestones, the successes. From the day she and Jax created Babel, she'd been working to make it the success it was today. By all accounts, she had succeeded. And then what? Surely this tower was the answer. If she built it, she would do a great thing in the world. She could never doubt her success, her worth, her reason for living. The tower would stand as a testament long after she was gone. People would never forget her.

Thoughts of the tower got her mind back onto normal Liz-track. A goal-oriented track. It was more comfortable for her there. What was the next step to get this land for her tower? She put it to Jake:

"Look, I see I haven't persuaded you. But I do think selling is best for you. This huge tower is going to be right there..." she pointed again in the general direction. "What can I do to get you to reconsider?"

A long pause. Again the breeze and the quiet entered her consciousness. "Do you need some time to think it over?

Would it help if I came back?"

She had no idea why she offered that. She was way too busy to be flying back to Nebraska with everything else going on with Babel and plans for the tower. It just slipped out before she could stop it. Surely it was because she was reading him so well and it was what he would need in order to sell. Right? Surely it was because she could tell he wasn't going to sell today, and she couldn't bear to lose the negotiation. That must be why.

But for the first time, her offer seemed to ruffle his calm. His eyes flickered, looked at the sky behind her, like he was listening to something, then came back to hers. When they did, she caught her breath. It was like they looked straight into her core. His words, when they came, were quiet.

"Yes. I'd like that. Come stay for a while."

Liz's breath caught. The intensity in his eyes made her hesitate. "Stay?"

"I don't mind much about the tower," he said. "People build things, things fall down. But you're a mighty interesting lady."

There was no hiding the crimson in her face now. She wasn't thinking straight, and she didn't trust herself to respond. "We'll be in touch," she managed to say before spinning off and walking away, with the strand of corn silk still clutched in her hand.

12

Jacob Conrad lifted a tin cup of coffee to his lips as the day's first light touched his face. He licked his thumb and pointer finger, then clamped them over the candle flame. The gray light played in the smoke curling up to the wooden rafters. He looked down at the thick book open before him. He closed his eyes and prayed.

When the sun crept over the flat horizon, he knew it was time to work. His tanned, calloused hands folded the book carefully. It would probably be his hands' last delicate moment until he returned to the book tonight. Those hands would be wielding tools and ploughs and tractor wheels. Jake would spend this Wednesday feeding, weeding, watering, and maybe even harvesting. He thought of the best watered corner of his land, where the sweet corn grew tallest and produced a few early ears every year. Fresh corn would be good with dinner.

Jake mouthed the words again. *Awake, O north wind; and come, thou south; blow upon my garden, that the spices thereof may flow out. Let my beloved come into his garden, and eat his pleasant fruits.*

He shook his head. He'd only met the woman once, just yesterday. This had nothing to do with her. But still her face was imprinted in his mind. He tried to wave it away, as if it were a fly buzzing past. He failed. Try as he might, the words from the wise man's ancient love song entwined with the brief memory of her, making a single encounter somehow feel infinite.

There was only one way to deal with a nuisance like that. Jake pulled on his hat, went outside, and began to work.

First he fed the chickens. Then he sharpened his axe. The wood didn't need chopping yet, but Jake needed to slam into something, split into the grain, and divide it. He dragged the axe blade against the hairs of his arm, satisfied as the metal shaved like a razor. He set his feet and raised the axe.

Whack.

The thick wood split in two. He grinned a little as he set the next piece on the stump. Up went the axe again, down it slammed.

Whack.

He laid the split pieces onto a stack. He kept hammering his axe down until his arms ached.

After a while he'd built up the pile. He leaned the axe against it and wiped the sweat off his forehead. With his first deep breath, the woman's face came back into his mind.

"Corn silk," he muttered. He walked to the tractor and started the engine. The thrumming pistons drowned out the face in his mind's eye. He rode the lengths of the field's edges, inspecting. A few times he stopped to pull out the victims of his traps. Two rabbits, one groundhog. He checked a few stalks to make sure growth was on pace. He eyed the clouds, smelled the rain coming. He tinkered with the irrigation valves, adjusting for the coming wetness.

Jake spent the whole day like that. He found escape in the work. Only when he was sweating and concentrating over some familiar task could he keep thoughts of the woman at bay.

By evening he was exhausted. He soaked in a tub of water and let his eyes close. She was still there. She was everywhere.

Why God? he mused, half-asleep.

She is yours.

Those exact words had come to him before she'd visited. But who could be sure about the source of words drifting into the mind? The mind was a tricky thing. He asked again, *Mine?*

She is yours.

Twenty minutes passed before Jake's mother knocked on the door. "You okay in there?"

He awoke with a start. He never fell asleep like that. "Yeah," he grunted.

"It's six o'clock," she said. "Dinner's on the table."

He listened for footsteps walking away, but didn't hear any. He climbed out of the tub and quickly dried and put on clean clothes. His hair and beard were still dripping when he opened the door.

His mother was standing there. "You sure you're okay?"

He nodded.

She smiled and motioned for him to follow. "It was hot out there."

Jake didn't respond. He greeted the others at the table—Pops, Grandma, and his sister, Annie. He sat down, blessed the food, and dug in.

His Mom and Annie talked all about the news of the tower. They talked about the woman who had visited the day before. They didn't bother asking Jake about her. They knew he wouldn't answer.

And if he'd had to answer, he wouldn't have known what to say. None of it made any sense. The way her face plagued his mind. *Not plagued*, he corrected himself. *She isn't ugly.* But it was still a nuisance. And then he kept thinking of those lines from his morning reading. Words about a garden and pleasant fruits. Words about love. Normally the holy words were his reprieve and sanctuary through the day. Now they were a haunting, unmet desire, and the desire was the face imprinted on his mind.

Worst of all, though, was the half-dream, the half-thought: *she is yours*. It made him almost afraid. She was a billionaire from Silicon Valley. How could he possibly get along with a woman like that?

A while later he finally lay in his bed. He feared hearing the words again. He feared believing them. No more words came, but they didn't have to. Jake fell into deep, dreamless sleep. He'd battled today, tried to resist the urges of emotion and desire, and for the first time in years, he'd lost.

13

Katarina Popova held her arms out to her sides, tense and straight and parallel to the San Francisco Bay. She tensed her leg muscles, finding her balance, then leaned over and stretched one of her arms overhead. The salty air filled her lungs with each deep breath. The movements warmed her core in the cold, foggy dawn. She still found it hard to believe that August felt colder in San Francisco than in Moscow.

"Downward dog."

The words translated into motion. Katarina's hands planted on the mat in front of her, heels behind her, shoulder length apart. Her gaze fixed on a blade of grass underneath, as she pressed her heels down. The pose formed a perfect triangle, her body two sides and the ground the other.

"Plank. Chaturanga."

She lowered into the position, her core strong.

"Upward dog."

Her back arched, her gaze raised. The man in front of her held the pose well. The muscles of his back glistened under a light sheen, like the dew around them in the rising sun.

By 6:45, Katarina's body and mind were awake. The instructor thanked them for coming: "Namaste."

Katarina rolled up her yoga mat and walked off. The man who had been in front of her casually fell into pace beside her.

"Good class," he said, in Russian.

"I like how the instructor pushed us," Katarina agreed,

speaking the same language and taking a brief glance back. No one was close enough to hear them. They would have a few blocks to walk, like every Friday morning.

"How was your meeting?"

"It went as expected. The board agreed that I could begin observing the target for potential transition into her role after the IPO. Three voted no, but only for general concerns. None of them know, or even suspect. I've been shadowing the target for a while now, anyway."

"And the target?"

"The same." Katarina smiled. "All she thinks about is this new project, the tower. I know her every move, and she's happy to let me run the operations. I do it better than she would."

"Our friends will be pleased. They want to know how long it will be."

Katarina had prepared for this question. Russian spies were known for precision, but not patience. "No changes," she said. "Construction should begin soon. The servers will be moved. But I won't get access until after she sells."

"When?"

"Next May, according to plan."

"Some want it done sooner. Some suggest that we…get rid of the target. It could speed things up."

"No, no one needs to die, yet. I've got it under control."

"Can't it move faster?"

"We have to deal with the company going public. Lots of laws, and we don't want suspicions." Katarina had earned Liz's trust. The last thing she needed was someone else meddling with her plans or killing the CEO while stock prices were rising. "I can handle this."

"The prize will be divided evenly whether you use the help or not."

Katarina had long accepted this, but she alone would have access to the data and the power it gave. The door to her building was fifty feet ahead. "I have one request."

"Yes?"

"Monitor the GC, Owen Strand."

"Anything to watch out for?"

"I'm not sure. I think he knows something. He might lead us to any risks."

"Understood. You still have the asset who is close to the target?"

Katarina nodded. She hadn't needed Dylan yet, but she could make use of him whenever the timing was right. He'd hate for Liz to find out about their night together. "He has agreed in principle about the data, but he won't go behind the target's back. He is clueless about the depths of this. He plans to pitch some idea to her about conquering death. He'll at least be an able distraction for now."

"Anyone else of concern?"

"You know about the prince."

"Yes, of course. We have assets in Dubai who are handling it."

"Then I think our pieces are in place."

The man stopped in front of Katarina's apartment building and pulled the door open. "Another good practice!" He spoke in English, with no trace of an accent.

"One day at a time," Katarina replied. "See you again next Friday?"

"See you then." The man gave her a friendly smile and waved. Just a cordial neighbor. "Have a great day!"

14

Liz woke up angry. Intense emotions were no stranger to her, but anger was unusual, especially on a Friday morning. She prodded at the lump of feeling while she sipped her morning coffee and looked out over San Francisco. Clouds were rolling in through the Bay with the day's early light. The water stirred darkly. The Babel office tower across the street was dark. Only one window, Katarina's, had the lights on. Nothing strange there—the woman was an early riser.

Liz's gaze dropped to the streets below. A few cars wound up and down the hills, but most of the city was brushing its teeth. She felt nothing as she watched the sun rising. She felt nothing as she looked around her home. The space was spotless. The concrete walls were bare and the bamboo floors gleamed under the ceiling lights.

No, the source of the anger was not here.

Liz made her way to the shower. She stepped under the water and the thought hit her.

Jake Conrad.

She remembered the conversation, the obstinacy. The fool of a man had turned down enough money to live like a king, just to keep his acres of flat land in the middle of nowhere. He could spend his life in the shadow of her tower. He could thumb his thick beard and watch the corn grow, dwarfed by what she would plant.

As she stepped out of the shower, goosebumps bringing

her skin and her mind to life, the anger raged only harder. She felt lost to it. She stared numbly into the mirror at her pale face and golden hair. The cool of her eyes hid the storm coursing through her. How had this man gotten to her? *How could he not care about the tower, and how could he refuse that much money?*

Liz put on a yellow sweater, grabbed her bag, and headed for the elevator. She left the building, crossed the street, and rode another elevator up. One minute later she stood in her office, looking at the windows of her condo across the way. A smile came to her face. A short commute never got old.

She began scanning the news headlines. Nothing interested her. She pulled up the news brief on Babel. The same reporters were reporting the same stories. Increasing presence in the global market. High expectations for the IPO. Questions about the CEO: *Could she handle the public scrutiny? Would she stay with Babel?*

Her PR people would have another busy day.

She started to open her email, then stopped. It would only bring questions and demands. She needed to start with her own questions. Owen's report had found nothing online, but she couldn't resist: she ran a search for Jacob Conrad.

Over one million hits came up. Nothing on the first page had anything to do with a farmer in Nebraska. Nor on the second page, the third, or the fourth. Apparently a Canadian hockey player named Jacob Conrad was a big deal. She tried searching for Jacob Conrad in Nebraska. Again there was nothing about him.

Every way Liz tried to search, she got zero. Apparently the man didn't exist for purposes of the digital world. She even felt tempted to breach protocol and check the Babel data, but she didn't expect to find much there either. Liz hadn't seen a trace of a Babel near the Conrad farm. She figured the family spoke only English, King James Version.

Liz had failed to learn anything about the farmer when Katarina showed up at her door. She wore a slim black suit and a white silk shirt with one button too many unbuttoned. *To each her own*, Liz thought, as long as Katarina kept doing such a phenomenal job.

"Good morning, Liz." Katarina fiddled with the pen behind her left ear. Liz had never seen her do that before. Maybe she was nervous. "The board meeting is scheduled for this morning, you know."

"Right. Is there a problem?"

"Owen and I have been talking to the directors. Off the record, of course. We don't think you'll have enough votes."

Liz leaned back in her chair, hands folded behind her head. When they'd decided to take Babel public, she'd agreed to let the board have more oversight leading up to the IPO. She'd come to regret that decision a hundred times over. Now she needed nine of the twelve board members to approve either Babel paying for the tower or moving the company to the tower. She couldn't raise enough cash to fund all the construction without selling most of her stake in Babel. Nothing like a multi-billion-dollar project to make a billionaire feel poor. "Who's against me?" she asked.

Katarina named five names, her poker face hinting at a smile. "I have an idea that might get two of them to change their minds."

"Fire away."

"You could try using the tower for Babel's publicity. Let people follow builders from every country working together. It's free marketing. We could put on quite a show. The board would like that."

Katarina had a point. The construction teams from around the world would showcase Babel's technology. The thought made Liz's gut swirl. She'd already been in a tail-spin this morning. It wasn't like her. She needed some time and space to get grounded again. "I'll think about it."

"Of course, we have time. Just think of it as an experiment. Perfect advertising leading up to the IPO. I think this could convince the board to approve company funding for the tower. It is an impressive design."

Liz nodded. She reached for the blueprint, the original draft that Katarina had delivered from Dubai. She unrolled it again, spread it over the desk, and gazed down at the drawing. Her eyes read over the same scribbled words for the tenth time. *This is the last of my vault. Behind the veil, the girl, and the hope—lost and gone forever.*

The vault. The veil, the girl, and the hope.

The same memory came to her: her dad standing in his study, and behind him was a large framed picture of Liz as a girl, with a veil. She rubbed her temples, trying to understand what the message could mean. She felt like she had to see that picture again, even if it meant a trip to Chicago. She wasn't up for another normal day at work anyway. "So do you suggest that we reschedule the board meeting?"

"Yes," Katarina said. "I recommend it. If we're going to pitch this marketing idea, I need a little more time to prepare. Maybe one week?"

"Okay, move the board meeting to next week. I'm going to make a quick visit to Chicago."

15

Liz pulled up in front of her family's old home in the Chicago suburbs. The house matched every other sprawling brick rambler on the block. Daddy had insisted, *keep the façade. A building must fit in its place.* He had been like the house—everything tidy and normal until you looked inside.

She climbed out of the car and moved up the stone path to the front door. It was a fine September day. Blue clouds and a cool breeze rustling the first fluorescent yellow leaves of the two oaks lining the path. But a tunnel of memories enclosed her vision with each step.

She could still see Mom's body lying peacefully in the bed, a year after they'd lost Daddy. After that Liz had sealed up the house and hadn't been back. She could feel the old wound pulsing, the scab ripped off again.

But now she was here, even when Babel expected her to be a million other places. She wanted to figure out Daddy's message about the girl with the veil. Maybe there were more detailed plans, more sketches.

She took a deep breath and turned the handle. Locked, of course. She pulled out her key—the key she'd never managed to take off her key ring—and unlocked the door.

The entry was stale as a tomb, but it wasn't dark. Nothing Daddy designed would ever be dark. The entire back of the little house was glass, and it offered a sweeping view of the city skyline and Lake Michigan. A little bump of a hill, a little trick of design would do that in Chicago. The sun shone into the house like a crystal kaleidoscope around the steel support beams. *Each shaft is like a sunbeam*, Daddy had said. Not even the layer of dust over the furniture or the kitchen counters could dampen the glow of the place.

She slid open the glass sliding doors to her left, walked down the hall, and entered the studio. She went to the desk and glanced over the dusty blueprints still stacked there. They were untouched and unfinished, as if waiting for someone to return.

One design was a university building. Another a museum. None of them a tower. Daddy prized his towers above all. She rifled through the desk drawers, flipping drawings of houses, of schools, of clubhouses and sheds. He'd done so much of this for free, never able to say no. Except to her. *Too busy. Design's due tomorrow. I'll make the next game.*

Liz stepped back from the desk. Her gaze lifted and found the three pictures on the charcoal-painted wall, the only wall of the room that wasn't glass. The picture on the right grabbed her—it was Mom, blonde and beautiful and newly married. It swept Liz back to when her dad died.

Liz still felt the anger. She'd fled from despair and poured herself into work, more intense and unyielding than ever. Her grades improved. A's became A+'s. Her track times were faster. She ran her fastest mile ever.

Harder, harder, harder, she'd thought. *I can overcome this. It's what Daddy would have wanted. Move on. Do something great.*

Liz couldn't bear the sight of Mom then, wearing only black, staying in the house, drinking herself to sleep. Liz had tried to ignore her. She stopped going into the house. She stuck to the garage. She showered in the high school gym.

School, track, garage.

School, track, garage.

Days became weeks. Weeks became months. Fall became winter. Every house on the street but hers had Christmas lights out. It was dark when she returned one Thursday night. She hadn't seen Mom waiting by the garage door until the motion-sensor lights blazed over them, mother and daughter, outside together in the cold. They hadn't spoken in weeks.

"Hey Mom. You okay?"

She wore a faded pink bath robe with little black flowers. She nodded and blinked her puffy eyes. "I'm sorry I've been so out of it."

For once, Liz did not smell liquor on her breath. "We deal with loss in our own way."

"Can we talk?"

"Sure."

The two of them had walked into the garage, Liz's makeshift bedroom and laboratory. Her twin bed sat on the floor in the corner closest to the house—the warmest corner. A table filled the center of the room, with three computers sitting on top of it. Their screens beside each other looked like a battle station. But when they were off and dark, they looked like black holes ready to suck in everything in the room.

Mom sat on the end of the bed and rubbed her bare arms. "It's cold in here. Will you come and sleep in your room tonight?"

Liz sat on the purple beanbag across from her. "I like it here."

Mom scanned the posters and computers and books scattered around. She eyed Liz and opened her mouth in a familiar I'm-your-mother way, but paused. "I saw that piece in the paper about you."

Jax had insisted on making the news with their software. "Which one?" Liz asked.

Mom reached into the pocket on the front of her robe and pulled out a clipping. "It says your translating software could be the next big thing."

"It is."

Her mom smiled weakly. "I'm proud of you…"

Liz had heard that before. It was her mother's wind up to do *real parenting*. "But?"

"I heard you won the mile race at the county meet. Your coach called. He said some college teams have noticed. Your teachers have been calling, too. They're concerned."

"About perfect grades?"

Her mom laughed a little at that. The first time Liz had heard the sound since her dad died. "You've always done well at school."

"So what's up?"

"People think you're working too hard. Not dealing with… You know, it's not normal for a girl who just lost her father."

Normal. The word made Liz's blood boil. "What's normal, Mom? Staying in the house and drinking myself to death?"

Mom did not wince. "I haven't touched anything in two days."

"That's a start."

"This isn't about me."

"Right. This is about making sure you have a *normal* daughter."

"I've never had that. Your father made sure of it." Jealousy tinged her Mom's voice. "Not everyone has a mind like yours.

in bold, block letters:

REGINALD AUGUST TRAMMEL

The scribbled words below were simple.

Build it, please build it.

A sketch of a building filled most of the page. It showed bowed edges at the bottom, pillars like legs stretching to widen the foundation. Unlike the blueprint from Dubai, it showed detailed drawings of the underground mechanics. But the overall motion of the design was the same. Shafts of steel curved up from the wide base and stabbed into the sky like a ladder to heaven.

A small person was drawn at the pinnacle, as if standing on top of the building, leaning over, as if ready to jump.

Liz knew what the person meant. It was her father. And now it was her.

Build it or jump.

Maybe those were the only options for the Trammells. She leaned back in her father's chair, hands covering her moist eyes.

"I will build it," she announced to the empty room, so any ghosts could hear. "No matter what it takes."

16

You have to see this. Swing by my lab?

It was a simple text. A shot in the dark. But Dylan felt desperate to see Liz and show off his idea.

Okay, she'd responded. *Tonight? 10 pm?*

Dylan had cancelled his dinner with students. Liz almost never had time any more for this kind of thing, and he wasn't going to miss the opportunity.

He readied his research station while he waited for Liz to arrive. He loved the space late at night. With the students gone, the high ceiling and concrete floors gave the feeling of a cave, and in the heart of it was the light shining on his work. He'd read enough Plato to feel like a shadow dancing on the cave wall.

His phone buzzed. Liz was outside. Dylan rushed to the front doors of the research building.

Liz stood there in blue jeans and a green sweater. She looked like the same girl Dylan had fallen for back in school.

"I'm so glad you came," he said.

"I just got back from Chicago." Her voice sounded heavy.

"Why'd you go there?"

"I went to the house."

"Oh." Dylan wasn't sure what to say. He didn't want to pry, because he knew what that house meant to her. He'd spent so much time there, working with her and Jax on Babel's early designs. But he'd always known that the place weighed on

Liz. She rarely left her room in the garage.

"I had to go," Liz said. "I found some more details about my dad's design for the tower."

"Where?"

"My dad had some papers hidden where I hadn't seen them before."

Dylan hadn't heard her sound so somber in years. "It must've been hard going back."

"Yeah." Liz stared down at her feet. "I guess that's why I came. I thought it might be nice to see someone who understands."

"I'm always here for you."

She met his eyes. "Thanks, Dylan. I know. But I don't really want to talk about it much... What did you want to show me?"

"Come on, it's amazing." Dylan led her through the empty and quiet building, their footfalls echoing together.

They reached his research station, which had a clean, sterile feel, with a large white table in the center of the room. On the middle of the table sat an enclosed cube of glass, with two holes for gloves so someone could reach the two mice inside.

"This is it," Dylan said, pointing to the mice in the cube. "The first step to living forever."

Liz leaned closer and peered at the mice. "They're cute, cuddling while they sleep."

"Not quite." Dylan reached his hands into the gloves, then gently nudged one of the mice. As the mouse moved, it revealed that the two animals were connected. "See, they're stitched together."

Liz stepped back. "That's awful."

"It's not so bad. We can undo it later. We have a strict ethics code." Dylan motioned to a computer by the wall. "Let me show you what we've found."

Liz followed him to the screen. It was full of biometric details about each mouse, comparing them across two columns.

"This is Roscoe." Dylan pointed to the left column. "He's the old mouse. He's been alive four years, but most mice live only two or three years."

"And the other one?" Liz asked.

"Chip. He's our youngster. Six months old. His blood is pumping in Roscoe's veins. That's one secret to Roscoe hanging around."

Liz moved back to the glass cube and the mice. "What does it do to Chip?"

"Ah, well, he's aging fast. But we'll separate them soon."

"So, you're showing me this because…?"

"Because I think you should make this idea part of your tower. You said you wanted to tackle the world's biggest problems. What's bigger than death?"

"Nothing." Her voice was quiet, her eyes fixed on the mice. "You want to use my tower as a place to…stitch humans together?"

Dylan laughed. "No, not at all. This is just an example with the mice. We can use blood transfusions for humans. It's totally legit, and it's only the beginning. Blood is basic stuff. Our geneticists are matching this with DNA studies. They're making progress on gene design. We can really start to help people live longer."

"It's impressive, I guess," Liz said. "But…you're already doing the work here. Why make this part of the tower?"

"You still need to convince the board about the tower, right? And to convince the world to get excited about it? Well, what better way than a research contest for the holy grail—living forever?"

"It might help. Katarina is also developing a reality TV show to get more attention." Liz leaned against the table, looking down and shaking her head. The room fell quiet.

Dylan hadn't seen Liz so troubled in years. He wondered if it was all about her dad, or if it had something to do with Katarina. Did Liz know that Katarina wanted to make the data accessible? Dylan found himself agreeing more and more with Katarina's idea, and not just because of their night together. Liz didn't need to know about that. It wasn't like a relationship or anything. Katarina was just right—the data shouldn't be kept locked away when it could be used for so much good. They were like modern nobility in Silicon Valley, with a responsibility to use their success for the benefit of the world. But Dylan didn't think there was much chance of Liz allowing it, and now wasn't the time to bring it up anyway.

He made his voice soft, gentle. "Liz, you okay?"

"Yeah." She looked up with moist eyes. "I just…I want to do the right thing for my Dad."

Dylan reached for Liz's hand. She didn't resist. "How better to honor his memory than research about life?"

"Maybe you're right…this is harder than I thought."

He moved closer and slowly wrapped his arms around her. "You've never let anything hard stop you before. You can do this."

She buried her face into his shoulder, her body shuddering lightly.

Dylan held her tight, amazed that this unstoppable and

unreachable girl of his childhood dreams was right here in his lab, crying in his arms. He said what he thought she most wanted to hear.

"You can do this, Liz."

17

Twelve people sat on Babel's board of directors. Seven women, five men. They lined the glass conference table, with Liz at the head, wearing jeans and a red sweater, because it was Thursday. Katarina sat to her right. She had spent the past week laying the groundwork and preparing the presentation. Now Liz just had to nail the delivery. So far so good.

She rose from her boardroom chair. "The tower will captivate the world's attention." The design projected onto the wall behind Liz. "It will be the largest in the world. It will rise almost a mile high, dwarfing the tallest buildings of New York, Dubai, and Shanghai."

Liz glanced at the image. The simple, steep lines of its steel and glass façade were the hallmarks of the architect. *Don't think about Daddy*, she told herself.

"But of course it will be more than a building," Liz said. "This will secure Babel's hold on the market. We'll bring workers from around the world, equip them with Babels, and follow the most fascinating crews. We'll televise it like reality TV. We've consulted with Hollywood and producers. We've tested the idea, and people are going to love it. No one will be able to think about translation—or even about building something epic—without thinking about Babel."

"Why would anyone want to watch you build a tower?" The question came from a grey-haired woman who wore pearls and a stern face: Susan Deschamps, the leader of the board's opposition. She'd never liked Liz much, because after a career climbing the corporate ranks, Mrs. Deschamps expected more respect for tradition.

"We're not just televising construction," Liz said. "We're capturing drama between the workers and their cultures. Imagine welders from Iran and Israel having to work together."

The older woman shook her head. "I thought you wanted to build it, not start a war."

"It will all be carefully monitored. We'll have team-building competitions as outlets for conflict. That brings me to another reason why this is going to be huge hit." Liz took her seat again at the head of the table. She leaned forward, meeting the board members' gazes.

"We're going to tackle the greatest challenge of humankind." She used the words as Dylan had explained it. They were as audacious as they were enticing. "We will invite the world's best scientists—geneticists, biochemists, doctors—and we'll ask them to work on conquering death." Liz noticed looks of surprise and confusion, but she marched ahead. "We'll provide the best research facilities. We'll offer millions for anyone who makes advances. And, of course, they'll be wearing Babels as they work. Can you think of any project people could care more about?"

The room was quiet, until the old lady in pearls let out a snort of dismissal. "It sounds a bit...silly. How much will it cost?"

More questions like hers came.

"Why would anyone believe it's possible?"

"Will this be funded out of the operating budget?"

"You can't use the equity from the IPO for this..."

Liz listened to the questions. She smiled in response, nodding, letting more challenges come. She had learned more than body throws in jiu jitsu. Let your opponent make a full first move before reacting. The conference room eventually grew silent.

"I understand your concerns," Liz said. "We have two options."

They eyed her skeptically.

"First, we start our plan for ad revenue early."

A few of them shook their heads. One man spoke up: "You know the market isn't ready. It's a year away, minimum. The saturation estimates…"

Liz held up her hand. "You may be right. It's a big step for people to start hearing ads from their devices. That brings us to option two." *The only option.* "I will sell my shares in the company to fund construction entirely by myself."

"You can't," one woman said.

A man nodded agreement. "The company needs you. You're our Steve Jobs."

"I will stay with Babel to lead our new business ideas, and as a figurehead for the translation work." Liz motioned to Katarina, who had been sitting quietly at her side. "You've already approved Katarina to take over day-to-day operations. And those operations will continue at the new headquarters."

The business minds gathered at the table did not need much time to process the implications of her proposal. "You would own the building?"

Liz nodded.

A woman asked: "And, what…lease space to Babel?"

"Exactly," Liz said. "But the payment would be nothing more than the agreement to operate exclusively from the headquarters."

A few of the hard stares softened. This was the key to the deal. This made business sense.

Katarina spoke up. "It would cut costs by millions, hundreds of millions over time. Imagine explaining to the shareholders why you turned that deal down."

A few members of the board exchanged glances, heads starting to nod in understanding. "We'll need to see the figures."

"Of course," Katarina said. She walked them through the numbers, an elaborate presentation that she navigated with ease. Her logic was hard to resist.

The oldest man in the room had not broken his gaze away from Liz. He was Paul Fielder, and he had been a CEO before Liz was born. His wrinkled eyes studied hers. "You really think the staff will move to Nebraska?"

She smiled. "Yes, Paul. It may take some convincing at first, and we may lose a few. But they will come. Our people joined Babel because they love exciting ideas, changing the world. This tower will be a phenomenon. A whole new Silicon Valley in one building. Who wouldn't want front row seats to conquering death?"

"You won't be the first to try..." Paul said.

"It's different now." Liz had had her doubts, too, but Dylan had convinced her that the idea was worth trying, or at least worth selling. "This is the first time in history when we have the human genome mapped, *and* when the smartest people in the world can work side by side regardless of their language. Here's the thing. Whether we get someone to live to 150 or not, can't you see how inspiring it will be to try? Babel's translation work is just the beginning. We can't always be a company that does only one thing. We'll take on the biggest challenges humanity faces."

"Sounds nice," Paul said. "But Liz, why do you want to build the tower?"

Liz had prepared well for this question. "When I started Babel, I wanted it to be something different." She looked around the group, playing her audience, giving them the piece of the truth that they wanted to hear. "We're not just another Silicon Valley start-up. With this tower, I want to see if we can build a place that's a world unto itself, a place where people can stay and they can shine. It will have everything anyone could need. Its own schools, a hospital, you name it."

Katarina stood by Liz. "Can you imagine what this pitch could do for stock prices at the opening?"

The board's attention stayed on the design on the wall. The building's base spread wide, like the Eiffel Tower. But it rose from there in block cascades, the edges like steep stair steps.

Liz explained how she wanted the bottom floors to be open and hollow. The lobby would be high above the ground, because this would not be an office building. It would become a home.

The board posed a few questions, but mostly listened as Liz spoke. Her passion for the plan flooded the room. No one could doubt the impressiveness of the design. None of them knew the architect who inspired it.

When Liz finished, Katarina called for the vote. They went around the table. Nine said yes, three said no. But nine was all Liz needed. She would build the tower.

PART TWO

And the Lord came down to see the city and the tower, which the children of man had built. And the Lord said, "Behold, they are one people, and they have all one language, and this is only the beginning of what they will do. And nothing that they propose to do will now be impossible for them."
Genesis 11:5-6

18

Liz sat in a folding director's chair in a cornfield, legs crossed, grey Sunday sweater, blue sky. She faced a reporter named Nancy Drake. Katarina had insisted on the interview and the location. *We need to get out in front of the press. It has to be you. Charm them.*

Nancy Drake was a legend, old enough to be Liz's mother. Her hair had an unnatural blonde glow. Her back was too straight, her face too made up. A coral flower pin adorned her suit lapel.

"You guys ready?" Nancy asked the row of cameramen. They gave her the thumbs up, and she turned to Liz. "Any questions before we start?"

Liz shook her head.

"It'll be streaming live immediately around the world," Nancy said. "That's what the people like. It's real, it's honest." She looked at a guy standing beside a camera man. "Joe, what are the numbers now?"

"About ten million, and rising," he said, glancing down at his tablet. "Over half from outside the country."

Nancy nodded, turning with a smile to Liz. "Impressive. The President rarely draws that much, but I guess everyone with a Babel has heard of you, and that's half the world now." Nancy leveled a more serious look at Liz. "Let's make this good, okay?"

"You're asking the questions."

"Great. Joe, let's get rolling."

The man nodded and held up his fingers. Three. Two. One.

Nancy smiled into the cameras. "Welcome, friends, to western Nebraska. I am Nancy Drake with Global News, and it is my pleasure to be hosting the first, excusive interview with Elizabeth Trammell, the CEO of Babel and the driving force behind what will be the tallest skyscraper in the world." She turned to Liz. "Tell us, Ms. Trammell, how did you first get the idea for this tower?"

"From my Dad." Liz knew at least the first question, and her answer. "He was an architect, and the basic tower design was his. Ever since he passed away, I've wanted to honor his memory." Liz's expression remained calm, unemotional.

"A daughter's tribute to her father. Many of the world's wonders were built to honor a lost loved one. The pyramids, the Taj Mahal, and now your tower." Nancy paused, a show of drama. "But why *here*, with nothing around for miles? You're not from Nebraska are you?"

"Actually, I was born near here, in Arthur, Nebraska."

"What can you tell us about your hometown?"

"It has about a hundred people, mostly farmers. I left when I was eight years old. I grew up mostly in Chicago. We considered building in Chicago, and lots of other locations. We even looked at building somewhere in the ocean, with pylons like a drilling rig. But in the end this place was the best fit."

"Now that's interesting. A skyscraper in the ocean! How did you decide against that?"

"I wanted a place that would be safe from disturbance."

"That's all?" Nancy asked.

"We're also above the largest aquifer in the country."

"What can you tell us about the tower itself?"

"The tower will be unlike anything you've ever seen," Liz said. "It will be self-sustaining, a world unto itself. So it's better not to think about it like a skyscraper. The lobby will be about as high as the fiftieth floor in a normal building. But that won't quite be half way up."

"There've been rumors about this lobby." Nancy gave a conspiratorial look to the cameras. "Some say there won't be a ground floor at all."

"That's right." Liz held up her hands, pressing her fingers together, with the palms expanding outward. "Think of the Eiffel Tower. The base has to be wide to allow the tower to reach higher. And when people come, most will stay. They won't go in and out much, so we won't need a ground floor. They'll have everything they could want right there. They will live in the tower."

"For how long?"

"How long do people normally stay in their own city?"

Nancy laughed. "That's quite the ambition. Are you planning to move in and stay?"

"I am."

"The top floor?"

Liz nodded, for the first time feeling a touch of warmth in her face.

"How high will that be?"

"A mile—twice as tall as anything ever built."

"I can only imagine the view from up there. Now," Nancy spared a glance for the camera, "how much does a building like this cost?"

"Too much, Nancy."

The reporter laughed again. It sounded slightly fake. "How

does that translate into dollars?"

"Around five billion." The words came out casually, honestly.

Nancy's eyes opened wide. "That's nearly your entire fortune, if the estimates are right."

Liz nodded. "I'd build it taller if I had more to spend."

Nancy breathed in deeply, then smiled, as if she liked where this was going. "You know what they say about money. The way you spend it says a lot about you."

"This is important to me."

"Because you could be spending this money so many ways, right?"

Liz shrugged.

Nancy pressed her. "Like feeding the poor, or funding cancer research." She turned to the camera again. "Five billion dollars folks, imagine what you would do with it."

No emotion showed on Liz's face as she gazed back.

"That leaves the big question," Nancy continued. "Why is this tower so important to you?"

"Many reasons."

"Like your father?"

"That's one. But this is for all humanity."

"When people see your tower, when they hear about it, what do you want them to think?"

"I want them to join me."

"That sounds like an invitation." Nancy scooted to the edge of her chair. "Please, tell us more."

"I've traveled the world and talked to people of every nation and culture. What Babel has shown me is that people everywhere feel the same yearning deep inside. It's a sense that this world is not what it could be. Our translation devices are a step in the right direction, bridging language differences and bringing people together. This tower is the next step."

"That's quite a vision. But the world has many towers. How is yours so different?"

"It's taller," Liz joked.

"And?"

"It's what will happen inside the tower that's amazing. Anyone may visit the lower floors to see for themselves. There will be libraries and hospitals and gardens. There will be beauty and excellence and peace."

"You mentioned lower floors," Nancy said, eagerness in her eyes. "What about the upper ones?"

Liz smiled. "No comment."

"How many floors are we talking about?"

"Yet to be determined. But we're counting in hundreds."

"You're quite a saleswoman. Who will be invited?"

Liz fixed her eyes on the camera. "Everyone. I believe the right people will come. The people who care about challenging the status quo. People who want to push the frontiers of the human spirit. My tower will remove the cap that society has placed on us throughout history."

"What cap is that?"

"Everything that holds people back—government and culture and poverty and sickness and fatigue. We will work to solve these limits for our tower residents. No doors will be closed. We are going to assemble the world's greatest minds."

"How will you convince them to come?"

"For starters, I'm pleased to announce that we're opening an exclusive contest to solve the puzzle of aging. We plan to conquer death."

"That's something you don't hear every day," Nancy said.

"Some scientists might be interested...what's the prize?"

Liz leaned forward. "Fifty million dollars." She paused to let it sink in. "There's more information to come, but here's the point. This is just the beginning. We've cracked the problem of language, right? So now we're going to fight back against death and everything else that holds humans back. The possibilities are endless. Maybe next we'll beat gravity by launching into space from the tower. This tower has unlimited potential, because *we* have unlimited potential."

"Fascinating, Ms. Trammell. Can you tell us when construction will start?"

"We break ground tomorrow."

"And people can watch?"

"Absolutely. Babel's website will be streaming the live video feeds constantly." Liz pointed behind them, where lines of temporary construction housing were beginning to fill the landscape. "People have come from all over the world to build this tower. They'll be working side by side, from every culture and language." Liz looked into the camera again, envisioning the millions of viewers like a crowd sprawled before her on the cornfield, a crowd eager to believe in something new and special. "You don't want to miss this," she said. "History has seen nothing like it. Prepare to be amazed."

19

The Crown Prince of Dubai, Nasir bin Muhammad, had exotic tastes. At twelve it was Maserati race cars. At fifteen it was girls; at twenty, academic degrees; twenty-five, buildings; thirty, one building and one girl. She was on the screen before him. Blonde hair and a face like Venus. He wasn't supposed to like this. He was supposed to like veils and dark eyes. He liked her even more.

She said she would build the tallest tower in the world, and his heart fluttered.

She's like me, he thought.

He already planned to buy the company, with the Russian's help, but was that enough? Katarina wanted to take over Babel. She had promised access to the data, but the prince knew better than to trust her. His American intelligence friends had warned him that she was a spy. That would not stop him from using her to acquire Babel.

But now he realized: *Babel needs Liz Trammell.* Shouldn't he try to keep her around? He couldn't buy her, couldn't woo her. But he could meet and impress her. He would have to proceed carefully. She would be watched.

His agents had acquired her personal cell number. He typed an encrypted message: *Saw the interview. Heard about your tower. Mine is bigger.*

A reply came within a minute: *I always win pissing contests.*

He laughed and typed: *Women are not so foul in my country.*

Liz: *Who is this?*
You face many risks.
You must be scared. My tower will be taller.
I fear no man.
I'm not a man.
The prince smiled. He replied: *That is your problem.*
And am I your problem?

The prince wasn't sure how to respond. He glanced up. The stars were countless above his palace courtyard. No one was near. But it didn't feel that way. It felt like this voice—from a woman in a faraway land—had entered his world, amusing him with secret conversation.

He typed: *You want to know me?*
Liz: *Maybe.*
We'll meet in London.
When?
Whenever you'd like. Maybe when you need my help?
It'll be a long wait.
I have much cash. If you need it, we can meet. We can talk.
A pause.
Will you be wearing pink?

The prince laughed again. This Liz was different. *I will find you*, he typed. *You will wear black. You will cover your hair.*
Unlikely.
Not orders, offers. I know things you need to know. And I have funds.
So do I.
I will wait for your text.
Enjoy the wait. Have a long life.
See you when the time is right.

No texts followed. Excitement swirled in the prince's

chest. He began thinking of a way to make this woman, this muse, want to see him. Maybe the American spies could help.

20

"Mom thinks you should sell," Annie said.

"I know." Jake didn't look up at his little sister. He knelt on the dark soil, inspecting the wire fence around the blueberry bushes. He knew what his mother thought. He also knew there was a hole somewhere in this fence.

Probably a rabbit. The most destructive, soft, and innocent-looking creature God ever made. *Other than humans.* The thought made Jake laugh a little.

Annie knelt beside Jake. She poked his side, and he laughed again. "What's so funny?"

"Rabbits," Jake said, "and you."

She smacked her chewing gum, poked him again.

"Quit that and help." He tried not to laugh again. He pointed to the wire. "You see any holes?"

"Only in your head. I was talking about Mom."

"Well, I don't want to talk about her."

"Yeah, we know." She planted herself in front of him, pulled at her ponytail. "Come on, stand up. We need to talk about this."

"I'm trying to fix the fence." But he stood all the same.

Annie looked up at him, now towering above her and smiling. "You know what I think?"

"I'm sure I will soon."

"You're stubborn. I mean, that's nothing new. But they're offering *a lot* of money."

"Land's not—"

"Yeah, I know, land's not for sale. But things are tight around here. I heard what you said to Pops about the corn prices. Not good this year, right?"

Jake gazed back at the fence and spotted a little hole. Just big enough for a rabbit. He bent down to patch it.

"Well," Annie continued. "Have you thought about the rest of us? Grandma has medical bills, and I'm sure Pops will too. They're not getting any younger. And what if I want to go to college?"

Jake sighed as his hands twisted new wire into place on the fence. "I want you to be able to go to the best school you can. We'll make it work."

"Oh yeah? How?"

"You're smart. Maybe you'll get a scholarship."

"*Maybe*? You think that's good enough when someone is offering enough to guarantee it."

"Nothing in life is guaranteed."

"Come on, at least consider her offer."

Jake tied off the last of the wire and stood. He smiled down at his sister. "Maybe for you..."

"You think this lady, Liz Trammell, will come back?"

"I...yeah, probably."

Annie's eyes locked onto his. Her question had caught him unarmed. "Do you think she's pretty?"

He shook his head, trying to hide his expression. Annie could see into him better than anyone—like she had a homing device for anything that ruffled his calm.

She just chewed her gum, studying him, waiting.

"The blueberries were good this year, weren't they?" He poked her playfully in the side and turned toward the house.

"Hey!" She rushed to catch up. "I'm not done with you. You're avoiding the question."

He shrugged. Guilty.

As they walked beside each other, Annie pointed to the west, where the sky looked like a painting. "This Liz, you know, her tower could be beautiful against a sunset like this."

Her tone was of admiration. Jake knew she was baiting him, but he couldn't resist. "It's a fool's errand," he said. "An idol made by man."

"Mom and I listened to her interview. She's making a statement for the world, a monument to potential. Why does that bother you so much?"

"Think about it, Annie. A monument to *whose* potential?"

"Humans, I guess."

"Exactly. This tower's setting up humans like they're God. It's been tried before—to build to the heavens, to prove there are no limits to *our* potential. You know how God responded. He gave the people different languages and scattered them across the earth. So now Liz Trammell has solved the language barrier and will build a tower to our potential, to try to defeat death? It's all pride, Annie. Don't be fooled by it. Whatever the new technology, God is still God. He's the creator and we are the creation. Anytime we try to set ourselves up like God, it ends badly. We do *not* want to be part of this."

"Well then…" Annie let out a little laugh. "Now I know how to wind you up for the Tower of Babel lecture."

Jake grinned and raised his hand like a professor. "You're welcome in my class anytime. It's all about the pride of man. Pride cometh before the fall…pride gets no pleasure out of having something, only out of having more of it than the next man." Jake paused. "Should I go on?"

"I think I got it." Annie's laughter faded into silence. The first sounds of crickets filled the evening, stirring with the distant sound of engines and construction vehicles.

Jake felt sure he was right about pride, but not about Liz. He didn't want to care about Annie's hints. But it was true. He didn't understand women. He knew the Lord and the land. Not women. He sighed. "Alright, tell me what you think about Ms. Trammell."

Annie wore a big grin that stretched the freckles of her nose and utterly disarmed him. "You're not as smart as you think."

He shrugged. "None of us are."

"So... you really wanna know what I think?"

"I'm not going to beg."

"Here's the secret." She stepped closer and spoke in a lower voice. "Liz Trammell is surrounded by people who want something from her. It's like the pretty girls who date old guys for their money, but backwards."

"She has friends."

"You're such an idiot sometimes."

Jake wasn't smiling, but he wasn't mad. His sister was probably right.

"She didn't have to come here by herself," Annie said. "She's a billionaire. She lifts her finger and people do whatever she wants. Come on, Jake, why would she want to see you?"

"Because she wants me to sell my land."

Annie shook her head, without any fading of her freckled grin.

"You think Liz came because she wanted to meet me?"

"Duh. She's intrigued by a man who says no to her."

Jake shook his head. "She's a proud woman. Her lawyer

failed, and she thinks she can't. She came to knock me down."

"Yeah, apparently you're both stubborn," Annie mumbled. "But anyway," she held her arms out wide, "opposites attract..."

Jake ruffled his sister's hair. "Maybe that's why you and I get along so well."

Annie laughed. "Yes, but I'm not letting you off there. What will you think if Liz comes back again?"

"I'll let you know if it happens." Jake didn't know what else to say. Questions like Annie's were the kind that filled his mind but never escaped his lips. Just thinking them made him feel like a hot summer day. It was foolish, though. No use speculating. Better to focus on what was in front of him. One day at a time.

Once they reached the house, the smell of fried chicken drifting from the door, Jake glanced back at the horizon. It was midnight blue above, but a yellowish glow of light had started to pollute the view.

His new neighbors were moving in.

21

Ken Thornburg invited only ten entrepreneurs to his monthly dinners. Much of the group stayed the same from month to month, a top-ten list of Silicon Valley VIPs. Even disruptive industries settled into hierarchy after time.

Three of the regulars were social media titans. Others had revolutionized everyday industries: taxis, airports, hotels, and even laundromats brought into the digital era. Unlike the others, Ken had not started his own company. He'd inherited a fortune and used it well, funding start-up after start-up, hitting a few jackpots. One of those recent jackpots involved fire hydrants, which is why Jackson Wong had the honor of attending the past two dinners.

Tonight's dinner was even more important to Jax, because of his guest, the blonde beside him in the deep bucket seat of his fire red Ferrari. They wound their way up the hill overlooking the valley.

Liz eyed the mansions lining the road. "So you think they'll ask me about the tower."

"Definitely," Jax said. "Ken finds the entrepreneurial mind fascinating. We won't talk much about business. It's more about life and stuff."

Liz didn't answer.

"But your tower has him really intrigued." Jax turned off the road before a wrought-iron gated driveway. "Ken knows all about Babel, and he's impressed with what you're doing."

The car hardly stopped before the gates swung open. Liz studied the hedges lining the driveway. "Anyone with bushes this manicured has a complex."

"I never said Ken was normal."

Liz breathed out a faint laugh.

"Be thinking about how you'll explain Nebraska," Jax said. "No one really buys what you said in the interview. Ken will be dying to know all the little details under the surface of what you told the public."

They pulled up to the front door. Jax gave the keys to a valet, and they walked through immense glass doors into the house. The inside was bare and beautiful, with concrete floors, white walls covered in Jackson-Pollock-like paintings, and a sweeping view over the valley.

A man rushed up to them. Liz noticed he was barefoot.

"Jax!" He pulled Jax into a friendly embrace. Then he turned to Liz. He looked barely older than she was. He wore jeans and a plain grey t-shirt. She had learned not to give much weight to first impressions, but he was exceeding her expectations.

"Elizabeth Trammell," he said, extending his hand. "It is a pleasure to finally meet you. I'm Ken."

She shook his hand, cool and solid. "Call me Liz. Thanks for inviting me."

"Of course, of course. I can't wait to hear about what you're up to." He turned and motioned for them to follow.

The wall to Liz's left was nothing but glass. Instead of chairs and couches, the vast space had little sitting areas with mats and beanbags.

Ken stopped before sheer, Japanese-style doors. "Shoes off, please. We want everyone to feel comfortable here.

Anything you want, just tell me. Can I start you with a drink?"

Jax asked for kombucha.

"Vodka martini," Liz said.

Ken smiled and touched his watch a few times. He looked to Jax. "I've upgraded the house with Lawrence's software. Just watch."

In moments a waist-high robot with shelves on its head rolled up. Two drinks sat there—a bottle of kombucha and, apparently, a vodka martini.

"Go ahead," Ken said, "try it."

Liz took the martini from the robot and sipped it.

"Good, right?" Ken didn't wait for a response. "Just wait till dinner. We're having truffled sea bass. All my fish are caught by my fisherman, Marco, off Baja. Very sustainable, very delicious."

He led them through the doors to a very small room. The table was sunken into the floor, so that the floor formed a bench around it. Seven vaguely familiar guys sat around it. They stopped talking and eyed Jax and Liz as they entered. Their gazes stuck on Liz.

"Surprise guest!" Ken announced. "You all know Jax, and I've invited Elizabeth Trammell to join us. Jax, do you want to introduce her, or shall I?"

Jax smiled. "It's all yours."

"As most of you know," Ken began, "Liz and Jax founded Babel together. We've had Jax before as a coding guru, but I thought Liz would be a great addition tonight. Our focus is building the future, and no one is building something quite like Liz. You all know about her tower, right?"

The group nodded. "Tallest tower in the world," said one of them. He wore a black turtleneck and a mocking grin.

"Exactly." Ken stepped forward and motioned to two empty seats on opposite sides of the table. Jax headed to one, so Liz took the other.

The group fell into pockets of small talk, and Liz introduced herself. The guy beside her seemed pretty normal, with curly brown hair and gentle eyes.

"Sam Woolrich," he said. "We met once before, at a conference on coding and diplomacy."

"Oh, right." Liz felt bad, she did not remember him at all. "How's your company doing?"

"Well, the one I had started when we last met did great. It's Narwal—the geotracker for the whaling industry."

"Remind me, did you sell it?"

"Yeah, I sold it to a big oil company. Now I'm working on something similar for the farming industry. Early phases, but promising."

Liz sipped her martini as he spoke about the innovative ways people could use modified corn species. She found it interesting. Her tower would be in farm country after all.

The tenth dinner guest arrived late. It was another woman—slightly older than the rest of the group. She took the open seat beside Liz. After a brief hello, the woman turned her back to Liz and spoke cheerfully with the man to her other side.

The sea bass arrived, along with a second martini. Liz passed and asked the robot for wine instead, "something red, you pick." The robot seemed as pleased as a robot could be.

Ken stood and raised his glass—something green and bubbly. "Thank you all again for joining tonight. This marks my seventeenth monthly dinner. So I'd like to raise a toast to another rich discussion. May we grow tighter and brighter together—cheers!"

Everyone clinked glasses and drank.

"Tonight's main topic is building the future. I introduced Liz Trammell earlier, but Liz, would you mind leading us off? Tell us more about your tower, and what it means for our world?"

Liz nodded and set her drink down.

Ken smiled graciously. "Remember, this is among friends. Whatever is said here stays here."

And stays in the Babel servers. Liz gave a faint smile to Jax, grateful for the heads up about this. She didn't want to say too much. "As many of you know, I'm building a tower. And as you may have heard, it's going to be tall."

The group laughed.

"As for what it means for the world, well, two things for starters," she said. "We can build faster and stronger than ever before. Only the raw materials have to be shipped. We're going to forge it all together right there at the building site, 3D printing most of it. The second point is that we can build this anywhere. I wouldn't be surprised to see more towers popping up in rural areas around the world, instead of just in cities."

"But why?" It was the arrogant-looking guy in the turtleneck. "If you could build anywhere, why build in the middle of nowhere?" Liz had learned from Sam that he was Lawrence Clint, who had coded the latest search algorithm upgrades. Some said he was as good as Jax. His grin suggested he knew this. "Why not here in the valley?" he asked. "Why not New York?"

"Too expensive, too crowded."

Lawrence beamed. "I watched your interview. I'm sure many of us did. We know you're not worried about the cost.

Why Nebraska?"

Liz felt all the eyes on her. For some reason the face of Jake Conrad appeared in her mind. She couldn't imagine anyone who would have been more out of place at this dinner. But she almost felt like she'd enjoy getting to know him more than this Lawrence guy. "I could give a hundred reasons," she said. "You heard them during my interview."

"I heard a nice PR pitch. But seriously, Nebraska?"

"You all make lots of decisions," Liz said. "For the big ones, doesn't it come down to following your gut?"

"For a multi-billion dollar project?" Ken asked, brow raised.

"There's also the nation's largest aquifer underneath," Jax piped up. "The land is wide open. And the governor gave us freedom to do what we want."

"I'm asking you, not your spokesperson." Lawrence's eyes had not shifted from Liz. "I don't believe in gut instincts. We all know the stomach can't think. You want us to just nod along while you throw good money after bad ideas. The world expects more from us." He paused. "So I'll ask again: *why Nebraska?*"

My father, she thought. The edges of her vision went blank. The room wobbled a little. She saw only Lawrence's sharp, severe face and his cap of jet black hair. She was not going to think about her father now.

"Take it easy, Lawrence." Ken had leaned forward, his hands folded. "This isn't an interrogation."

Lawrence's gaze turned to the host. "You knew she'd face questions like this. We have to challenge each other if we're going to keep building great things. Look, I like the tower idea. But it has to serve our world. I've seen too many of us run

around chasing our own pet projects. It gives us a bad name."
He turned to Liz, eyes intense. "You understand?"

Liz kept a straight face. Now she knew the guy's game. He
was the enemy. He was the force that grinds down freedom
and independence and joy and creation. He was like the men
who rejected her father's designs. He was a murderer of
ideas—all in the name of benevolence and the common good.
How dare he achieve his own dreams and then tell her there
was something wrong with hers. She would *not* let him push
her around.

"I understand you." She pronounced each syllable
deliberately, slowly. "I didn't come here to explain myself. I am
building the world's tallest tower. It will be a monument to
human potential. It will change the world. And I want it in
Nebraska. My motives are my own."

The room was perfectly silent. Lawrence took a long drink.
Ken took a bite of sea bass.

Liz gazed around at the others. A few uncertain smiles.
"Something drives us to where we are," Liz said. "We can try
to explain it, to rationalize it. But I know that, deep down, the
fire inside of me defies explanation. I will not sell myself short,
and neither should you."

"I ain't sellin' anything short." A large man with small
glasses patted his chest. "It's just about the money for me. I'm
a businessman and down-home man, a simple man. No one
wants you to waste your cash."

"Money is not simple, Cody," Lawrence said, then turned
back to Liz. "You must know what drives you or it will
consume you. Listen, I've tried what you're doing, pretending
it can't be explained. It's nothing but running from your
demons. It doesn't work."

"She has no demons," Jax said. "Maybe you're just jealous of the attention she's getting."

"Oh? No demons?" Lawrence grinned at Jax. "How about her father? The failed architect, Reg Trammell. Didn't he have something to do with a tower?"

"Hey," Jax warned. "That's out of bounds."

"Just because he killed himself?" Lawrence taunted. "Couldn't handle the pressure...maybe like his daughter?"

Jax did not hesitate. He hurled his glass straight at Lawrence's head. The man ducked the missile and surged to his feet. "You—"

"*Enough!*" Ken slammed his fists on the table. "Both of you. Get out. Now."

"What about *her*?" Lawrence growled.

"Lawrence." Ken spoke the word like a death sentence. "That's enough. Jax, I apologize for my friend's rudeness, but you have crossed the line. You have to leave now."

Lawrence shook his head, muttering "waste of time," and sauntered out.

Jax began to leave but paused behind Liz.

"Liz, you are welcome to stay," Ken said. "Please, Lawrence probably just had too much to drink. The conversation will be much more cordial."

Liz carefully folded her napkin and set it on the table. "Thank you. But it's late."

Ken smiled warmly. "You're welcome back anytime."

"Thank you." Liz rose and walked out with Jax. Her arm curved through his, leaning on his sturdy support. Her thoughts were years in the past and miles away. She couldn't feel Jax's heart thumping hard beside her.

22

Katarina sat at her desk, staring at the screen. She'd gotten her inbox down to zero again. All messages responded to and filed for the day. She turned to the stack of purchase orders next. Any contracts for more than a thousand Babel units had to be signed by the CEO, which meant Katarina had to review them and sign on Liz's behalf. She flipped through the pages, signing each one on the bottom. Deals in Iran, Mongolia, and Indonesia. They were going to need more chips from the factory in China. She went back to the computer and dashed off an email to the factory manager. She glanced at the clock. 12:24.

She'd been at it for five hours straight since her day's last meeting. At last she could step away.

The office was perfectly silent as she rose and turned to the wall of glass. She loved the way the city looked at night, with its few remaining lights dotting the horizon and glimmering in reflection over the water.

She slowed her breathing, making it deeper. She reminded herself, as she had to after every day, that this boring work served an immensely important purpose. She had earned Liz's trust and the board's trust the hard way. No tricks. No shortcuts. Just years of grinding through the work, and doing it well, making Babel's operations hum.

She was getting so much closer to what she wanted. She'd have unique access to the data. She'd have so much power that even the one calling the shots, the Russian president himself, would have to take her calls. And with that leverage, she would protect herself in a way her parents never could. Their reward for a lifetime of service was being abandoned after they were caught as spies and executed. The data would be her insurance policy. If she alone could access it, she would become indispensable.

She jumped at the distant sound of footsteps. Then she laughed a little inside at her moment of fear. No one in Babel's office was a threat to her.

As the footsteps came closer, she could make out the familiar click against the floor. It had to be Owen. Only he would be here this late, wearing his wingtips.

He showed up in the doorway moments later. His black skin looked particularly dark against his slim-fitting khaki suit. He wore a bright blue tie and a leather messenger bag over his shoulder. Katarina might have found him attractive if she didn't despise his nosy meddling with her business and constant warnings about whatever securities laws he worried Babel could risk violating.

"Hey Kat," he said. "Got a minute?"

She put on her practiced smile. "Sure, come on in. I was just wrapping up."

"Another late night." He took a seat in front of her desk as Katarina sat opposite him. "What's keeping you busy?"

"The usual." Her smile didn't budge. "What can I help you with?"

"I thought Liz was going to be in today, but I never saw her. Will she be around tomorrow?"

Katarina shook her head. "She changed her plans and left this morning for Nebraska. She'll be out through Sunday."

"Again?"

"I think it's going to stay this way for a while. You know how much Liz cares about the tower."

"Yeah, but it's not exactly a slow time around here. I guess that leaves a lot of work on your shoulders, right?"

Katarina shrugged. "Same as you."

"Just doing our part." Owen smiled. "Do you know why Liz decided to go back to Nebraska so soon?"

"I'm not sure," Katarina said. "She seemed tired this morning and said she'd been out late for a dinner last night. I tried to talk to her about the IPO, but she just wanted to know if I'd learned anything about that farmer."

"And?"

"Nope, haven't learned a thing. It's not a big deal though. Their farm slowed down construction a bit because the crews had to re-route the access road around them, but now things are moving along fine."

Owen laughed. "Liz just can't stand that the farmer wouldn't sell. And I get it. I tried too. He's very frustrating."

"How so?"

"He doesn't talk much. He wouldn't even engage with me. I could have offered him a billion dollars and I bet it wouldn't have made a difference."

"Very odd."

"Yeah, the only interesting thing I found after some digging is that the farmer's grandfather had a reputation for being the same way during the Vietnam War. He had a long military career."

Katarina was suddenly intrigued. Her agent had warned her to be on the look out for former military involved in any way with the tower. There was some intelligence about government interest, especially if they moved the data servers. "What's the grandfather's name?" she asked.

"Isaiah Conrad."

She made a mental note to look into it. "Okay, well, anything else you came by to discuss?"

"Yeah, just one thing. I saw that the Dubai Sovereign Wealth Fund arranged to buy more shares. It seems odd. Know what it's about?"

Nosy Owen. He needed to stay focused on his own issues. "No clue," Katarina said. "Why is it surprising though? They have more cash than they know what to do with, and our valuation keeps going up."

"You're probably right. I just need to keep an eye on this for reporting purposes. With the IPO coming up, we have to inform the government of any major foreign acquisition."

"Got it. I'll keep you posted." Katarina would do no such thing. But maybe she'd keep a closer eye on this Conrad family. She could have cameras installed. It could even give her an excuse to test how far Dylan would go to help her. He still seemed like the best tool for prying into Liz's secret method for accessing the data. Jax certainly wasn't going to help. Or Owen. She suddenly remembered he was still standing there. She caught his eyes. "Anything else?"

"Nope, that's it. Thanks for talking, and sorry for holding you up so late." He gave a friendly wave. "See you tomorrow?"

Katarina smiled. "Another day in paradise."

23

The dead tree needed only a few more good hits. Jake wiped the sweat off his brow and let the afternoon breeze cool his skin. He glanced up at the branches against the sky. They were barren, but the nearby trees were full of leaves and ripe apples. A good harvest.

But not this tree. He aimed the axe at the trunk and steadied himself. He swung hard. Five swings later he heard the crack deep in the wood. He stepped back as the tree began to lean and fall. It crashed with a thud.

All went quiet. Jake stood still, axe in hand.

"Ever heard of a chainsaw?"

Jake jerked toward the voice.

Liz. Hand on her hip, smiling.

His already quickened pulse raced faster. How long had she been watching?

"I work with my hands," he said.

"It looks more like an axe to me."

"Is there something I can help you with?"

"I think you know why I'm here. Please, take your time."

He knelt down and picked up a shovel. He began digging a circle around the thick stump, wide enough to get to the deeper roots.

He dug for ten minutes, then paused for a drink of water. He glanced to Liz. She was still watching.

He picked up his pickaxe and started in on the roots. He

felt her gaze on him, but he managed to work a while longer before turning to Liz again.

This time, when their eyes met, she approached him. "Mind if I help?" she asked.

He couldn't resist a look of surprise. This would be interesting. He nodded to a second shovel on the ground. "There's plenty of dirt to move."

She picked up the shovel and started digging. Jake watched in disbelief as she shoveled scoop after scoop of black earth from the growing hole. Then he went back to it.

They worked on opposite sides at first. They came closer and closer as they removed the last of the dirt by the underground trunk. The sun was setting.

"That should be enough," he said.

He smiled as Liz climbed out of the small pit. Her jeans and sweater were filthy. Her face showed streaks of sweat through the dirt.

"Thanks for the help."

"I can work with my hands, too." She handed him the shovel. "What's next?"

He pointed to his tractor. "Drag it out and burn it."

The sky darkened as he tied a chain around the stump, climbed on the tractor, and pulled away, yanking the last of the roots out of the ground. Liz followed him on foot to a pile of wood by the river.

He added the stump to the pile and lit it, wondering how long Liz planned to stay. They stood beside each other as the flames licked up the edges of the wood.

Minute by minutes the fire spread and rose into a red and orange blaze as tall as they were. The warmth of it wrapped around them, as if separating them from the world outside this conflagration.

"This night," Liz said, her head tilted to the stars above. "It's so quiet. It's beautiful."

"It is," Jake said. "I'm glad you came."

Liz faced the fire again and rubbed her hands together.

"How are your hands?" he asked.

"They'll be fine. Maybe a few blisters."

"You know, you're not so bad," he said, "for someone from Silicon Valley."

"I was born near here."

He looked to her, surprised. Her face was aglow in firelight, and it held his gaze like a magnet. He'd never been so transfixed by anyone.

"So I guess we're stuck with each other," she said, meeting his gaze evenly.

"Is that so bad?" he asked.

She smiled, revealing nothing, and slowly walked off into the night.

24

Veruca knelt beside the fire hydrant, gleaming under the bright Palo Alto sun. She ran her hands over the iron surface. It showed no damage. No reason for the camera to go out.

This wasn't her normal job, but she needed fresh air. She'd worked three straight nights for Jax after he had returned from some meeting and said they'd picked the engineer who would lead the construction. He had set the final deadline for the contest with Roger and Beck, the FireSpy group. They had four more hours before they would each present their best ideas for the tower. One million dollars for the winner.

Veruca had come up with plans for stronger steel, a deeper foundation, and other little improvements. But nothing seemed like a million dollar idea. She knew her competition. Beck and Roger were brilliant in their own ways; they'd have something good. She needed to do something better. Not for her, but for Jax.

Her blood rose at the irony of it. Jax was diverting his own company's time and money for Liz Trammell's pet project. Veruca had seen it over and over. Everything Jax did was for Liz. All his software, all his fortune, all his brains—he'd sacrifice all of it on the altar of Liz.

It had been a year since she met Jax, just a block away from this hydrant. When she'd shown up for her first interview, she'd been surprised by how short he was. With a reputation as big as his, she figured he'd be six feet tall or more. He was almost a foot shorter than that. And his thinning black hair was no match to Veruca's flame red curls. But Veruca didn't care much about how he looked. It was his mind that attracted her.

In the interview, he'd sat perched on his stool, studying her across the table. His eyes had shown their ever-playful amusement. His first words: "I don't hire redheads."

"I think you'll make an exception for me," she replied.

"What's seventeen squared?"

She answered instantly: "Two hundred eighty-nine."

"When did you write your first code?"

"I was nine."

"How long before that code changed the physical world?"

"Is there any difference between physical and digital?"

He had paused then. She'd felt his stare prying into her. It had been the longest twenty seconds of her life. "Come here," he'd finally said, turning to the thin computer screens on his desk.

She'd walked around the desk and stood beside his stool. Complicated code filled the screens. He slid a keyboard over to her. "Follow my lead."

The next hour had changed her life. Jax had led her through a few simple coding patterns. She hung with him. Then he added a dimension, then another. Each step blew her mind, but she managed to keep up. By the time they finished, the two of them, working side by side, minds melded, had reverse engineered the security algorithm at the heart of Jax's new company.

Jax had smiled at her and said, "That was good."

They had produced amazing work together in the year since that interview. Veruca's feelings had only grown, but Jax

131

treated her as nothing but a business partner—a very efficient and sharp engineer, but nothing more.

Maybe that would change when Liz moved to Nebraska, away from Jax. Veruca needed to help with the tower for that reason alone. The million dollar prize would be icing on the cake.

Her attention turned again to the hydrant and its faulty camera. The lens was almost impossible to see at a glance. She had to lean close to the thick bolt screwed in at the top of the hydrant. It was solid steel, connected to the valve stem below, running from the underground pipes. The lens seemed fine. The problem had to be inside.

Veruca pulled out her heavy wrench. With her red hair cascading over the operation, she began to loosen the bolt. Each turn was careful and practiced. A stray twist could break the lens. Finally the bolt slipped off, and she studied it in her hand. The little camera that would forever change national security.

But this one still wasn't working. She found a new bolt with an embedded lens in her bag. She tried it on the hydrant. Still no activity. It had to be the power source.

She wiggled the whole hydrant in its place. It was too loose, as if disconnected from its base. And something was rattling inside. The force of the water line underneath powered the camera, so if anything wasn't connected, that would explain the problem.

She lifted the casing at the top of the hydrant. Inside there should have been a smooth metal connection running from the ground to the cap, but instead there was corrosion and a few loose bits. She tilted the fire hydrant from one side to the other, and the parts shifted with it. They should have stayed steady, centered. They should have counterbalanced the motion.

Veruca dropped the wrench and stood.

Counterbalance.

That was the key, the million-dollar idea. A tower that was a mile tall would sway too much in the wind, regardless of the foundation. It needed a counterweight high in the tower—something that would shift the opposite direction when the wind blew the tower one way or another. It would have to be huge, with enough mass to pull the building back toward equilibrium when it leaned.

She dashed off a note for someone to replace the pipe inside the fire hydrant and hurried back to the FireSpy office. The idea poured out of her into a design—immense weights of steel plates suspended from the ceiling of a high tower floor by a series of cables. And like the hydrant, a connection to pipes deep underneath the tower, stabilizing it from top to bottom. It would require a few exterior changes, but it would work.

She scanned several studies of counterbalances. She found examples in other skyscrapers, the largest in Taipei 101. But this would have to be far bigger, over 1,000 metric tons, like 1,000 cars strung on cables a mile above ground. Poles would have to extend out from the tower at steep angles to suspend all the weight, to balance how much the tower might sway in a Nebraska wind, even a tornado.

She sat back and admired her sketch. She couldn't wait to show Jax.

25

"I can't believe this pollution." Dylan eyed the overflowing trashcan beside him. It was foul stuff. Empty food containers, a few used needles, and even a prophylactic used by someone in a recent escapade. A needle had fallen out on the ground in front of a fire hydrant under a streetlight. Certain parts of San Francisco just weren't worth visiting anymore. It was freedom gone bad.

"You should move to Nebraska," Katarina said, her Russian accent thick. She could hardly be seen in the night, wearing all black, snug yoga clothes, with the hood of her sweatshirt up.

Dylan laughed. He'd take the worst of San Francisco over empty cornfields any day. "I'll visit," he said. "But this is home. How about you?"

"I'll move there if the title is right."

"You think Liz will be okay with you as CEO?"

"Why not? What do you Americans say? Better the devil you know?"

"I guess so…"

"I'm already doing most of the job. I make sure the company stays on track for the IPO. I manage our teams, analyze our inventory, approve our suppliers. It all keeps stock prices high so she can build her tower."

"Sounds like a win-win." Dylan paused, feeling a bit awkward. This was the first time he'd seen Katarina since their night together. "So, why did you want to meet?"

Katarina waited before answering, as a group passed in front of them on the sidewalk, talking and laughing and obviously drunk. "I need your help."

"Is it about the data?"

"That's part of it."

"You still want to make it public?"

"Yes, and we're getting closer to that. Liz has agreed to move the servers out of their desert stronghold and into the tower."

"But you know she'll keep it locked away there, too."

"That's fine for now," Katarina said. "What I'm worried about is the transition. Hundreds of engineers and workers are involved in the tower's construction. They're building a whole new security system for the servers, but that creates risks. Who exactly will set up the system? What if someone tries to get access to exploit the data? Imagine what they could do—sell the data, blackmail, you name it."

The word *blackmail* sounded odd in her accent. Dylan had worried about that exact thing. That's why it was better to just make the data available to everyone. But it wasn't his decision. "Have you talked to Liz?"

"Of course. She says she trusts the new chief engineer. His name is Hunter Black. Jax helped her pick him, but I have reasons to believe Mr. Black is a risk."

"Why?"

"He used to work in the government. His resume said it was the State Department, but you know that's often a cover for the CIA. And his engineering work was in places like Tehran and Moscow. I think he might still be an agent. You know how much the government would like to get its hands on Babel's data."

Dylan leaned back, considering the conspiracy theory. "I guess it's possible. Why are you telling me all this?"

"Wouldn't you want to protect Liz?"

"Yes, but I'm not really involved with the data. I'm just helping design the research contest. Why not talk to Jax or Owen? They talk to Liz more than I do."

"I've tried. Jax said he picked the engineer, and he's not worried about it. Owen said he understood the risk, but he defers to Liz. You know he'd never challenge her."

"If they're not worried, why should I be?" Dylan knew Liz wasn't going to let her guard down about the data, and he doubted the government would really try to hack its way in.

"The government has lots of surveillance, like phone call recordings and emails. But we have recordings of almost every conversation in the developed world. The Feds can't stand it when someone has information they don't have. You know how many times we've turned down their requests for Babel data?"

"I saw the story earlier this year about the murder investigation."

"Yeah, and remember the headline: *Killer Goes Free After Babel Refuses To Turn Over Data.*"

"That looked pretty bad," Dylan said.

"The prosecutor talked to the press. He probably would have lost the case anyway, but he blamed us. People got over it. They want their own data private, too. But the government didn't get over it, because that's just the tip of the iceberg. They want the data for lots of noble things: stopping terrorism, money-laundering, *and*...anyone who's against the party in power."

"I see."

"We turned the FBI down seven times in just the past month."

"If they really want the data, can't they find a way to get it? Issue a warrant or something?"

"It would be a PR nightmare. They might do it if they had to, but I think they're trying to find another way to access it. Some way that nobody knows about."

Dylan shook his head. She was probably right. If any group had exclusive access to the data, it gave too much power. Better to spread the knowledge. Make everyone equal. "This is why Liz should just make the information public."

"Which she won't, but I'll be able to do it if I become the CEO."

"You get access just by being CEO?"

"Yes, through the board of directors. The company's data encryption can be bypassed by nine of the twelve directors. We set that up a year ago. I suggested it, because otherwise what happens if Liz or Jax die? They were the only ones who can access it. So if they were gone...?"

A chill coursed down Dylan's spine. Katarina sounded so casual about it. "How does the board get access?"

"They all show up at the data center, and nine retina scans later, the CEO and the board can access it. Liz agreed with it as a backup plan to let the board override the system and get to the data."

Dylan had mixed thoughts. Maybe he should have told Liz weeks ago about what Katarina had said. But...if it was just company politics leading the data to be released, would that be so bad? It's not like it would hurt Liz. He turned to Katarina. "It sounds like you don't need my help."

"Unless the board doesn't agree. Then I'd need to figure out Jax's code. Any ideas?"

Dylan remembered what Liz had mentioned at his lab, about her DNA. He started to tell Katarina, but something in him resisted. "Not really," he said.

"I figured." Katarina leaned back and sighed. "It's too bad, because as long as Liz is the only access point, she could be a target."

"A target?"

"Yeah, because like I said, if she's gone, then the board can override the system. Owen and I told her she should get a security detail. It's not unusual for a person in her position. But she wouldn't agree."

It was true. Dylan couldn't stand the idea of Liz being at risk. Maybe...he should tell Katarina. It would probably be safer for Liz if access to the code required her being alive. "You know, now that I think about it, Liz mentioned that Jax uses her DNA to store data. The code might have something to do with that. If we let that idea spread a little, it could keep Liz safer, right?"

"Fascinating." Katarina tapped her lips, thinking. "You're right. But how would the DNA be used?"

"They could do it a lot of ways. Maybe Jax embeds a unique encryption code in the DNA?"

"If that's true, then you're right. It would keep Liz safer. Could you look into it more?"

"Okay... But you're the one who works with them. There's not much I can do."

"Anything would help." Katarina was quiet, staring ahead. "One other thing. You know about the farmer in Nebraska?"

"The one that won't sell his land?"

"Yes. Something about him doesn't make sense. He wants us to think he's a simple farm boy who doesn't want to leave home. But no one's that simple. Maybe he's working with the Feds or someone else."

"I don't buy it. Liz said he's just stubborn."

"Liz finds him interesting," Katarina replied, a touch of annoyance in her voice. "Apparently she visited him one day and helped him with digging or something. People at the tower said she returned covered in dirt. Can you believe that? She's made me look for every scrap of information I can find on Mr. Conrad."

"And?"

"That's the thing. I've basically found nothing. There's zero trace of him online. He's never had a credit card. Never had a passport. Not even a birth certificate. It's possible that he's legitimate. Home birth, homeschooled, and that's it. But I doubt it."

Something about Katarina's idea didn't add up as Dylan thought back to what Liz and Owen had said about the farmer. But he also couldn't make sense of why Liz would have helped the guy with digging. "What about the family? Weren't they there before?"

"Bingo. That's what got me worried. I did some research on the grandfather. He fought in Vietnam, won a purple heart. It's not certain, but some of his background suggests CIA. What if the government is using its old connection with him to monitor something from their farm?"

"I don't know…" The whole thing seemed like a stretch. "What are you planning to do about it?"

Katarina tapped a small package on the bench between them. "I want to monitor the farm—to protect Liz. I got these cameras to place around there. They look like flecks of dirt, undetectable, and they'll show us whoever comes and goes. Think you could visit and stick them in good places?"

"Me?" Dylan was shaking his head. "No, I'm not going to Nebraska."

"Suggest it to Liz. Tell her you'll try again to buy the land. She'll agree. She's spending a lot more time out there, and she's fascinated with the guy. I've never seen her so driven to learn about somebody, and she's met with world leaders. Just don't mention the cameras."

Dylan had to laugh at the thought. "So I just say, *Hey Liz, do you want me to visit that farmer about selling his land?* That's your idea?"

"That's it. Trust me."

Dylan didn't like it. He took a deep breath. "What's in it for me?"

"This buys us more time. I need to figure out who's trying to access the data. Oh, and I think Liz has a crush on this guy. So you may want to check out your competition."

"Liz is like a little sister," Dylan said, his reddening face thankfully hidden by the night.

"Right...and you wouldn't mind in the slightest if she found out about us?" Katarina's voice sounded like she was smiling.

Dylan swallowed. "She wouldn't care."

"Well let's keep it between us for now, okay?"

"Agreed."

She nudged the package closer to him. "The cameras are tiny, won't be noticed. Just stick them on the front porch and anywhere else that makes sense. We'll see whoever comes and goes."

"You really think this will be good for Liz?"

"Absolutely. It's possible the farmer is just a boring guy that Liz happens to find interesting. But it's also possible he's trying to cover up something."

Dylan looked again at the pile of trash and the fire hydrant beside their bench. The city had so many messes. Now the tower was creating messes, too. He'd never imagined himself hiding cameras around somebody's home, but he'd also never thought Liz would be at risk. It was just cameras...

He turned to Katarina again. "Okay," he said. "I'll do it."

"Thank you." She leaned closer. The lines of her face were soft and seductive in the shadows. "Thinking about inviting me over again tonight?"

26

Jake gazed up at the dead apple tree. The third he'd lost this year. He rubbed his hands over the crisp, dry bark. No bugs, no worms, just rot. The exact same thing had taken the others.

It wasn't lack of water, he knew that. Good apples required good water, and his irrigation and filtration system meant only the best for the orchard. It wasn't the soil, either. He knelt down and rubbed it between his fingers. The brownish dirt crumbled in his hand. The color and texture hadn't changed in his lifetime.

It had to be the heat. He'd never seen a summer this hot, or last this long. September should have brought more cool mornings. It hadn't.

And now another tree had to be pulled out. He grimaced at the work before him. First he'd chop it down. Then he'd split the wood. Then came the hard part: removing the stump.

A smile spread across his face. He still felt like it was a dream when Liz had come and helped with the last tree. She hadn't contacted him since, but he hadn't stopped thinking about her. Now even a dead apple tree was making him smile. Part of him hoped beyond reason that she'd suddenly show up again to help, as if felling apple trees was his invitation to her. But he knew better.

He'd be on his own with this one. Most of the time, he didn't mind working alone. He preferred it. It's just that some jobs were better with four arms than two, especially if two of those arms belonged to Liz Trammell. But he could handle the tree himself—tomorrow, after a good breakfast.

He turned back toward the house. The sun had just dropped below the horizon. The sky before him lit up in red and purple streaks. It was beautiful, except for the cranes stabbing into the sky, dipping and turning and rising. He let his eyes get so lost in the wonder of it that he didn't notice the motorcycle parked in front of the house until he was almost on top of it. He read the name on it: *Ducati*. The gleaming black machine seemed utterly foreign.

His gaze lifted to see a man talking to his mother on the porch. They were both smiling, laughing.

"Jake, come here!" his mom said. "You've got to meet Dylan."

No, Jake thought, *I don't have to meet Dylan*. But the two of them blocked the way through the front door.

Dylan held out his hand. "Great to meet you, Mr. Conrad. Your mother is marvelous." She giggled at that. "I'm Dylan Galant."

Jake nodded.

Dylan paused, waiting for him to say something. When he didn't, Dylan continued. "Your mother invited me to stay a while longer, but I just wanted to see your place. It's become quite the legend in my circles."

"We make legends of what we don't understand," Jake said.

"I guess we do." Dylan smiled. "Well, I'd heard your grandfather was sick. I'm a doctor connected with the tower, so now we're like neighbors and I thought I'd pay a visit."

Jake held a straight face. Pops had a simple cold. He didn't need a doctor. And how did this guy know about it?

"I brought some medicine with me. Your mother has the details. It should help him recover quickly." He reached into the pocket of his leather jacket and produced a little white card. "This has my contact information. Call me if he has any setbacks, okay?"

Jake took the card, eyeing it suspiciously. He knew he wasn't supposed to judge a man based on his looks, and really not at all, but he didn't like this guy. He felt like he could never like this guy, but he'd pray for God to help him. Eventually.

"Oh, thank you again, Dr. Galant," his mother said. "We will call. And please, next time you're here, you must stay for dinner."

"I'd love that," Dylan said. He gave her a friendly embrace. "Bye, Ms. Conrad." He glanced at Jake, and nodded. "Mr. Conrad."

"Goodnight."

The man stepped off the deck, zipping up his leather coat. He fired up the motorcycle, sounding like a little jet plane, and rode away with a cloud of dust.

"You don't have to be so rude," Jake's mom said.

"That man seems like the type to sell snake oil. I hope you didn't buy it."

She smiled, putting her arm through his and walking him inside. "He brought medicine, not snake oil. This could be just what Pop needs."

"I doubt he'll take it."

"Oh, we'll see about that." They paused at the foot of the stairs. "Evening reading soon?"

"I'll wash up and be down in a few minutes."

"What'll it be tonight?"

"Something from Proverbs. We need a dose of wisdom in

this place."

She laughed and gave him a friendly shove up the stairs. "Try to smile when you look at yourself in the mirror. It'll do you good."

He climbed the stairs two at a time. "Just what the doctor ordered," he muttered.

27

Liz stood on a platform facing the huge crater in the ground. It had been two months since the televised interview. Jax's team had come up with a brilliant idea to build the tower even higher and safer in the atmospheric winds. Katarina had the company making more profit than ever, and the projections for the stock price were rising.

In the meantime, the tower had consumed Liz's time. She'd selected the builders and the suppliers. She'd signed the media contracts for the reality show—*Building Babel*. And, most importantly, she'd picked the chief engineer.

There had been five finalists for the lead role. "The best in the world," Jax had said, after his team combed through hundreds of applications.

And Jax's favorite had won: Hunter Black. He'd showed up for the interview alone with a backpack, chinos, and a button-down shirt. Liz liked that. The other finalists came in large teams and pinstripe suits—from New York, Tokyo, and Berlin. But Jax recommended Mr. Black, from Kansas City. The engineer had the right resume, having built towers around the world. Katarina didn't like him, but for the tower, Liz would follow Jax's recommendation. She approved him for the job.

Now Hunter joined Liz and Jax at the edge of the pit. The three of them walked down the viewing platform that extended over the giant hole in the earth. The flat metal surface was like a diving board under Liz's feet, except it had no spring. She felt like an ant on the edge of a swimming pool.

"Will it get any bigger?" she asked.

"Not much." Hunter held out his large hands and formed the shape of a square. "The foundation will be five hundred feet deep, and about three thousand feet on each side. "It's like nine football fields put together. And it goes deep enough to hit water." The engineer pointed to the bottom of the pit. "That's the aquifer bubbling up down there."

Liz studied the muddy surface below. Shafts of metal rose out of the brown water, reaching for her like fingers. They went all the way around the pit, each one angled toward the center. Six thick shafts rose up in the center, coiling around each other like DNA. Liz pointed down to them. "That was my father's idea, right?"

"It was," Jax said. "He scribbled a little note beside it in the drawing. He called it the wind helix."

"Brilliant idea," the engineer added. "Wouldn't have been possible ten years ago, but this synthetic steel bends and molds. Those six shafts go down another five hundred feet, and a block of concrete the size of the White House anchors them down."

"How'd you get the concrete down there?"

"Our team from Norway is leading that. They have the drilling technology to reach deep under the North Sea. We imported one of the drills and used it to pump the concrete in. We let it set around the steel shafts, then pumped more concrete in all the way to the bottom of the pit you see."

"So the tower will stand no matter how hard the wind blows?"

"Exactly," Hunter said. "These roots aren't going to

budge, and the counterweights above keep it balanced. The team from Korea built a computer model to test it. Even with a direct hit from a tornado, the tower will stand. All twenty million square feet of concrete and two hundred thousand tons of steel—it'll stand. There could be damage, of course, but nothing is going to knock this tower down."

"Good." Liz's head was spinning a little from the height. She turned back. "Let's take the picture. I want to meet more of the building teams."

The three of them posed for a line of press cameras. Flashes. A few questions from reporters with CNN, BBC, Al Jazeera, and more. Liz answered them with a smile: *Yes, all is on schedule. We're 3D printing the supplies on site. Record speed and the best quality. Watch the show! You'll see!*

They journeyed back to the makeshift town. Lines of pre-fabricated buildings like motels housed the thousands of workers. A renovated barn served as the town hall, where groups streamed through to meet with the head of the operation. Liz greeted them with smiles, feeling like a politician.

The Babel board had insisted she do this often. Her friends were behind the idea, too. "Good for morale," Dylan had said, flashing his bright smile.

Liz knew it was true. Jax's suggestion of free drinks once a week also helped. As the workers finished their day, they crowded around the barn for cold beverages and a chance to see the woman behind all this.

A group of Egyptians greeted Liz. One of them cracked a joke about the pyramids, and how they had some work to do to catch up with the tower. Next came the drilling team from Norway, the modeling team from Korea, the Brazilian ecosystem team, and the Russian welders.

After a while Liz took her leave and walked outside. She gazed up at the stars, imagining the tower reaching up to them. She tried to envision the day when she'd reach the top. She'd be the first to stand at such heights, and she had a sense that she would find something there, something that had been worth striving for all along. It's what her father would have wanted.

Then Liz looked east, over the cornfields, and she thought of Jake. He kept showing up in her dreams, usually holding a shovel or a bright red apple. He was surely on his farm now, within earshot of the construction but oblivious to it all the same. He didn't even own a TV. Probably not a radio, either. How could the man live like that, in such blissful ignorance of the world around him? Her tower was changing things. She was bringing the world to his backyard. She wanted to see him again, more than she cared to admit. Maybe she would pay another visit and ask how he liked the new neighbors.

28

Rachel Conrad scrubbed the dried breast milk off the bottom of the bottle. She rinsed it, put it in the sanitizer, and picked up the next bottle to clean. Her hot pink kitchen gloves protected her hands from the scalding water. The television on the wall distracted her from the boring work.

It was episode two of *Building Babel*.

An army of workers covered the bottom of the tower's foundation pit. They wore white construction hats and fluorescent orange jackets with yellow reflector strips. Cranes lowered steel beams down into the subterranean world, and the workers guided the beams into place. The narrator's voice said: "The crew has the largest cranes in the world—from Dubai, Saudi Arabia, and Japan. Last night they finished pouring the massive concrete slab, the tower's foundation. It is over fifty feet thick and the size of nine football fields. It will support a mile of glass and steel. Today we see the dangers of working with such huge materials, all for the sake of building the next great wonder of the world."

The televised feed zoomed onto two of the workers. One was crouched down, positioning a beam into a perfectly fitted hole within the concrete. A flag was stitched onto his sleeve— white and green with a crescent moon and star. Another man stood beside him, looking up and holding the top of the steel beam, keeping it steady. The flag at his shoulder had three bands—orange, white, and green—with a symbol in the center.

"These two workers hail from India and Pakistan," the narrator said. "The two nations have fought multiple wars, with millions of deaths. Kabir, the one who is standing, his parents were killed seven years ago by Muslim jihadists from Pakistan. He speaks Hindi. Abbas served in the Pakistani military. He claims to have killed dozens of Indians. He speaks Punjabi. They have agreed to work together today."

The camera paused on Kabir. His gaze was tilted up, and a look of surprise crossed over him.

"Kabir has just seen this." The view switched to a steel beam suspended in air over the pit. It was slipping, in slow motion, out of the chain hanging from the crane. "Watch what happens," the narrator said, as the view switched again to the two workers.

The action returned to normal motion, and things happened fast. Kabir began to lunge out of the way, but he paused to glance down at Abbas. He suddenly knelt down, wrapped his arms around the other worker, and dove with him to the side.

The beam crashed onto the concrete, missing them by inches.

"*What*—" Abbas yelled at Kabir, his lips forming the word in his native tongue. But as he stood and saw the beam and realized what had happened, the look on his face flipped from anger to relief. "You saved me..."

Kabir nodded. He was breathing fast.

Abbas clasped his shoulder. "Thank you. I must repay you..."

The show switched to a dinner scene. Groups of Pakistanis and Indians sat across from each other, talking and eating. The sound of their conversation faded out, and the sound of Liz's voice overlaid the scene: "This is just the beginning. We've cracked the problem of language, so now we're going to fight back against death and everything else that holds humans back... This tower has unlimited potential, because *we* have unlimited potential."

Rachel recognized the words from Liz's interview about the tower—it was all about publicity. She turned off the TV. She had already finished cleaning, and she had not meant to watch the rest. It was just a silly show, even if the idea was pretty good. And maybe the filming, too.

She went to the living room and lay on the couch, staring at the ceiling. Her husband was on call tonight. The kids were asleep. She knew she should just go to bed, but hearing Liz's voice had her mind racing. She picked up the phone and called Owen.

"Hey Rachel."

"Hey Owen. Got a few minutes?"

"Sure... How are you? It's been a while."

"I'm fine. Just watched episode two of your new show."

"Cool, I like that one. You didn't know if Kabir would save him or not, right?"

"So he wasn't just an actor?"

Owen laughed. "No, it's the real deal. They film hundreds of hours and pick only the best moments for the show. They hire interesting workers, too. Can you believe millions of people actually watch the live stream every day?"

"No."

"I know, it's crazy. Great for publicity before the IPO. And just wait until episode three. It's even better."

Rachel paused. "I wanted to ask about Liz."

"What about her?"

"Is she doing okay?"

"Yeah, she's great. Why?"

"I just worry about all the attention she's getting. Hard to stay grounded, you know?"

"She's the same as ever. It's not like a Silicon Valley star stays grounded, anyway."

"That could be good or bad. What about the tower?"

"She spends most of her time focused on it instead of the company. But you know how she throws herself into whatever she's doing."

"Yeah."

"I guess there is one odd thing. She's fixated by this farmer who lives near the tower."

"A farmer? Why?"

"I'm not sure. I mean, he lives right by the tower and he slows down construction vehicles that have to go around the farm, but it's not that big a deal. I guess she's just frustrated that he won't sell."

"Liz has always been fascinated by things she doesn't understand."

"No kidding. And this farmer is…different. Liz and I have both met him. He's about our age, but very old school. He hadn't even heard of Babel."

"Welcome to the Nebraska heartland."

"Right… I bet Liz will eventually get the Conrads to sell, and then she'll be onto the next thing."

Rachel sat up on the couch. "Conrads?"

"Yeah, you know them or something?"

"I'm related to them. Is the farmer Jake?"

"You got it, Jacob Conrad. Man, that's crazy. Small

world."

Rachel rubbed her eyes, trying to make sense of it. *It can't just be a coincidence.* "Owen, are you still going to church?"

There was a pause. "Every now and then. Why?"

"I'll be praying for Liz, and I think you should, too."

"I'm not really the praying type."

"Maybe you should start," Rachel said. "You remember what I told Liz about the Tower of Babel story?"

"Not exactly. God knocks down the tower or something?"

"No, God sees the people building and says that if they continue, nothing will be impossible for them. So God makes everyone start speaking a new language. People got confused and scattered around the world. Don't you think that could mean something for Babel?"

"Not really. This is the 21st century."

"I'm worried about Liz."

"Okay…but maybe you should get some sleep."

"I know it sounds crazy." Rachel sighed. "But just remember what I said, please?"

"Sure, you know I'll do whatever I can to protect Liz and the company."

"Thanks, Owen. Give me a call if I can help with Jake."

"Will do. Goodnight, Rachel."

She said goodnight and hung up. She went to the fireplace mantle and picked up an old picture from a family reunion. Fifty Conrads gathered around Pops, with a teenage Jake standing by his side. Rachel shook her head and closed her eyes. It was too much to be coincidence.

29

Jax and Veruca stood in the center of a sprawling underground parking garage, encased in concrete and steel. The ceiling was almost low enough for Veruca to touch if she jumped. But it was high enough for the hundreds of vehicles that would fill this space once the tower was built. Now it had an eerie feeling—dozens of thick columns, unmarked pavement, and exposed ductwork above. It didn't help knowing that they were fifteen floors under the earth.

Veruca climbed up a small ladder to inspect one of the pipes running along the ceiling. She studied the head of a small sprinkler attached to it.

"Can you see the camera?" Jax asked.

"From this close, yes." Veruca looked down. "But you can't, right?"

"It's invisible from here."

Veruca pressed a small button to the side of the sprinkler. Then she pulled out her phone and checked the feed. The video showed the top of her head, Jax standing below, and a fifty-foot radius around them. She waved her hand, and the video followed immediately. So far, so good.

"The tower's first camera has been activated," she said with mock formality as she climbed down the ladder.

"How many more to go?" Jax began carrying the ladder to the next sprinkler in the row.

"Just a few thousand." She grinned. "But you don't pay me

enough to do this for all of them."

"Hey, you won the million dollars. Spent it yet?"

Veruca held out her arm and pointed to the old Timex watch with a velcro strap. "Yeah, on fancy watches and stuff."

"Seriously, you should take some time off. Treat yourself to a vacation. Somewhere tropical."

"You know my skin doesn't take to the sun."

"Life must be hard for redheads."

"Oh, harder than you know," Veruca said. "But I could wear sunscreen. The problem is that if I took a vacation, you'd get lonely. So…I guess you'll have to join me."

Jax laughed as he set the ladder down under the next sprinkler. "Sure, let's go to Cabo. I know a great place overlooking the Pacific. But first we've got to finish this project—a couple hundred floors of sprinklers. Maybe after the tower and the IPO are done?"

"Cabo it is." Veruca passed closely by Jax and stepped up the ladder again. She began inspecting and testing the undetectable camera attached to the sprinkler above.

Jax's phone buzzed. He checked the text. The contact name appeared as "Agent"—it was Hunter Black.

Liz incoming.

How long? Jax replied.

5 minutes.

Jax took a deep breath and pocketed the phone. He looked up to Veruca. "Hey, almost done with that one?"

"Yeah." She began climbing down. "I'd like to check a few more. We'll leave it to the construction crews to activate most of them, once I've confirmed the system is working."

"Sounds good. You can check the next floor later." Jax folded up the step ladder. "Liz is swinging by, so let's head back to the stairs."

The two of them began walking down the long garage, between the columns of concrete. Jax's shorter legs shuffled quickly compared to Veruca's long strides.

"You seem nervous," Veruca said.

Jax stopped. "Me? Why?"

"You're walking fast. And you're not talking."

"I'm fine. Just thinking."

"About Liz?"

"No...well, yeah."

"You think a lot about her."

"We've been friends forever."

"I know. So does everyone else. The story of how Babel started is pretty famous...with you two working together."

"Kind of like how we work together." Jax smiled. "Except you're better at coding."

"Thanks, but I still don't understand. Why are you doing so much work for this tower?"

"Liz needs my help. And I'm...worried about her."

"So you've decided to spy on everything she does here?"

Jax laughed. "You know it's not just me. Our clients are the spies."

"Liz agreed to let us install the cameras, right?"

"Of course. But not about who will have access to the video streaming. That stays within FireSpy."

"I know. It's none of my business." Veruca looked down at her feet. "I'm just the technician."

"You're more than that." Jax paused, studying her red curls. "Seriously, V." He put his finger under her chin and lifted her gaze. "You're—"

"Hey!" Liz's voice echoed through the garage. "There you

157

are."

Jax and Veruca exchanged an awkward glance and turned to walk toward Liz.

"We were just wrapping up," Jax said.

"How are the cameras working?"

"Great," Veruca said, coming to a stop in front of Liz, meeting her blue eyes levelly. "We'll have live video covering every inch of this garage."

"Excellent." Liz smiled and pointed to the ground. "You both know what will be stored underneath here. We want to make sure no can get down there without us knowing it."

"And even if they do get down there," Jax said, "no one will get past my code."

Liz looked to Veruca. "Does he brag like this at FireSpy?"

Veruca grinned but didn't answer.

"Anyway, yeah, I'm feeling good about moving the data. With our encrypted code and these cameras as security, it'll be safe here." She turned to go. "Let's head back. I didn't want you to miss the latest episode of *Building Babel*. We'll be showing it for the first time in the main hall tonight. You're going to love it."

"Let me guess. More close calls? More bickering foreigners?" Jax asked, following after her.

"Hey now." Liz glanced back, then continued ahead. "People are loving it. We had 33 million viewers last week, and thousands have requested to visit the construction site. I knew the world would understand once we got started. You know what they say—if you build it, they will come."

Jax caught Veruca's gaze and rolled his eyes. Her smile in return was more genuine than it had been in weeks.

30

The Friday morning yoga class ended with *Namaste*. Katarina rolled up her mat and began the usual walk back to her place. Her agent fell into pace beside her.

"All clear?" she asked, in her native tongue.

"Yes." The man glanced around, then nodded to confirm. "The boss wants the data now."

"We can't rush this."

"There's an issue with Ukraine. We have a target there who's using a Babel. The boss needs to know what's being said. Lives are at stake. Our agents' lives."

"The IPO is only a few months away."

"They might not wait. They'll kill to speed this up."

Katarina knew it was true, but this would all go smoother if no one died, especially not Liz. "Not the target," she said.

"You don't have the final say on that."

"I learned something. The encryption is related to her DNA. It'll be easier to get that if she's alive."

"Not if we have the body."

"You don't think that'll raise suspicions?"

He shrugged. "You can guarantee access after the IPO?"

"Yes. Liz is definitely on her way out, and she's actually fine with that once the IPO is done. The board knows I'm the one running the company's translation business. As soon as I'm CEO, I can get into the vault. Even if I don't get the board's approval, I will figure out the encryption by then."

"You're sure?"

"The DNA part should be straightforward. We just need to figure out where the coder stores it. Probably in her hair... So there's only one other piece."

"What?"

"It's almost too easy. I need a password."

"Whose?"

"The coder's."

"Should we bring him in? Rough him up?"

"No, he's close to Liz. Too many questions. We just need to have him followed for a while."

"Okay, what are we looking for?"

"Not sure. Just collect information. Try to drop a camera in his office...you know, the usual."

"Alright."

"Be careful, though. This coder is pretty good. His company is FireSpy."

"Ah...their clients are not our friends."

"Exactly, and we know the government has placed assets who are working on the tower. I'm still trying to figure out where. So like I said, be on your guard."

The man smiled. "We're always careful."

31

The steel beams began to rise out of the ground. The bright spotlights and welding torches lit up the sky every night. Fall turned to winter and a new year as workers poured more tons of concrete into the pit, building up the massive foundation, like a giant's fist clenching into the earth. Even more cranes arrived, so that a dozen of the birdlike metal creatures sat around the pit, hoisting beams and materials and men.

Tonight, as the tower's steel facade loomed two hundred feet over the pit, Jax and Owen sat together at the construction site bar. Like everything about the tower, the bar was huge. It stretched from one end of the old barn to the other, with dozens of workers lining up for drinks. Jax and Owen had found a small table looking out toward the rising tower, where lights gleamed on the machines in action. The work had not stopped since it began.

Owen had come to Nebraska to meet with Liz. She spent so much time out there that if anyone wanted to see her, this is where they came. Owen was managing the IPO process, making sure all the legal pieces were ready for Babel to become a public company in the spring, just a few months away. It would make most of his friends very rich, and Liz most of all. She had already sold stock options to a Middle Eastern investor to fund this construction, and she wanted to sell more. But the regulations limited how much she could sell before the IPO, so Owen had to figure out how to make it work.

Jax was sipping green tea. He had been working with Liz constantly on the tower technology, everything from building materials to the computer system. "We'll be ready to move the data servers soon," he told Owen. "That's what I wanted to talk with you about."

"The data servers?" Owen asked.

Jax nodded. "Will anything need to change about their security once Babel goes public?"

"No, the company will still have its privacy policy." Owen thought through the many requirements for a public company. "We'll have to report on that, but it should stay the same. The access rules could change if Liz isn't the CEO, and if Katarina is."

"That's what I'm worried about."

"Katarina?" Owen hesitated before saying more.

Jax glanced around at the crowded bar, then back at Owen. "Up for a walk?"

They pulled on their jackets and left, walking along a well-lit path toward the tower. Jax stopped when they reached a rope near the edge of the pit. A sign read: "Helmets required beyond this point." The sound of clanging metal and machine engines roared in the night. No one was close to them.

Jax slipped off his Babel device and pocketed it. He motioned for Owen to do the same. Owen had never seen Jax take it off, but he followed Jax's lead.

"In a couple months, the servers will be right there," Jax said, pointing to the base of the tower. "I've been here overseeing the preparations, making sure security is ready. The chief engineer has made this a priority as well."

"Mr. Black?" Owen watched his breath drift off into the cold night air.

"Yes. He's more than an engineer. He's on our side."

"What's our side?"

"I'm not completely sure," Jax said, "except that we support Liz. And I'm realizing some people are supporting Katarina instead."

"I don't get it. You're acting like there's some battle between them. I work with them both most days. They get along fine."

"Maybe that's what Katarina wants Liz to think..." Jax handed Owen a small, unmarked memory drive. "Watch the video. You'll see. It's from one of my fire hydrants in San Francisco. I just discovered it a few days ago. I don't know what it means, but Dylan and Katarina are up to something."

"I guess I have worried about how much power Liz is giving Katarina. She could be some kind of corporate spy for all we know."

"Or worse." Jax met Owen's eyes. "The government is monitoring this. The professionals. We need to be careful. No need to show that we know anything...yet."

Owen studied Jax's expressionless face. "Who are the professionals?"

"The engineer, Hunter Black, he's one of the agents. I don't know who else. But you know the types we work with at FireSpy."

"CIA? FBI?"

"That's the idea. I'm giving you this video so that you can be on the lookout. See if you can learn anything more about Katarina, and try to protect Liz. Just be quiet about it."

Owen could be discrete, but he still didn't understand what was going on. Something about Jax's tone made his heart beat faster. "What do you think Katarina is trying to do?"

"I think she wants the data. She may have others working with her. A few people on my team have reported suspicious things."

"At FireSpy? Like what?"

Jax nodded. "One of my engineers found someone dressed as a janitor trying to install cameras in our office."

"Why target you?"

"Who do you think controls access to the data?"

"You."

"Exactly. And if Katarina becomes CEO, Liz and I may be the only ones standing between her and the data."

"What about Liz? Does she know about this?"

"I told her that I'm worried about Katarina and the data, but not about Hunter."

"We have to tell her," Owen said.

"It's safer if she stays out of this for now, and I don't know what's actually going on yet. No one is being watched more closely than her with the IPO coming up. Think about what happens if she's not around anymore. Who takes over Babel?"

"Katarina. It's not a secret."

"Maybe not, but what if things don't go the way Katarina wants? There's one clear path for a new CEO." Jax paused, a look of concern in his eyes. "The former CEO disappears."

"You think Liz is in danger?"

"The government is not taking this lightly. You keep doing your job on the legal front, okay?"

Owen shivered in the cold. "Do you know what Katarina wants to do with the data?"

Jax shook his head. "I don't need to know the details. I'm just trying to do my part to keep that from happening."

"What's your part?"

"The coding."

They said goodbyes, and Owen found his way back to his room in the construction housing. He pulled out the memory drive and played the video from Jax.

It started with Dylan and Katarina sitting together on a bench, under cover of the night. He could hear every word they said. When the video finished, he booked the next flight back to San Francisco. He needed to talk to Dylan.

32

Owen tightened his tie, the only tie in sight. The elite design school where Dylan taught seemed to have a dress code: jeans and hoodies. Owen stuck with his suit. Students eyed him warily as he passed, his wingtip shoes clicking loudly on the concrete floor. The ceiling arched high above, supported by interlaced white beams. There were no signs of individual offices. It was a vast expanse, filled to the brim with students and post-it notes covering massive white boards.

Owen approached two students huddled over a cardboard formation, maybe a molecule. "Do you know if Dylan Galant is here?"

They looked up, neither hiding surprise. "Dr. Galant?"

"He teaches here, right?"

"Absolutely, man." One of the guys rubbed his week-old stubble. "I took intro to medical design with him. Blew my mind."

"Do you know where he is?"

"Yeah." The guy turned and pointed to the far corner of the room. "He's teaching the newbies over there."

"Great. Thanks."

A cluster of students surrounded Dylan. Owen slipped into the back of the group—maybe twenty strong, enough so he didn't think Dylan had noticed him.

Dylan held up one finger. "If you remember one thing from today, remember this: human values are at the heart of our approach. It's collaboration, not cubicles. We want to give you a spectacular experience. You should lose your breath every day. You should be transformed. Along the way, you'll think outside the box and solve the hardest challenges facing our world." He paused, studying the group, spotting Owen, smiling. "Any questions?"

A girl near the front raised her hand.

"Yes?" Dylan asked.

"I just want to say, Dr. Galant, thank you! This is so amazing. My only question, and it's silly, I know, but you didn't say anything about how you'll be grading this class."

Dylan grinned. "Let me guess. Harvard undergrad? Or Yale?"

The girl smiled. "Yale."

The group laughed.

"Well, look, no offense to them and grading and all that, but if you thought that *I* would be telling you if you learned something, you might focus more on *me* than your own creative self, right?"

"I guess so."

"So we'll cover this more later, but basically, your fellow students will be grading you. It's how we ensure everyone works for collaboration. If we're not building together, we're not building at all. Okay?" Dylan clapped his hands together. "Great! Now I see a friend is paying a visit, so we'll wrap up a few minutes early. See you tomorrow."

The group scattered and Dylan approached Owen. "To what do I owe this surprise visit?"

"I need to talk to you."

"Go for it."

Owen glanced around. The concrete floors amplified the

sounds around them. "Somewhere private."

"There are no walls here. It's an open community."

"I'm serious, Dylan. Maybe outside?"

"Alright, no problem."

Dylan led Owen out through wide glass doors into a courtyard. They found an open bench overlooking the fountain in the middle. The sculpture rising out of the water looked like the solar system, each planet connected by thin metal bars.

"It's called *Beyond the Planet*," Dylan said. "It reminds the students to not get stuck on normal models of thinking."

"How long have you been meeting alone with Katarina?"

"What do you mean?"

"I know you've been meeting with her."

"And? What's it got to do with you?"

"I'm Liz's friend, like you, but I'm also Babel's lawyer. I need to make sure Katarina and Liz are on the same page."

"What makes you think they aren't?"

Owen sighed. "I know Liz is okay with Katarina succeeding her at Babel, but they're very different. Katarina has been meeting with important people, major investors." *Like that prince in Dubai.* Owen had been urging Liz to visit the Babel servers and check what Katarina had been saying and hearing in all these meetings. But Liz had been too focused on the tower.

"Liz asked Katarina to take all these meetings," Dylan said, relaxed. "You know that."

Owen formulated his question carefully, staying focused. "Why have you been meeting with her?"

"It's not a big deal. It's personal." Dylan looked away, to the sculpture in the fountain. "What's this all about?"

168

"Look, I want to believe you," Owen said. "But the pieces don't add up." He pulled his phone out of his pocket and held the screen out to Dylan. "What am I supposed to make of this?"

The video began. It showed two figures approaching each other on a dark street in San Francisco. It was late at night. No one else was around. The sound was pristine, revealing even the shuffles of their feet. The two met almost exactly in front of the camera.

Owen felt Dylan tense beside him. The video played their conversation on the bench, then showed Dylan taking a package from Katarina. After a while they stood and walked off together.

"What was in the package?" Owen asked, pocketing his phone.

Dylan met Owen's eyes. "It's like I told you. We have a thing going."

"A thing where you meet on the street in the middle of the night and exchange a package?"

Dylan shook his head, smiling. "She's into some weird stuff, man."

"Like sabotage? Corporate theft? What?"

"It's not what you think. It's...kinky. And yeah, you caught me, but everyone has their romantic thing, right?"

"I'm celibate for a reason."

Dylan shook his head, sighed. "You can understand why I wouldn't broadcast this kind of thing, right?"

"Because it's illegal?"

"Lighten up! We're consenting adults. There's nothing criminal about it. But it's pretty weird, and I have a reputation to keep up." Dylan's tone had turned sheepish. "Promise you won't leak this? For a friend?"

Owen didn't buy it. "You're mixed up in something bad."

"Katarina's…different, but she's good. I swear."

"Good for who?"

"Look, I'm telling the truth. It's been a secret. You caught me, and I've confessed. What else do you want?"

"What was in the package?"

"Something to spice up the love life, that's it. Seriously."

Owen shook his head. "Fine. But as your friend, I have to say, you're playing a dangerous game."

Dylan flashed his most convincing grin. "That's what makes it—makes her—so exciting. I wouldn't expect you to understand. Trust me, she's amazing."

"Anything else you're going to tell me?"

Dylan shook his head. "Nothing more to say."

The two of them stood and said their goodbyes. As Owen began to walk away, Dylan called after him. "Hey, how'd you get that video anyway?"

Owen smiled. *Jax's fire hydrant.* "You have your secrets, and I have mine."

As soon as Owen had reached his car, he fired off a text to Liz. *We need to talk. ASAP.*

* * *

Once Owen was out of sight, Dylan dashed inside. He ignored the students who tried to stop him. He went to his workstation and tried to slow his breathing. He didn't want to tell Katarina, but he had to. This was too much risk.

He texted her. *A friend knows about the package, but not the contents.*

The reply came within moments. *In meeting with Liz. Talk tonight?*

Yes. Dylan tried to think of a safe location. *Not outside. Your place?*

Fine. 10 pm. Keep your hood up.

See you then.

33

"I can't believe we're meeting here." Liz sat beside Owen in a wooden pew in the huge church.

"I wanted privacy," he said. "This is important."

Liz glanced around the room, feeling small. A few people sat scattered around the room. The place hardly had the feel of a real church. It was like those European cathedrals that hosted more tourists than prayers. She didn't like it. She shifted in the hard pew. "Let's make this quick."

"You know this church is named after St. Ignatius?"

Liz nodded.

"Ignatius started somewhat like you. He was talented and ambitious. He rose quickly in fame among the Spanish elite. At the time, this required serving in a royal court and…"

"You said this was important."

"Is your Babel on?" Owen asked.

"Of course."

"Turn it off."

Liz raised her brow.

"Please?"

"Fine." Liz pulled off the earpiece and held down the power button. The device's faint blue light faded. She laid it on the wooden pew between them. The clean metallic lines looked alien on the old, grainy surface.

"The point," Owen continued, "is that St. Ignatius later experienced a conversion. He developed spiritual exercises that are still used today. It's why he has churches like this named after him. He's remembered, like you want to be." Owen paused, but Liz didn't react. "Anyway, I've talked to Rachel about all this, and about the Tower of Babel. And then came this farmer."

Liz felt her cheeks flush. "What about him?"

"Did you know he's Rachel's cousin? She thinks it could be a sign."

"Her cousin? Seriously?" Liz knew Rachel had a big family from Nebraska, but this seemed like too much.

"That's what she said."

"Well, you know I'm not worried about her warnings." But maybe she'd give Rachel a call to see what else she could learn about Jake. They hadn't spoken in months, ever since their meeting in San Francisco. She almost felt bad for not even calling Rachel when she was within a stone's throw in Chicago. Rachel would only have complained about the tower... "Don't tell me you're on her side now."

"I'm on your side," Owen said. "That's why I've been in here, thinking. I've been worried. I didn't know what else to do. I went through the spiritual exercises that St. Ignatius developed. They're supposed to help us discern the spirits, to determine the path forward."

"Super."

"I'm serious, Liz. And I'm not telling you to stop building the tower."

"The company's name is no coincidence, you know. Babel is undoing the mess God started because of that tower in the old story—giving everyone the same language."

Owen smiled. "So modest."

"You know my favorite book, right?"

"The Fountainhead."

"Yeah, my dad gave me a copy when I turned twelve."

"It's the books we read early that leave the biggest impact."

"I didn't read it until the year after my dad died. I decided he was Howard Roark. The world didn't understand his genius." Liz paused. "They're starting to understand now."

"You haven't been paying much attention to the company," Owen said. "Our legal team, including the DC lawyers, we have everything on track for the IPO. But the board wants you more involved."

"I'm involved enough. It's not like I'm leaving the company."

"Yet."

"What does that mean?"

Owen's eyes dropped to the device. "I think Babel is under attack."

"We have a lot of competition."

"I mean, from the inside."

"Really?" Liz felt the first grip of surprise. This was not what she expected. *Stop building the tower. Get more exercise. Give more money to the poor.* Owen would say all those things. He would not point fingers at people. It wasn't his way. "Attack by who?"

He leaned closer to Liz and whispered a name into her ear. "Katarina."

"Oh, a Russian spy?" Liz mused. "Is that what you dragged me here to tell me?"

"You already know something?"

"Yeah, I know she's been doing a great job for me for years. The company's performing better than ever. Revenues

174

are up. Costs are down. I work closer with her than with anyone else. Don't you think I'd notice if she were doing something against Babel?"

"What if she's helping Babel, but not in the way you think?"

"Like what?"

"I'm not sure, but did you know she's been meeting with Dylan?"

"Jax mentioned it."

"Well I've looked into it more. They've met many times, and every time it's in some dark place…and they both turn off their Babels."

That's odd, Liz thought. She hoped it wasn't some kind of tryst. They weren't each other's type. And why turn off their Babels? Katarina knew the policy. Everyone inside the company was supposed to keep their device on, at all times. They had to show how easy it was, and how they believed the company would protect their privacy.

"What else?" Liz asked.

"The first time they met was the night before Katarina flew to Dubai. Remember that, last summer? Guess what happened to the projected stock prices after that."

"They went up?"

"Look." Owen pulled out his phone and brought up a chart. He pointed to a sharp little downturn, followed by a much larger jump. "This was the day after she returned from Dubai. There was a press release about Babel's earning projections. They had dipped and so the price dipped. Then, within minutes, guess who bought a billion stock options?"

"A competitor?"

"The sovereign wealth fund of Dubai."

"Okay?"

"It's the slush fund that the ruling family uses. You can imagine what would happen if Dubai had a controlling interest in Babel."

"It's a free world. Why should I care if they buy it?"

"It's free for now." Owen picked up his Babel. The metal gleamed in his hand. "But what if they used all the data collected by these devices?"

"You know it's encrypted. Only Jax and I can access it, and we don't. Our security is better than the CIA's."

"For now, but it all depends on you. I worry Katarina is planning something, something bad, once you're out of the picture."

"Why?"

"She's being groomed to take your job, Liz. I think she's courting investors, like that prince in Dubai, to buy the company and give her complete control sooner than we think."

"I'm not leaving Babel."

"You're going to lose control of the company when it goes public."

"But Jax and I will still control the data."

Owen's voice dropped to a whisper. "As long as you're alive."

Liz kept her face steady, but then she laughed. "Seriously? This again? You've got to be kidding…"

"I'm not," Owen said. "Just think about it. If you or Jax were out of the picture, then whoever was in control of Babel could access the data. They could know most of the words spoken and heard on earth. People have been murdered for far less. And now you could have the Russians and Middle Easterners involved. What if you're the only thing standing in their way? Can't you see the risk?"

Liz had stopped laughing. "I guess so, but I'm still not convinced. What would I do about it, anyway?"

"Look, I told you about Dubai. I think Katarina tipped off the prince. Not sure why. And I told you about her meeting with Dylan. Here's one more thing I learned. She's been disconnecting her Babel device every Friday around the same time."

"When?"

"6 am. Every week for two years, no exceptions."

"Okay, that's weird…" Liz went quiet.

Owen held out the Babel to Liz. "I think she's hiding something. Why not at least check out her data? See what you learn?"

As a company executive, Owen could see basic data, like when Babels were on or off. But he couldn't access the words spoken. Only Liz could. She'd managed to avoid the data center for almost a year. "You've discussed this with Jax?"

"Yes, we're both keeping an eye on her, and on Dylan. Whatever it is, I don't think it's good, and I think you're the target."

"When did you become a conspiracy theorist?"

"This tower is only putting you more in the spotlight."

"I can handle it."

"I don't doubt that, but why not use the tools you have? Check the data and see what you find."

Liz agreed to do it soon, and then she left. Owen sat alone in the basilica for a little longer, his sense of dread rising. He felt like he was being watched, that they all were.

34

"Hey Rach."

"Hey Liz."

"I know…it's been a while. You doing well?"

"Yeah, we're good."

"And the kids?"

"They're great. Full of life. We had a big milestone this week: Tyler pooped in the potty."

Liz laughed. "Congrats, I guess?"

"Yeah, it's a big deal. For us, anyway… I've seen your show."

"How do you like it?"

"Not bad, but you already know what I think about the tower."

"That's not why I called. Owen told me Jake Conrad is your cousin."

"Yes. He's a good guy. I haven't seen him in years."

"He's quite a character. And not bad looking. But he lives near my tower and won't sell his land."

"Not surprising. He's one of the most thoughtful and faithful men I know."

"What could change his mind?"

The line went quiet.

"You know him, Rach. What do you think he wants?"

"Not much. He's always been content where he is… You sure you're not just trying to prove that you can get whatever *you* want?"

"You know it's not that simple."

"Maybe it is. Why not spend more time on the farm with him? It might do you some good."

"I did. I helped him dig out a dead tree stump. I actually kind of enjoyed it."

"I guess that's a start…"

There was a long pause. "You know, I'm sorry about what happened when you were in San Francisco."

"Thanks. I'm sorry, too, about what I said about your dad."

"It's okay. You weren't all wrong. I found his design, along with some old letters and a family Bible. I'll admit now I'm building the tower for him. At least, that's one main reason."

"It's quite a memorial."

"It's not just about the past. It's for the future, too."

"That's what I'm worried about. I'm praying for you."

"Thanks… Well, good talking to you."

"You too, Liz. Take care."

35

The security guard's hand rested on his gun as Liz rolled the window down. "Step out of the car."

Liz opened the door and stepped out. "I don't remember seeing you before," she said. "What's your name?"

"Mike." The guard held up a small scanner. "Glasses off."

Liz pulled off her shades. The sun was blazing, making her head throb after last night's dinner and drinks, courting investors. She was growing tired of Bay area billionaires. Two hours east and now she was in the land of scorched earth desert. It was warm even on this January day. Not the best place for keeping the servers cool, but Babel had to keep the data safe and no one stumbled by this facility by accident. She'd still be glad when it was closer to her, in the tower.

The guard kept the device steady in front of her eyes. It was as thin as a pencil, and looked about as threatening. But the guard's hard stare made Liz feel like he was ready to blow her head off.

"Any other visitors today?" she asked.

He didn't answer. It was quiet except for a steady mechanical hum from the warehouses on the other side of the fence. A green light flashed on the guard's wand.

"Stay there," he said. "Hands above your head."

Liz raised her arms in the air while the guard stepped into a small gatehouse. She pushed away slight annoyance. It was good that they stuck to protocol, even with her. She stretched her arms and gazed up at the fence. Twelve feet high and barbed wire at the top. She hated to be the cause of more barbed wire in the world, but it served its purpose. This data had to be kept secure. No one was getting in without a struggle, and the cameras every twenty feet would detect anyone who tried.

The guard walked out a different man. He was smiling shyly. "Ms. Trammell?"

"Yes?"

"I'm sorry, I had no idea. I've called the boss. She'll be here any moment."

"You're doing a fine job, Mike. How long have you worked with us?"

"Two months. It beats the prison where I used to work."

"Easier keeping people out than keeping them in?"

He laughed. "Got that right."

The gate began to swing open. A roofless Humvee pulled up on the other side. A woman stepped out, dressed in fatigues. She had short-cropped gray hair and a thick build.

"Ms. Trammell, we're delighted to have you."

"It's good to see you, Alice."

"You want to access the servers?"

"I need to visit the vault."

Alice nodded, all business. She glanced to Liz's car. "Keys?"

Liz handed them over, and Alice tossed them to the guard. "Park it close, Hunter. Keep an eye on it. No one else enters as long as Ms. Trammell is here. Understood?"

"Roger that."

As Alice escorted Liz to the Humvee, she reported on the latest activity at Babel's data center. No security incidents. Four new hires. A better camera system installed around the perimeter.

The wide gravel road passed through a half dozen low warehouses. Each one was huge, the size of a football field, and separated by just as much space. Giant water tanks loomed beside each one.

They pulled up outside the smallest building at the center, a concrete shed the size of a bathroom. "We've never had a breach, or even an attempt here."

"Good," Liz said. "And the preparations for moving?"

"We're on track, but…"

"Go on."

"With respect, Ms. Trammell, it won't be as safe there."

"Why's that?"

"You can't control access the way we can here. No one just happens to pass this place. We're in the middle of nowhere. Costs are low. Security is high. There's a reason the government puts its most important data out here instead of in Washington, DC."

Liz smiled. "Nebraska isn't Washington."

"From what I hear, your tower won't be Nebraska."

"*Touché!*" Liz clasped Alice's shoulder. The woman was built like a tank. "I need you to make sure this data stays safe. I want you to come to the tower."

Alice hesitated. She didn't look away, but she didn't answer.

"What'll it take, Alice? You have family, roots here? Is it about the pay?"

"No. I'm from nowhere. After I left the service, I just wanted quiet. The desert gives me that."

"You can have quiet at the tower, I promise."

Words appeared on the screen: *Welcome, Liz.*

An outline of her hand's shape was below the words. Liz pressed her hand to it.

"Success," said a voice from the computer. "What is your favorite color?"

"That's a stupid question."

"Who do you love the most?"

"Myself."

"Why are you here?"

"To discover the meaning of life."

"Access granted."

The last question made Liz smile. She hadn't been here in so long. Her answer had almost changed. She was here to find out if somebody was betraying her. But maybe that related to discovering the meaning of life. Everything did, one way or another.

In the text box on the screen, Liz typed "Katarina Popova."

Thousands of individuals with the same name appeared. Liz thought of different ways to narrow it down. One seemed obvious.

"Employee of Babel," she said.

Only one hit. Liz selected it and scanned the typical data feed from the Babel device. Thousands of words every day. Katarina averaged 113,423 words heard, and 24,943 words said. Both well above the world's average.

Liz pulled up the graphic display. Katarina's words were evenly spread over each day, seven days a week. She worked the same hours that Liz did. 8 am to midnight, or later. It was a job requirement.

But as Liz looked closer, one thing was odd, as Owen had

said: almost every Friday, around 6 am, there were a few words, followed by silence for the next hour. Katarina's device stayed in her condo building over the whole time. Liz figured maybe she got up early and had some quiet time. She didn't think Katarina was a religious type. Maybe it was meditation, yoga or something.

Liz picked one of the days from last week. She read the transcript of the early morning words, just before the device was left behind.

Morning, Charles.

Good morning, Ms. Popova. The path is clear. A nice day for yoga.

Thank you. Here's the unit.

Your shake will be ready when you're done. Banana-kale today.

What would I do without you?

Oh, I don't know, banana-strawberry?

[Laughter.] Be back soon.

Enjoy, Ms. Popova.

Then came an hour of complete silence. The Babel device did not move an inch over that time, but it stayed on, detecting nothing.

Liz guessed that this Charles person held the device for Katarina, maybe put it in a drawer or another quiet place. It meant Katarina was violating company policy. Never turn off the device, and never take it off. Not even for yoga.

Liz eyed Charles's words again: *The path is clear.*

What did that mean?

She started reviewing the data from Katarina's feed every Friday around 6 am. It was the same every time, except that the smoothie flavor changed.

She did a few spot checks of Katarina's data at unusual times. Occasional conversations in the middle of the night were with customers in Asia. It was all normal business and hard work. She ran searches through the data for dozens of keywords—like *Russia*, *spy*, and *data*. She read through pages and pages of conversations but came across nothing suspicious.

She stood from the computer. She walked to the food cabinet at the far end of the room. The concrete was like a glacier under her bare feet. She grabbed a bottle of water and downed half of it. Then she remembered there was no toilet down here.

As she moved back to the desk, she thought about Katarina. The woman was a genius in her own way. She was an operator, a control freak, a master of details. But could she really be a spy, a Russian agent? It was possible, but Katarina had been a godsend. She'd been Liz's best employee from the start. She'd never let Liz down. It would take more than a regular morning with her Babel off to make Liz doubt her. She might as well just ask Katarina about it.

Then Liz remembered what Owen had said about Katarina and Dylan meeting. She decided to pull up Dylan's data. It was clear he'd been meeting with Katarina, and they'd both turned off their devices when they talked. Only their first meeting— just before Liz started with the tower—had any words recorded. The conversation was:

Liz told me what you said, when you met with her.

And?

You told her to stay with the company and use the Babel data.

Liz shook her head, thinking back. She'd never told Katarina that Dylan had suggested using the Babel data. Katarina had lied to him.

The conversation went on, with Katarina telling Dylan she

agreed that it was a waste to keep the data locked up.

Then the recording had stopped.

Not good. Why would Katarina talk about accessing the data with Dylan? And why hadn't he mentioned it to her?

Liz checked the prince of Dubai next, but no single device could be tied to him. Finding any of his conversations would be like finding a needle in a global haystack.

She quickly scanned a few others—Jax, Owen, Rachel, even her own. She ran searches and used the system's algorithm to spot anything unusual. But it was mostly ordinary talk. Rachel rarely used her device, and when she did it was with her French-speaking au pair. Jax and Owen had turned off their devices a few times, but that wasn't too strange. Even Liz turned hers off every now and then. Company policy aside, everyone deserved a few minutes of complete privacy once in a while.

She stood up and stepped back from the computer, feeling dirty. It still felt wrong, like a voyeur looking through a peephole, to eavesdrop on others' conversations. What people said had to stay private. That's why she'd vowed from the beginning to keep this data safe. That's why she hated to make exceptions for herself.

The guilty feeling made her think of Jake, the man who'd never wear a Babel and showed nothing but indifference about it. She almost envied him, or at least the carefree life he lived on his farm. She knew there would be no data from him, but what if someone else with a Babel had talked to him?

She sat down again. She found the exact coordinates of his farm, which was easy to find just a few miles from her tower. She then ran a search across the entire database for any mentions of "Jacob Conrad" within 200 miles. The search began combing through the millions of recorded conversations just within that area and the few years of Babel's existence.

There was one hit. From just weeks ago.

The system showed the location as a bank called Farmer's Trust, in the closest town to Jake's home. She played the conversation.

Hey, I'm Chuck Frazer. The guy had a friendly voice.

Jacob Conrad. Nice to meet you.

Likewise, Mr. Conrad. What can we do for you today?

I'm…interested in a loan. He sounded uncomfortable, almost nervous.

Sure, have you worked with us before?

My grandfather has.

Okay, let me just check the system. There was a long pause. *Isaiah Conrad?*

That's him.

He took out a loan, with a farmhouse as collateral, about thirty years ago. Are you looking to do something similar?

No collateral, Jake said, his voice firm. *It's to help my sister, Annie, with college.*

Oh, well that's easier with collateral, Mr. Conrad. But there are other special loans for education.

Okay, tell me about the options.

The banker gave a long explanation about all the loans, and then asked, *So which one sounds good?*

They're…expensive. She still has another year, and she's smart. Maybe she'll get a scholarship. I'll think about it.

Just come by when you're ready, Mr. Conrad. We're always here for you at Farmer's Trust.

The two said their goodbyes, and that was the last mention of "Jacob Conrad" in Babel's records.

Liz leaned back and smiled. Jake had made a trip to the bank just for his sister. She hadn't expected him to support her going to college, or to admit that he needed money. It was kind of touching.

Another idea struck her. What if other people wearing a Babel had visited his farm? She searched for any data from the exact coordinates.

A few results came, but nothing surprising. There was Owen's first visit, then hers and Dylan's. She scanned the words. Jake said little in the conversations, but she played the audio from their meeting anyway.

Corn silk...Hard to see the silk in your hair. It takes to you.

Liz found herself sinking into the sound of his voice. It was deep, rugged. He was bold in his own way. After a while came her question: *Would it help if I came back? Give you some time to think it over?*

A pause. *Yes. I'd like that. Come stay for a while.*

His answer made Liz feel even more confused than before. Rachel said he meant what he said. But why would he want her to come? And why did she *like* that?

She shook her head and studied the screen again. The last blip of data near the farm caught Liz's attention.

Hunter Black, the chief engineer of the tower construction, had traveled from the tower toward the farm, then turned off his Babel device when he reached the fence in front of the Conrad's farmhouse. An hour later he'd turned the device back on at the same spot.

Liz couldn't think of any reason why Hunter would visit the farm, except maybe to try to buy the land. But then why would he turn off his device? Was he trying to keep something secret?

Too many questions. And the data, powerful as it was, did not have enough answers. She needed to talk to Katarina, to Dylan, to Hunter. Maybe she'd even pay Jake a visit. He didn't seem to fit in her world, but Liz felt like he was the oddly shaped puzzle piece that could help her see the bigger picture.

She would be back in San Francisco soon, and she could start with her friend. Dylan was like a big brother. He would look out for her. He would have answers.

She returned to the elevator to begin the long trip home.

37

Dylan's stomach roiled like the ocean in a storm. He'd woken up with a headache and a text from Liz. *Come to my place at 9. Need to talk to you.* Liz had invited him over before for breakfast, but it had been a long time and she never said things like "need to talk to you," especially on a Saturday morning. The elevator slowed and stopped. The churning in Dylan's belly didn't.

He walked down the hall to her penthouse unit. He knocked on the door.

The door unlocked before he heard steps approach. *Barefoot steps*, he figured. When it swung open, Liz stood there in all her unadorned beauty. Purple V-neck sweater and faded pajama pants. No shoes, no makeup. *Gorgeous.*

"Morning, Dylan. Thanks for coming."

"Of course," he said, stepping inside.

She eyed him with a playful smile. "You look tired. Coffee?"

"Absolutely. It was a late night. I came as soon as I got your text."

"Right on time." She walked to the small kitchen and poured him a mug of coffee.

He glanced around and saw nothing unusual in the open space. It was clean and spartan and breathtaking. He walked to the glass wall overlooking San Francisco and the Bay. "You're going to miss this view in Nebraska."

She came to his side and handed him the mug. "Oh, I'll have a view. Sure you don't want to come?"

He took a sip. It was hot and black. It did not settle his stomach. "I'm not ready to leave SF."

"The tower needs good scientists and doctors."

"You'll have them lining up once it's built."

"Hope so…" She trailed off, and he turned and met her eyes. "I bet you're wondering why I asked you to come."

He smiled. "You missed me?"

"You wish." She gave his shoulder a friendly shove. "But it does kind of have something to do with that."

"Yeah?"

She looked back out over the city. "I was talking to Owen a few days ago."

"Always a dangerous idea," Dylan joked, but it confirmed his fears. Owen would have told her about the video.

"He seems to always know what's going on," Liz said, "like how you've been spending time with Katarina."

Dylan figured there was no use denying it. He sipped his coffee, then nodded.

"How much time?" she pried.

"Enough to get to know her better."

"You like her?"

Dylan shrugged, unsure how much Liz knew. He hadn't done anything really wrong, anyway. He just should have told Liz about Katarina earlier, and about how she wanted the data. "Maybe," he said. "It's no big deal."

"Then what is it?"

He smiled, playing it cool. "She's pretty, ambitious, kind of like you. But it's a little too early to know where it's headed."

"Too early in the day, or in your relationship?"

The way she said *relationship* made Dylan tighten, like she'd just grabbed his heart and squeezed. Jealousy was the last thing he'd expected from Liz. She'd laughed off his subtle advances for years. He didn't know what to say, or what to feel. He fought to keep his expression blank.

"I mean, whatever it is, good for you. Katarina is great."

"But we're not…"

"Seriously, it's fine," Liz interrupted. "We're friends, Dylan. Always will be."

Always friends, always out of reach—that's just how it was with Liz, he told himself.

"Come on," Liz motioned to a small table, "let's sit down. I asked you to come for a different reason."

"Yeah, what's up?" he asked.

They sat across from each other by the window. Liz motioned to his mug. "More coffee?"

"Sure."

She poured a refill, unusually quiet. Dylan sensed she was delaying, maybe struggling to say whatever was on her mind. He couldn't remember her being this hesitant. His stomach started turning again.

"I have a question about a guy." She kept her eyes on her mug, where her fingers tapped idly. "Let's say there's a guy who lives in the middle of nowhere, works all the time, doesn't talk much, and is more stubborn than a rock. What do you think drives a man like that?"

"Hypothetically," he smiled, "a farmer in Nebraska might be ignorant."

"Let's pretend he's not ignorant."

"Okay, so what's the motor inside every man?"

She nodded.

"It's what drives me to pull all-nighters week after week. It's what pushes guys like Jax to try to change the world. And it's the same in you, because at bottom gender doesn't matter. The motor drives all us strivers: it's pride."

"You make that sound like a good thing."

"It can be," Dylan said. "But it takes many forms. It could drive men to want attention from women like you."

"I think it's something different here."

"With the farmer? What, like he's not who he says he is?"

She paused, then shook her head. She seemed disappointed. "I'll figure it out. Just like you'll figure Katarina out."

Her words gripped at him again. "There are no easy answers," he said, defensive.

"And there aren't any easy plots," she replied. "A real man faces his fears and calls them out, like a farmer who refuses to compromise his values." Her gaze bore into him. "I'm worried you've compromised, Dylan. What are you and Katarina up to?"

"I'm not—" Dylan hesitated, caught off guard by her directness.

"You know what I'm talking about. You and Katarina have been meeting and discussing Babel's data." Liz's voice went softer, sounding hurt. "And worst of all, you've kept all this from me."

Dylan's mind raced for a good answer. All he'd done was give Katarina some information about Babel and Liz…and planted a few cameras around the farmer's house, but maybe Liz didn't know about that. "You know what I think about the data. I wasn't hiding anything."

"Really?" She clearly didn't believe it.

"I told you how powerful the data could be, of all the good it could do. Stopping crimes, connecting brilliant minds around the world...maybe even changing the way people speak."

Liz's head was shaking. "No, Jax and I made a vow when we started this company. We told our customers: the data stays locked away. We have to use it to improve the algorithm, but not even the government gets access. We want to *help* people communicate. If conversations don't stay private, who would use Babel?"

"I get that." Dylan used his most innocent, peaceful voice. "But think of all the other things people do online. They post things, they share, they visit sites they'd never reveal to their mother. And they do all that knowing this stuff won't stay private forever. You're sitting on a treasure, Liz. You can't just keep it hidden."

"I didn't invite you here to debate this." She rose to her feet and crossed her arms. "I invited you here to give you a chance to tell me what you've been hiding from me."

Dylan stood and faced his friend. He didn't want to lie to her, but he couldn't tell her everything. It would only make it worse. "Look, you're right." He gave his voice the tone of confession. "It's not just a relationship with Katarina."

"So what is it?"

"We both agree that the data should be public, so we've talked about it. I promise it's nothing bad. We're just trying to prepare for it, but you're still the boss, right?"

Liz studied him, quiet for a moment. "What do you know about Katarina?"

"The same things you do," Dylan said. "She's worked with you for years. She's run your company like a professional, and

196

she's loyal to you."

"Loyal while she conspires with my friend to violate my orders and make my data public?"

"That's the problem, Liz. It's not *your* data."

A flush of red filled Liz's face. "Then whose is it?"

"The data is everyone's," he said. "It's a public good."

"The data is off limits. From you, from Katarina, and from everyone. If you're somehow working with her to try to make the data public, then you're working against me."

Dylan shuffled back, guilt and confusion surging inside him. "I just want the best for you…"

She laughed, and not in a friendly way. "You have no idea what's best for me. But if that's true, you should start by telling me the truth, the whole truth."

"I'm not lying."

She stared at him, waiting.

"I swear. I'm still on your side"

She stepped past him and pulled open the door. "I hope you're right. Bye, Dylan."

38

Jax met Liz at ground level, by the glass elevator shafts rising to the tower's lobby high above. Both wore hard hats, earplugs, and heavy coats. Their breath billowed out as steam in the cold air. Metal clanged around them, machines and cranes and men at work on every side of the edifice. The frigid February morning did little to cool the fires of construction.

One part of the tower was almost finished: the unseen foundations deep underground. A solid steel door by the elevator shaft had a retina scanner by its side. It was just like the door at the Babel data center, except surrounded by a tower and thousands of workers instead of a fence and an empty desert.

Liz leaned close to the scanner. The red light blinked green and the door opened. Inside were stairs going down. The door closed smoothly behind them, sealing away the light and the noise. Hard hats and earplugs were removed and placed on the ground, bathed in the stairwell's yellowish light.

"Where's Hunter?" Liz asked.

"He'll be here," Jax said. "He's never late."

Liz led the way down the stairs. Jax followed, feeling uneasy. He had already given her the detailed update on the data servers, but she wanted to see them in person. And she suddenly wanted to meet with Hunter about it. Jax felt awful about hiding Hunter's government connections, and now he worried that Liz had figured it out. He considered telling her now. He'd explain that he'd just found out about Hunter from a FireSpy contract, and that he'd wanted to tell Liz as soon as possible. He needed to ease into the revelation.

"How do you think Hunter's doing?" he asked.

"Great." Liz didn't stop her descent on the stairs. They had ten floors worth to cover. "The tower is ahead of schedule. The inspectors say everything is being built perfectly to plan. The workers are happy. The show is a success. Hard to ask for much more." Liz paused, glancing back at Jax. "Why do you ask?"

"Oh, no reason. I agree." Jax hesitated. "Sometimes though…well, he seems a little too perfect."

"You're the one who suggested him."

Jax smiled. "And I pick only the best."

"Did you know he visited the farmer, Jacob Conrad?"

"No." *Why would Hunter visit the Conrads?* Jax had felt nothing but annoyance about this farmer. It made no sense that Liz worried about him, even if he wouldn't sell his land. It wasn't stopping anything. "But Hunter covers all the bases. It's probably no big deal."

"I'll ask him," Liz said. "And I'm going to visit the farm again soon. There's some…mystery to this guy, Jake."

The way she said *Jake* made Jax's skin crawl. Liz never talked about guys like that. "It's probably better to just leave him alone," Jax said. "Why should we care anymore?"

"I don't know." Liz sounded distant, almost dreamlike. "He's not like anyone I've ever met."

"Why? Because he's a simpleton?" Jax said, his voice toeing the line between amused and contemptuous. He'd resigned to not having Liz love him back, but if anyone was going to capture Liz's attention, it shouldn't be this guy.

"Ha, I doubt it." Liz laughed off his question.

Four flights later they reached the bottom, two hundred feet underground, and Jax hadn't said a word about Hunter Black. Owen had already warned her about Katarina. Maybe it would be better not to tell her about the CIA yet, and to let them set up a few cameras in the tower. More protection for Liz wouldn't hurt, even if she'd never accept it.

Liz led the way down a short hallway to another locked door and retina scan. A red light turned green, and the door swung open to a small holding room with a desk. It was a security station, where a guard would be posted at all times once the data was moved down here.

Hunter Black sat alone at the station's desk. "Hey Liz, Jax. How was the trip down?"

"Not bad," Liz answered. "The security worked well."

"It should. You paid for it." Hunter stood and moved to the next door. It looked like a bank's vault. "This is the first time we've activated this final step. Ready?"

Liz nodded, and she and Jax went to Hunter's side. He pressed a button by the vault door, and a clear glass panel slid out.

"It works just like my code," Jax said, motioning to Liz's arm.

She held out her arm and Jax took it in his hands. It was not like their prior meetings, with Hunter looking on. The romance felt lost. But Jax followed their routine all the same. He plucked a fine, nearly invisible hair from Liz's arm and placed it on the glass tray. A blue light began to glow from the glass, and the tray slid back inside.

No one spoke as the system processed the data stored in the hair's DNA. Jax studied Liz, wondering if she might ask how much Hunter knew. Jax had already explained how it worked to Hunter. But Liz didn't know that. Not yet.

The door swung open without a sound.

Hunter smiled. "Lead the way."

Liz walked through the door into the cavernous room, Jax following close after her. He looked around in wonder at the place. The walls were hundreds of feet apart, the ceiling at least fifty feet high, with thick concrete columns extending for support. Along the floor were rows and rows of servers. Enough servers to store all of Babel's existing data and all that would be created. Enough data to hold every word spoken in the world.

They moved in silence down the center aisle. The hardware on either side was dark and inactive—blocks of metal and silicon that awaited life from their creators. As they advanced, Jax felt the sheer immensity of the room. The servers were over ten feet tall. Every twenty paces there was a cross-cutting aisle, revealing another line of data storage almost as far as he could see. The room had a sterile, brand-new smell.

Liz stopped when they reached the center. A large table sat as the centerpiece, with four screens facing out in different directions. A red bundle of wires, thick as an oak, descended from the ceiling to the center of the table.

"It's even better than I imagined," Liz said, wonder deep in her voice.

"I've never built anything like it," Hunter said. "Everything is ready for activation. All you have to do is order the transfer from the current data center."

"Not until I move to the tower, and after the IPO." Liz ran her finger along the edge of the desk, her eyes on the red bundle of cords.

"If construction stays at this pace, you could move in three, maybe four months."

Liz turned to Hunter. "So, June?"

He nodded. "If we get the funds to pull it off."

"Remind me how much more you need before then?"

"We've spent over a billion so far. We'll need another deposit soon to keep going, and four billion more to finish."

Liz's eyes closed as she breathed deeply.

Jax had seen her do it a hundred times—steadying herself before tackling a problem. He also knew what the money meant. She would have to sell her shares, as she'd known all along. But she also needed some of the cash before the IPO in June. Owen had told Jax that he thought Katarina was using this timing to plot against Liz somehow. And Jax had told Hunter.

Liz blinked open her eyes. "How soon do you need the next deposit?"

"Two weeks," Hunter said, "three weeks max."

"I'll make it happen. And you'll keep this place completely locked up?"

Hunter nodded. "It will be sealed up tight and under constant surveillance. I'll let you know if anyone even thinks about trying to get in."

Liz's gaze turned again to the desk and the red cord, her head tilting up to trace its long line to the ceiling. When she looked back to Hunter and Jax, her face was calm and focused. She smiled and turned back down the aisle of servers.

They made their way out of the room and up the stairs to ground level. No one said much. Jax's thoughts were on the funds—whether and how Liz could get that much money so soon, and whether they could protect her against whatever

Katarina was trying to do. At least the Babel data would stay secure.

Once they reached the surface, Liz turned to Hunter. "You know the farmer who lives over there? The one who won't sell his land?" Her voice was casual as she pointed to the east.

"Yes," he answered. "He's not much trouble."

"Then why did you visit him?"

For a moment Hunter looked surprised, but he answered plainly. "I wanted to meet the neighbors."

"Why?" The word left Liz's mouth with a blast of steam in the cold air.

"I've dealt with these situations before," Hunter said. "I thought maybe I could convince them to sell, now that construction is underway with all its noise and annoyance." The sound of clanging steel from above reinforced the point.

"And…how did it go?"

Hunter shrugged. "They said no."

Liz studied him quietly. "They? Who'd you meet other than Jake?"

"His grandfather, Isaiah."

"Why did you turn off your Babel for the conversation?"

Jax noticed a tightening around Hunter's eyes. Liz must have checked the data. That's the only way she could know. That meant she could also know Jax had turned his device off—and several times exactly when Hunter or Owen had turned theirs off. Jax felt fear creeping up, and annoyance. This farmer was like a grain of sand wedged in an uncomfortable place.

"You know these Midwesterners." Hunter laughed. "They catch a whiff of technology and they won't trust you. I figured I'd have a better chance if they didn't see me wearing a Babel."

"But the device is almost undetectable."

"Almost…" Hunter said. "But folks like the Conrads pick up on these things. It's not normal to them like it is to us."

"Fair enough." Liz smiled, as if she believed him, but Jax knew better. He knew Liz was onto something, and that spelled trouble.

39

Liz parked by the fence and cut the engine. She felt tired. Everything had gone sour since she'd accessed the data. Dylan had confirmed some of her fears, but there was still too much she didn't know. Jax had been more quiet than normal, like he was hiding something. Hunter Black had revealed nothing except that he'd met with Jake Conrad's grandfather and that she needed more cash soon. Lots of cash.

She took a deep breath and stepped out to look for any sign of Jake on the farm. He was nowhere to be seen.

She looked down at her phone. She remembered the odd texts she'd received from some guy who called himself "the man with the tallest tower." She felt sure it was the prince from Dubai. Owen had warned her about Katarina's meeting with him, and his country had the tallest tower, the Burj Khalifa. Tallest for now.

He'd offered to help. And Liz needed cash.

She found his message and typed: *Man with the tallest tower, the time has come.*

Liz looked out over the empty, frozen soil of the farm while she waited. It must get so boring here for Jake in the winter. What does he even do when it's winter?

The response came.

I knew that it would. Shall we meet?

You have $4B?

I have far more than that. Come to London.

When and where?

Heathrow Emirates Admiral's Club, Feb. 28, 5 PM Greenwich time.

That was five days. Liz could make it. *It's a date.*

An expensive one... you will wear a naqib?

If you wear pink.

Done. I will have the 4b.

See you in five days.

Liz was breathing fast, plumes of steam rising from her mouth. She needed to collect herself. She needed rest. She turned to the car and put her Babel device and her phone inside. Technology detox.

When she came back to the Conrad fence, she spotted Jake in the distance. He was riding a big green tractor in her direction. She climbed over the fence and walked toward him between two fields. The brown grass crackled under her feet.

Jake stopped the tractor. He climbed down and began to approach. Their eyes stayed locked on each other until inches separated them. Neither knew that their hearts pounded like locomotives.

"Hey Jake."

"I hoped you would come again."

Her breath caught. She hadn't expected that response, or how much she'd like hearing it. "We're neighbors now, aren't we?"

"And you're just in time for dinner. Will you join us?"

"I'd like that."

He smiled and motioned for her to follow. She fell into step beside him as they walked toward the white farmhouse. Neither of them spoke, but there was communication in their steady pace. The motion settled them into each other's company. Liz couldn't tell whether the rich, earthy smell was from the land or from him. Probably both.

* * *

Katarina was in her office in San Francisco when she received the encrypted text.

The target is onsite.

In moments Katarina had watched the video feed, showing Liz at the Conrad farm. She'd seen Liz texting but not the words. She'd seen her leave her devices in the car and walk toward the farm. Katarina couldn't stifle a laugh when she saw her boss walking close beside the farmer.

She texted back: *And the other pieces?*

She'll need the cash soon, and the trip to see the prince. The lawyer is our main threat now.

Katarina already knew that. She and Owen had been working together on the IPO, and he had started asking too many questions. The wrong kind of questions. Katarina needed him out of the way. Her fingers hesitated over the phone, but then she typed the words: *Take care of him.*

Any specifics?

Any available means. The sooner the better.

This was business. She was doing what had to be done.

40

Liz joined the Conrad family for dinner. There were five of them: Jake, his mom Beth, his sister Annie, Pops, and Grandma in a wheelchair. They crowded around a table covered with a well-worn white linen cloth. The plates had a blue toile design with farmhouse scenes. It seemed authentic and altogether foreign to Liz.

As Jake closed his eyes to say a prayer, Liz found her hands in the grips of the grandfather to her left and the sister to her right. The bony, weathered hand held hers as tight as the young, smooth hand. Liz looked on them in wonder as they each bowed their heads, eyes closed, in this religious circle. Liz had never experienced anything quite like it. They were so sincere. It was surreal.

Jake finished praying and met her eyes. His gaze was warm, even friendly. It made Liz feel comfortable, and she remembered how different she'd felt at her dinners with billionaires in Silicon Valley.

"Bread?" Annie asked. Her green eyes matched the bow in her hair.

"Yes, thanks." Liz took a warm slice and passed it on. She did the same with the meatloaf, corn, and peas.

The family talked about the farm and the day's weather. Cold but sunny, not much to say. But still they chatted, light and warm, until the grandfather asked Jake, "So tell us more about your guest."

The family's eyes all turned to Liz. "Miss Trammell's the one building the tower," Jake said, in about same tone that he'd used to describe the day's temperature.

Liz put on her best smile, refusing to let Jake's tone bother her. Could he still be so unaffected by what she was doing? "I came to give Jake another chance to consider my offer," she said. "He's a stubborn man."

The women at the table broke out in laughter. "He is that!" Jake's mother took in Liz with a smile. She had traces of grey at the temples of her brown hair. "I've heard you're no pushover, either."

"How so?" Liz asked.

His sister Annie piped up. "You're the richest woman in America. Richest woman in the world!"

Liz smiled. It was impossible not to like the teenage girl's energy. "And now I'm your neighbor."

"You wanted to buy our land?" Pops asked.

"Yes." Liz found it hard to believe that he didn't know all about it. "That's why I came before, with an offer to buy your farm at any price you name." The older man didn't react, but the mother's and sister's eyes opened wide. "Jake wouldn't give me a price," Liz said. "So I suggested one for him: thirty million dollars."

Annie dropped her fork. "You should have told us!"

Jake shook his head. "We aren't selling."

The grandfather held up his hand. All eyes turned to him. "I must tell you, Jake has the final word here. You understand?"

Liz nodded. "But you know he should sell at the price I'm offering."

"You seem like a smart woman," he said. "But smarts

don't mean much on their own." The old man pulled out a handkerchief and coughed loudly into it. The sound was like a death rattle. Then he folded it and continued as if nothing had happened. "I've known a lot of folks in my life. Met them in Vietnam, in New York, in Kansas City. And I've never known anyone as wise as my boy, Jake."

Liz looked to the younger man. His beard mostly hid the touch of color in his cheeks.

"And this is what Jake knows in his bones. When a family, heck, generations of family, pours itself into a plot of land, that land ain't no commodity anymore. It's a part of the family. We are who we are because of this place." He pressed his weathered finger into the table, as if to emphasize the earth under their feet.

"But this place is changing," Liz said. "I think identity has more to do with your genes than your dirt."

The old man's tender eyes twinkled. "It's all that. The genes, the faith, the dirt." He glanced around the table, coughed to clear his throat. "Let me tell you my story. Maybe that'll help you understand."

Liz did not object. She was eager to learn more about him, especially after the engineer, Hunter, had admitted to meeting the old man at the farm. Something about it didn't add up.

"I was born on this farm in 1929," the grandfather said, "the year of the market crash. While the country fought the Great Depression and a world war, I learned how to work the land. I chased chickens down rows of corn. I went fishing and picked fresh apples. And in the winters, I helped with firewood and other chores around the house, but mostly, I read. My mom loved books. You can still see a lot of her classics on the shelves here. They filled a farm boy like me with wanderlust."

"So you left?" Liz asked.

He nodded. "My father never liked it, but my mom said I should go off to school. We didn't have any money, but with all my reading, I got into West Point. I was one of two from Nebraska to start there in 1947. I played football. I wasn't the biggest, but I hit hard. Second team All-American. I studied hard, too. More of the classics. While my mind went incredible places, my roots stayed planted in this Nebraska soil.

"It was an odd time to become a soldier. The world war was over, but the military lived on. My first tour was the Korean War, leading men on the front lines. No one remembers that war anymore. But let me tell you, it was awful. There's nothing worse than a war of attrition. Ground troops like me sat there just waiting for a night ambush or a bomb to drop on us. Anyway, I survived, and they promoted me to colonel. After that I did tours in Okinawa, Germany, and finally, Vietnam. I don't want to talk much about that. I'll just say I thought that if we were going to go to war, we had to go all in. I wasn't in charge, though. It made us lose the war, and it sent me into retirement. And here I am."

Liz was quietly impressed. She'd forgotten how many stories came wrapped in old skin. "After all that, don't you get bored here in the middle of nowhere?"

The grandfather smiled. "Active minds are not easily bored. I have my family, my farm, my books." He reached over and squeezed Annie's arm. "And this young lady keeps me more than entertained."

Liz's eyes stayed fixed on the grandfather. "You traveled the world," she said. "Great adventures."

"You could say that."

"With what I'm offering for this land," Liz said, keeping

her voice quiet, "all of you could go around the world twenty times, then you could buy another farm."

Silence.

Liz focused on the old man. "Why did you meet with Hunter Black?"

He stayed perfectly still, except for the slightest pressing of his lips. Liz had spent enough time reading people that she detected his surprise. Apparently this wasn't something Liz was supposed to know.

"Hunter's an old friend," he said.

"From?"

"He fought under me in Vietnam."

"And you stayed in touch?"

"As much as men like us do," Pops said. "You picked a good man to build your tower."

Hunter had hidden this from her. He'd said that his visit to the Conrads was just about the land, about meeting the neighbors. But he knew this old man. He'd fought in Vietnam and worked in Tehran and...Moscow. The pieces were coming together.

Liz glanced around at the table, thinking, as the rest of the family watched her quietly. Even Jake seemed mildly surprised.

Liz turned back to the grandfather. He knew more than he was saying. "I have reason to believe that Hunter is more than just an engineer. Am I right?"

"Yes." The old man shrugged. "All I know is that dangerous people are interested in you, but good people are on your side. Hunter is a good one. He's an honest American."

"He didn't tell me knew you." Liz leaned forward. "He said he came here just to try to get you to sell your land."

"That's true," the grandfather said. "He warned me that

something was going on and told me I should sell the land and get my family away from here. But he didn't tell me more."

"Who does he work for?"

"You."

"And?"

The grandfather smiled. "That's all I know. But I'll tell you this, connections with the government don't just go away. Hunter served with me in some rough places over the years. He's proved himself reliable."

Liz studied the old man, considering his words. She believed him, and it mostly made sense. If Hunter was a friend from years back, he'd warn the Conrads but wouldn't need to tell them the details. They'd be safer if they didn't know. But that still didn't explain why Hunter thought they should sell their land, or why the grandfather had refused.

"So you've gotten some kind of warning, but you still won't sell your land?" Liz asked, wondering what Hunter could have meant. Was someone plotting to blow up the tower or something? "Don't you believe what Hunter told you?"

"All he said was there's a risk. But I think it's about your tower, not us. There's no reason for anyone to bother with our little farm. We're not giving up this land."

"If someone tries to hurt my tower, you might get caught in the way. Aren't you afraid of that?"

"Everyone's afraid of something," Pops said. "We don't let fears make our decisions for us."

Liz caught Jake's eyes, and a feeling of concern washed over her. "Look, I don't want anything bad to happen to you because of me. I can buy you land somewhere safe, somewhere further away. Please consider it."

Jake met her gaze evenly but didn't speak. His grandfather

did. "Tell me, Liz, how did you become a woman who can't accept no for an answer?"

Liz blushed.

"She's from Silicon Valley," Jake said, after being quiet for so long. "Those people think they can control everything."

"No," the grandfather said, eyes still on Liz. "It was before that. Everyone's naked and poor when they're born. Then things start to change. Annie said your last name is Trammell. What were your parents' names?"

"It doesn't matter."

"It always matters."

"My father was an architect. His name was Reg Trammell."

"Was. So he's passed away?"

"Twelve years ago."

"Sorry to hear that. I knew him. Bright boy."

Liz swallowed, her throat tightening. "You *knew* him?"

"Beth told me you had some family from these parts. There's only one Trammell family I've known. And only one boy named Reg. No one like him since."

"What do you mean?"

"He used to come over, play with my son, Titus."

"You mean..." Liz's palms had found their way to the table, seeking something stable. "Jake's father and...mine?"

"Yes ma'am. They'd hunt salamanders in the river, chase the chickens, and pick apples out of my orchard. They were good boys. In the evenings we started to see that your dad was different."

"What do you mean?" Liz didn't try to hide her curiosity. Rachel had been her only link back to Nebraska, back to her time here. She was even related to the Conrads. But this old man had met her dad.

"We kept a lot of books here." He looked at his wife, whose eyes were closed. She hadn't spoken a word. His voice rose. "You remember that Betty? All the books?"

She nodded without opening her eyes.

"Well," he continued, "when your dad laid eyes on 'em, he looked like most boys in a candy story. He started staying around more. I'd catch him reading in the middle of the night. He'd been through everything we had in about a year. He stopped coming soon after that."

"Why?"

"You know what happens after a caterpillar tastes its first leaf?"

"Um, no?"

"He eats another one, then another. Ain't nothing that can satisfy a caterpillar until he's stuffed himself. Then he piles up inside a cocoon, then boom—you know what's next."

"A butterfly."

He nodded. "I reckon your old man was like that. What ever happened to him?"

"He became an architect. He designed some impressive buildings. When I was sixteen, he jumped off one of them."

Everyone around the table was still. The mother put her arm on Annie's. "Let's go clean up."

"Why?"

"Come on now," her mother said.

The two of them slipped away, to the kitchen. Liz took her last bite of peas. The grandfather waited until they were gone, then spoke again. His voice had the low rumble of desperate lungs. "Our soil is stable and fertile. Your dad grew a little here, but then he drifted off. Maybe he sprouted too soon. His parents—your grandparents—weren't easy people. I won't talk to you much about suicide, but I'll say this: just like the land's part of us, that death is part of you, and it's poisoned soil. It can run in the family."

Liz's whole body was stiff, resistant. "I'm over it."

The old man smiled. "That makes it curious that you'd build your tower here, don't you think?"

"It's in his honor, that's all."

"A noble goal." The grandfather pointed to Jake, who had been sitting quietly, watching Liz. "My boy here wants the same thing. It's his decision about this land, just as much as it's your decision where to build the tower."

"I don't mind the neighbors," Jake said. "We're not moving."

"I know, Jake, I know. And she's not going anywhere." The grandfather stood slowly, then stepped behind his wife's wheelchair. "I'd better get Betty to bed."

41

Jake's mom returned soon after Pops left. She insisted that Liz stay the night. She said she had made up the bed in the guest room.

Liz started to object but stopped. Why not? She was trying to rest, to stay away from technology for a while. And it could be interesting to sleep in the same home where her father had been as a kid. So she agreed, and after saying goodnight to Jake, she followed his mother to the guest room.

Pops waited by the room's door. A small package bound in brown paper was in his hands. "This is for you."

She gazed down at the package. It felt like a book. "What is it?"

"Something your father loved. He read it many times here as a boy. I thought you should have it."

She gripped it tighter. "Thank you."

"You're welcome." The old man paused. "You know, I was thinking about what you said, about building the tower in honor of your father. Do you remember that you've been here before?"

"In this farmhouse?"

"That's right," Pops said. "Your family lived nearby, and one time your dad visited and brought you with him. I'd never seen a girl with such energy."

Liz felt like she was wading into a dream. She didn't remember any of that. She'd been five when they'd moved

217

away.

"You even played with Jake," Pops continued. "I remember you two sitting on opposite ends of a seesaw in a small park not far from here."

"That's...hard to believe."

He nodded. "I remember it like yesterday. It was one of those perfect summer afternoons, with corn tassels rustling gently, golden in the late day sun. Jake bounced up and down like he had something to prove. Your blonde hair could have made the corn silk jealous."

"You paint quite an image."

"So do you." He smiled. "Well, listen to this. You shouted to Jake, *I can go higher than you!* Then his skinny legs pumped harder. The faster you went, the wilder you laughed. It was like the sound spilled out of the park, over the prairie, and into the world, while the two of you stared each other down. Not so different than now, eh?"

"I guess not."

"I bet it would have gone on forever if Betty hadn't called Jake for dinner. He's always been obedient. He jumped right off the seat, making you fall to the ground. You bounced up again but quickly dropped. You couldn't stay up without him, you see."

That's how seesaws work, Liz wanted to say, but she couldn't bring herself to answer. She tried to ignore the image created in her mind of Jake sitting across from her as a little girl. She tried to ignore the impossible serendipity that they'd met again.

"So that package," Pops said, pointing down to the wrapped book in Liz's hands, "maybe it'll help you remember something. Well, goodnight."

Liz said goodnight, stepped into the guest room, and

closed the door. The little twin bed had a red-and-white patchwork quilt. An old fashioned lamp gave the room a pale orange light. She sat on the edge of the bed and began to open the package.

It was a worn paperback with a picture of a marlin and a fishing hook—*The Old Man And The Sea*. Seeing it put her back beside her father, reading at night.

She pulled it open and flipped through the pages. A picture fell out, then a note. She looked at the open page where the note had been held. A line was underlined: *"But man is not made for defeat," he said. "A man can be destroyed but not defeated."*

The picture was of two parents and a little boy. It must have been her father as a child. He looked maybe eight. He looked happy.

She looked at the note next. The crisp paper had only a short message, likely in her father's boyhood handwriting. It said: *Come, let us build ourselves a city and a tower with its top in the heavens, and let us make a name for ourselves, lest we be dispersed over the face of the whole earth. Genesis 11:4.*

Two memories hit her at once. She remembered Daddy mentioning that story as he first told her about the tower, while he worked over the design in his study. But she also remembered her last visit to that study, and the worn Bible she'd found there. Why would Daddy have left it in the safe with those last letters of his life? She hadn't cracked the book open then, but now she wanted to check inside. She felt sure there was some clue to be found, and maybe that Daddy wanted her to find it.

Liz carefully placed the picture and the note back in the book and closed it. Tomorrow she would go back to San Francisco and look inside the Bible. In a few days she would fly to London to meet a prince. But tonight she would sleep in this newfound home, under the red and white comforter, and down the hall from Jake Conrad.

42

The instructions came through the device in the shooter's ear. *The next car. The driver. You get one shot.*

The shooter waded through the corn stalks and checked the road. No headlights were in sight. He'd wait as long as it took. He stretched his legs, steadied his breathing. The key to a good shot was a stable base. If his legs wobbled, if his body shook in the slightest, he wouldn't be hitting anything. At least the wind was calm. Mornings were a good time for a hit. In an hour the sun would rise.

He brought the rifle up, leveling it just above the horizon. At this distance, he could put the crosshairs on the target and pull the trigger. No adjustment for distance needed. It was as easy as it came, except for the motion. Hitting a moving object never came easy. And a human head in a car called for a top-notch marksman. It called for Russia's best.

43

Jake bolted upright in his bed. Quilt thrown off, drenched in sweat, he shook his head violently, trying to make memories of the dream fall out. She had been there…immodestly. He'd never seen such a thing. He'd never wanted such a thing, and it was the wanting that terrified him.

He couldn't believe Liz was actually here, asleep in the house. He had to get some fresh air.

He swung his feet over the bed. He didn't bother putting on his jeans, coat, or shoes. The floorboards creaked in protest, but nothing stirred in the farmhouse. He stopped by the guest room door. It was closed. Liz was in there. It had only been a dream.

He slipped down the stairs and out the front door. The night air was soft but Jake was hard, every muscle tense as the dream hounded him. No rooster crows yet. Maybe an hour before dawn. Not long before he'd usually wake up. But he'd usually wake up eager for the day, not dreading the day. Images of Liz paraded across his mind.

He exhaled, threw his shoulders back. He focused his mind, eyes closed. Work, purity, diligence. *Keep your heart with all diligence, for out of it spring the issues of life.* He sucked in air, cleaner air, and envisioned rushing rapids washing away Liz's stained impression. He craved to be clean.

He walked to the river by the orchard. He stepped to the bank, a few feet above the river's deepest pool.

Straight as a board, he tilted his head back. The moon and the million stars swam above him. The enormity of it—the sky, the universe, the infinite folds within his soul—unraveled the tension. His jaw unclenched and fell open. He could not fight this. It had come from too deep inside. Could he be condemned for dreams he couldn't control? Why would God incite him with this woman? Or was it the devil's game?

His head lowered, a final deep breath. He sprang off the river bank and into the water. The shock of cold cleared his mind. He let himself sink to the muddy, sandy bottom. He found darkness and quiet there. It was a place he could hide, a confessional.

I'm sorry.

It was silent. The water numbed his skin, surrounding him, cleansing him.

His lungs thirsted for air. He blew out bubbles and tensed his legs. Then he surged up through the river's surface.

Moonlight danced on the ripples around him. He felt reborn. His dream spawned from sin, his own desire. That would be forgiven. He would keep this woman out of his mind. He would start this day fresh.

It wasn't until he turned to the shore that he saw the figure watching him.

Shock turned to shame as he recognized his grandfather, leaning on his cane on the river bank.

"How's the water?" Pops asked.

"Cold," Jake said. "What are you doing out here?"

"Age brings many losses. One of them is sleep. I was praying when I heard footsteps." Pops held out his cane, pointing it at Jake as he climbed out of the water. "It's been a while since you've done this. What was it this time?"

"A dream."

Pops nodded and handed Jake a thick overcoat. "They afflict the righteous and evil alike. You can't run from them, and sometimes they show things you would never let yourself admit. Sometimes, they're God's way of talking to us."

Jake was shivering as he wrapped the coat tight. "I didn't like this one."

"I can see that." Pops waited, as if giving Jake a chance to tell him more. Jake didn't. "You're already baptized, you know."

"The water helped me wake up," Jake said. "Thought I'd get an early start to the day."

Pops smiled. He didn't pry. His wrinkled face gazed up at the stars. "Our days are numbered, especially at my age. You ever wonder when He'll return?"

"Not really. Better to focus on today."

"That's right," Pops said. "But I look forward to that day. Down here, we've got our desires mixed up. We want what we shouldn't. We don't want what we should. Worst of all, I reckon, we run away from our heart's longings. We can even mistake them for sins."

Pops met Jake's eyes. Jake thought through Pops' words carefully. Something about it sounded right, confusing longings and sins.

"I know it's good to have a wife," Jake said.

"Sure is, especially for men like us. We're workers, Jake. We need a woman to make us remember those important things. Work's just the baseline. God offers us far more."

"The right woman?"

Pops laughed, then coughed heavily. "There's the vanity of youth! Ain't no man who can know the woman before God's put her in his path."

"How do you know?"

"Same way you know anything," Pops said. "You ask, you listen, you wait. But after a while, you just know."

Jake nodded. The two of them began walking back toward the farmhouse. When his mind drifted to Liz, Jake didn't force it away. She'd be there, in the house, and she'd be waking up soon.

* * *

Liz joined the Conrad family for breakfast—blueberry pancakes. Her eyes were puffy and red. The pancakes and butter helped. Jake even seemed a little talkative. He told her about his plans for the day. How the corn would be planted soon.

His mom got Liz to agree to come back to try her apple pie. Pops didn't say anything about the note. Liz didn't ask.

They walked out to the front porch together. Liz had to get back to San Francisco for a meeting. Then she had a meeting in London, and only a few weeks after that, before Babel would go public. And there were a hundred decisions every day about the tower.

But on the porch of the pretty white farmhouse, those decisions were far away. Liz hardly missed them. Annie and Jake walked with her down the steps, but Annie stopped at the bottom.

"Look!" she said. "It's a bird. He's hurt."

Jake knelt down beside it. The bird was small and dirty. Liz wouldn't have noticed it. It was flapping around a little, but not flying.

"Let's bring it in," Annie said, "take care of it."

Jake studied it, then met Liz's eyes. He was quiet a moment, as if conflicted. But eventually he nodded and reached down for the bird. He cradled it gently in his calloused hands, then carried it inside, with Annie and Liz following. They went to the kitchen sink, and Jake began running water over the bird's body. It protested at first but then fell limp, resigned to its fate. When Jake turned, he held the still bird in his open palms. "It's a dove," he said.

"It's beautiful!" Annie looked down at the white feathers and beady black eyes.

"One of its wings is broken. It's young, though, might heal." Jake met Liz's eyes. "Care and rest might do it."

"It was good being here," Liz said.

"You'll come back, right?" Annie asked.

Liz said she would and made her way out. She thought about her dad and the bird and the tower as she drove away in her car. She thought about the farmer, too, as she glanced at the white farmhouse in the rearview mirror.

44

Owen didn't usually check his phone on the road, but he was in the middle of nowhere, a straight and empty dirt road through empty fields in Nebraska. He was getting tired of this drive. Next time he'd take the helicopter to the new pad by the building site. But at least this gave him more time to think.

The first public trade of Babel's stock would be soon. He and Liz planned to field calls and talk to investors and reporters from the makeshift office near the rising tower. The early reports were not good. The stock price futures had plummeted yesterday. Investors cited concerns about leveraging the little devices for more profit. They cited concerns about government regulation of the data collection. They cited concerns about Liz.

Everyone but the Dubai Wealth Fund seemed to be turning away. It had bought another million stock options. International investment made sense—translation company, universal application, universal need—but no one had predicted such targeted interest from Dubai. Owen did the quick math again in his head. This wealth fund had been a pre-purchaser—among the select few groups who could buy shares just as the trading opened, before others had a chance. It was how investment banks made their millions. It was how companies gave favors. But with the wealth fund's early stock purchases, added to this late acquisition...it could give Dubai something close to a controlling majority interest in Babel.

He needed to tell Liz. He had been working an idea into the IPO documents. It could be a way to keep control over the company.

The car suddenly shook, one wheel slipping off the groomed dirt road. Owen dropped the phone and put both hands on the wheel. He focused his eyes ahead as he straightened back on the road. No more using the phone.

He checked the rear-view mirror. A cloud of dust trailed him. It looked ominous in the morning light, like some vaporous monster chasing him, ready to consume him. But no one was anywhere in sight.

He heard a gunshot.

He didn't get a chance to react.

As Owen slumped, lifeless, the car careened off the road and carved a path through the cornfield, not stopping until it hit an irrigation ditch half a mile away. It was over a day before a farmer found the body.

PART THREE

The Lord said... "Come, let us go down there and confuse their language, so that they may not understand one another's speech." So the Lord dispersed them from there over the face of all the earth, and they left off building the city. Therefore its name was called Babel, because there the Lord confused the language of all the earth. And from there the Lord dispersed them over the face of all the earth.
Genesis 11:7-9

45

Five feet of water separated Katarina from Dylan. Five feet, or a million gallons, if you counted the depths under their kayaks to the bottom of the San Francisco Bay. The sun was out. Katarina's bare shoulders had a golden glow. Dylan wore a black wetsuit. His skin did not take kindly to the afternoon sun. But Katarina had requested this. She'd said it was the kind of thing that dating couples did.

"We're far enough," Dylan said, continuing to slice through the water. "What do you want to talk about?" His Babel was stuffed into a ziplock bag in the front of the kayak, recording nothing.

"Any guesses?"

"The IPO?"

She smiled and swept her oar through the water, long arms tense, surprisingly strong. She was stunning.

"I thought Babel had finished the arrangements," Dylan said. "The prince is buying over half the shares, right?"

"He is." Katarina paused. "Liz will meet with him in two days."

"Why?"

"I think Owen may have suggested it."

Dylan's throat was tight. "Owen…"

"I heard the news, too. It's awful. He was a fine general counsel."

"You think it was a coincidence?"

"What?"

"You just said he was the one who suggested that Liz meet with the prince. And when I told you he'd seen us meeting, with the package, you said he was a problem. Now he's dead."

"It was a murder." Katarina shrugged, a corner of her lips turned up. "Terrible, I know, but these things happen. They found his body not far from one of the workers' camps near the tower. He probably got into a fight with somebody. Probably drinking, guns involved."

"Owen never fought anyone. He was shot in the head while driving."

"So a worker wanted revenge, I guess."

"For what?"

"It's under investigation."

Dylan stared at Katarina. Her eyes were straight ahead. Her arms continued pulling the oar through the water. Their kayaks were moving fast. Dylan was starting to sweat. "That's it? That's all you have to say?"

A spray of water glistened over Katarina's arm as she flicked the oar out and into Bay. "What do you want me to say? I don't know any more than you do."

Dylan felt sure she knew more, but she wasn't going to tell him anything, especially not if he freaked out. And he was freaking out. He bit his tongue, kept rowing, thinking. A flock of birds flew overhead in a perfect V. "You still think Liz will sell her shares and let you take over Babel?"

"Yes, as long as she's still involved. She's joined pitches to several investors about the IPO. That was before we heard about Owen."

Dylan swallowed. The way she said *Owen*—casually, warmly—felt like a threat. "Why do the pitches matter?"

"It's the last marketing before the IPO. There's only a couple more weeks, but the board is not as concerned about it now that the prince has already agreed to buy so many shares."

"The board knows about the prince, too?" Dylan asked.

"Of course, it will be in this week's filing."

"What filing?"

"Before an IPO the company has to submit a bunch of papers. Legal stuff. It lists potential buyers, so we included the prince. The one thing nobody knows for sure is how many of her own shares Liz is going to sell."

"What happens if she decides not to sell?"

"Then she runs out of cash to build her tower. She's burning through it fast. If this deal doesn't go through, construction could stop."

"She won't let that happen, not when she's so close. But I'm still surprised Liz is okay with the prince."

"Why wouldn't she be?"

"He'll have control over the company."

"Yes, and he'll make me CEO, and we'll make the data public." Katarina turned to him. "That was always my plan. You thought it was a good idea, remember?"

"Yes." Dylan paused. He was still thinking about Owen. He felt sick about it. The rocking kayak didn't help.

"So how is your end of the arrangement working out?" Katarina asked.

"It's fine," Dylan said. "Liz is pressing forward with my idea of a contest to conquer death. We're designing the research station. She's moving the servers to the tower, too."

"And you're working on how to get access?"

"There's not much I can do."

"Have you talked to Jax?"

Dylan shook his head. "No point. He's the same as ever. Brilliant and tortured. He'd never tell me anything."

Katarina fixed her eyes on him. They bobbed up and down on the waves, far from the shore, the San Francisco skyline behind them.

Dylan wiped the cold sweat from his forehead.

"You know," Katarina said, smiling, "Owen said something similar."

"Is that a threat?"

"We need access to the data," she said. "The world needs it. So...I just hope you can follow through."

Dylan thought of the device at his feet, momentarily deaf to his words. He didn't like his position, but he had little choice but to play along. If he had his Babel on, and Katarina knew her words could be heard by others, she wouldn't threaten him like this. No one would speak without considering their words. The world would be a better place. Maybe Owen would still be alive.

"I will do what I can," Dylan said.

"Who does Jax trust, other than Liz?"

"I don't really know. He's close with a few engineers at his company, FireSpy. One of them came up with an idea they're using in the tower."

"Name?"

"Veruca, I think."

"Good." Katarina dipped her oar into the water, and pulled. Her kayak came to the side of Dylan's. She put her hand on his arm. "Just a few more weeks, Dylan."

"I know."

"We're going to change the world."

"I know."

She squeezed his arm, leaned closer. "Some cannot bear the weight of greatness. Owen couldn't. But you've proven yourself so far. Finish strong, right?"

He met her dark eyes, keeping his face a blank mask. "Finish strong."

She smiled and gave his kayak a playful shove. Their vessels drifted apart, and she began the long row back to the city, with him following after.

46

Liz hesitated by the coffee pot. It was already late, maybe midnight. Katarina had left an hour ago. The building was deserted and dark, except for the light from her office. But she had so much more to do. Her hand shook as she poured. One more cup, a few more hours. This was the final stretch.

She walked back down the hall, her bare feet gliding silently over the bamboo floors. Strange thoughts occupied these corners of existence. Like how quiet seemed to be a cousin to gravity. The larger something was, the more it pulled. The deeper the quiet, the more it compelled silence.

Losing Owen compelled silence.

Losing Daddy compelled even more.

She remembered every word of the note she'd found inside Daddy's old Bible. It was just as she'd suspected, tucked in the page about the Tower of Babel. The note had been in Daddy's neat, drafting-pencil script. A suicide note. Tears filled her eyes as she thought of the words:

Hemingway did it, Van Gogh did it. I will do it.

Some say this thing I do is selfish. And I am sorry, about everything. But everyone will be better off without me. I have nothing left after the failures, over and over, of these late designs. I can't live, and none could suffer me, with them bound to paper. At least the other buildings stand. If anyone misses me (Meg? Liz?), look to them. Their glass and concrete and stone hold more of me than this poor flesh.

That was it. A lifetime reduced to a half page.

Liz wiped away the tears as she sat at her desk, in front of the screen again. No one was around to care if she cried, but she had work to do.

She was going over the company's IPO submission to the government. Katarina had told her not to waste her time. "It's just the details. It's like reading the fine print during a home closing." But Liz had always read the fine print. She couldn't stop herself.

And so she forced herself to focus on page 323 of the filing. Then page 324. Babel's balance sheet. Its leadership. Its expected investors. Its business opportunities.

One thing caught her attention. A supremely small thing.

A period in a sentence was in bold font, while the rest of the words were not. These were the details that appeared after midnight, after a fifth cup of coffee, in the immense silence of an empty office tower.

Liz knew Owen had worked on this filing. It was his final work. Maybe his masterpiece. He was not the type to make mistakes. She owed it to him to fix it.

She accessed his account on the Babel network. The folders and documents were immaculately organized. She opened the folder titled, *IPO - SEC filings*.

A dozen different versions of the same document were there. Each with a slightly different name. She opened the last one he had opened—the day before someone shot him.

She went to page 324, the one with the period. But now it was not just the period in bold. It was the whole line—a single sentence she had read once before without much thought. Now she read it again.

No notification is required under the Exon-Florio Amendment to the Defense Production Act of 1950, because no acquirer is deemed to be a foreign entity.

Liz had no clue what the bolded line meant, but the words "foreign entity" stood out.

She looked back at the final version. The one they would file with the government tomorrow. The last phrase was gone. No mention of a foreign entity. Only the bold period after "1950."

Weird.

Liz felt something roiling in her stomach. Maybe it was the coffee. Maybe it wasn't.

She searched online for the cited law and found a summary. As she read, she breathed faster. *When a non-US acquirer seeks to acquire a US target, if the target's business includes US infrastructure, technology or energy assets, the acquirer and the target may need to file a notification with the government. The President can prevent a foreign company from acquiring a US company if the President views the acquisition as a threat to national security.*

Liz had never heard of this, but for some reason somebody decided to delete a phrase from Owen's draft. Only a few people had been making final changes. Only one person cared about a foreigner buying Babel. Only Katarina.

Liz stood and began to pace.

Katarina had told her that the Dubai prince wanted to purchase shares in Babel at a premium. And Liz knew what it meant: if she met with him and sold her own shares, then he would have a majority of Babel. He would control the company. *A non-US acquirer seeks to acquire a US target.*

Babel's technology touched everyone, every day, in the United States. Her growing government relations office attested to the concern about it in Washington, DC. But she never thought the government could actually help her keep enough control to protect the data, even if she did sell and step down.

She turned her attention to the screen again. If Owen had included that line in the draft, he would have done more work on the issue.

She went to his files. The folders were again in perfect order. One was called "Foreign Investment." And in it, a subfolder: "Legal analysis."

There she found a law firm memo. She read the executive summary, and she knew. This was the answer, Owen's answer. This was how she could stop Katarina's plan.

Dylan had admitted that Katarina was somehow working behind Liz's back to make the data public, but Dylan probably underestimated her. Liz had to be careful. Katarina couldn't know about this, or she would fight back, find a way to stop it.

She looked up the bio of the attorney who had sent the analysis to Owen. His name was Christopher Planter. His pedigree was nearly as coifed as his grey hair in his website photo. Harvard and Yale. Supreme Court clerk and White House counsel. And now partner at this white-shoe firm, a partner who had left his cell number in the document.

Liz's office clock said 3 am. 6 am on the East Coast. Early, but a guy like Mr. Planter should be awake. Liz slipped off her Babel and laid it on the desk. She walked to the door and pulled her jacket on. She made her way out of the building, her body tired, her thoughts racing.

The streets were empty. She strolled down toward the waterfront and made the call.

"Chris Planter," he answered.

"Chris, this is Liz Trammel, CEO of Babel. You did some work for our general counsel, Owen Strand."

"Yes." He paused. "I read about what happened. I'm sorry for your loss."

"Thank you." She breathed in the cool air from the Bay, forcing herself to focus as she looked over the countless little waves rippling over the dark water. "I need to ask you a few questions about a memo that you wrote."

"About foreign investment in Babel?"

"That's right. I have new information. I need to make sure you're the right person to help. Your bio says you worked in the White House?"

"Yes, during the President's first term. I served three years as a legal adviser and left on good terms. The President and I remain close."

Liz was shaking, nervous energy coursing through her. She sat on a bench facing the water. The salty air washed over her. "Do I need to have you sign something before I tell you what I need?"

"No. Owen had me sign a retainer, with complete confidentiality. He said it was of the utmost importance. He even said you might call. I'm at your service."

Tears threatened to fill Liz's eyes. Owen. Of course he'd thought of this. He was always brilliant, but now he was gone.

She steadied her voice. "I'm going to tell you everything. Can you reach the President soon?"

"Is today soon enough?"

Liz leaned back and smiled, staring over the water. Then she started, telling him first about her planned trip to London to meet the prince.

47

It was 4:30 am when Liz walked back into Babel's offices. She rode up to the top floor and walked down the hall to her office. She felt more in control than she had in months. But her coffee was wearing off. She needed another cup to get through the morning.

She went to the break room and started brewing a pot.

"You really should get some sleep," said a voice behind her.

Hunter Black, the chief engineer of her tower, stood in the doorway.

"What are you doing here?" she asked. "And how did you get in?"

Hunter smiled. "I know my way around buildings."

"Who are you working for?"

"You. All was well with the tower when I left last night." His eyes went to the coffee pot. "Why don't you pour me a cup, too?"

Liz filled two mugs, and they went to her office. Hunter took a seat across from her desk without asking.

"Before I start," Hunter said, "you should know that your office is bugged."

Liz swallowed. "Who?"

"Two groups, last time we checked. My team, the Americans, and the Russians."

"How do you know that?"

"Because we're the ones scrambling the Russian signal. All they hear is occasional typing in here, and a few conversations that we let through."

"Thanks, I guess."

Hunter walked to the window, gazing out. He turned back to her. "Nice view. You remember when I came here to interview for the job?"

"Yes. You seemed...honest."

"Thanks. That's my job. Jax was the one who invited me, and he did it because we told him to."

"We?"

"You know about Jax's fire hydrants?"

"Of course."

"And his biggest customer?"

"The FBI?"

Hunter shook his head, smiling. "That's domestic."

Liz thought of what Jake's grandfather had said: *Hunter served with me in some rough places over the years.* "The CIA."

Hunter smiled. "Those fire hydrants have become mighty helpful around the world." He returned to his seat, relaxed. "We've developed a close working relationship with Jax. He knew we'd try to protect you."

"So your engineering credentials..."

"Every good agent has a track record."

Liz sighed, leaning back in her chair. *Jax.*

She felt anger and confusion welling up, overwhelming her. After losing Owen, Jax was the only one left who she could trust. *Was.* Now there was no one. But she had to stay composed. A spy was in her office. She fixed her eyes on him. "Why are you telling me all this now?"

"Because of what you discovered last night. You need to

241

slow down."

"Slow down with what?"

"Raising flags about the share acquisition. You've got to let that go a little longer. We know about it, of course. But we're not worried about Dubai. You have a much bigger problem on your hands."

Liz thought of Owen's warning months before. "Katarina?"

"Katarina Popova, aka Katarina Ivanovich, aka Sneaking Beauty. We've been onto her for a long time. She's as good as they come, but we have almost everything we need to bring her in."

"For what?"

"Espionage is my concern, but we don't want our enemies to know how much we know. We've found another way to put her behind bars. Conspiracy, corporate theft, and securities fraud."

"She's done all that?"

"Not yet. You need to let her advance with her plan. She's going to try to steal all the Babel data, and when she does, we'll be ready to take her down."

Liz tapped her desk. Even if Hunter was who he said he was, she had no reason to trust him. "I'm listening."

"Just assure Katarina that everything is going according to plan," Hunter said. "Let her keep plotting. We also need you to agree to sell your shares to the Dubai prince. You fly out today, yes?"

Liz felt exposed. He seemed to know everything. "Why?"

"Because Katarina expects it. She wants to make the whole deal look legit."

"What about the President?"

"Katarina will know about that little conversation you just had. We were worried about that. I got here too late to warn you." Hunter shrugged. "You weren't supposed to figure out that option, at least not so soon."

"A friend left me a clue."

"You know what they say, keep your friends close, and your enemies closer."

Liz put down her coffee. "I need to think this over."

"You'll need to think fast," Hunter said. "Katarina will be here in twenty minutes for your morning briefing. I have to go now."

"What if things don't go as planned?"

"They usually don't. But trust me, we're on the same side."

48

Hunter Black had been gone ten minutes when Katarina arrived for the morning briefing, prompt as usual. Her straight dark hair looked like a veil around her face.

"Hey Katarina." Liz walked around her desk and sat on the edge, folding her bare feet beneath her. She still hadn't slept. "What's on deck today?"

Katarina studied her. "You were here all night?"

"A lot stacked up while I was at the tower."

"Tell me about it..." Katarina rattled off quick summaries of the news. There had been a rough couple of days, but it was back on track. Babel was relisted as a hot stock, a company to watch. Opening share price projections were rising, with only three weeks until the IPO. "Most analysts have come to terms with the tower. Some are even getting excited about the research contests you've planned."

"I knew they would be."

"The only issue is liquidity." Katarina nudged her glasses up to the bridge of her nose. "You're spending so much on the tower. Cash is running low."

"I know. That's why I'm flying to London today."

"Today?" Katarina's eyebrows arched in surprise.

Liz wondered if she had known already, if this was another lie. "I'm going to meet with the prince from Dubai, the one you met with."

Katarina was quiet a moment, her face revealing nothing.

"It makes sense," she said. "He told me he'd like to meet with you before he makes the final decision about buying your shares. We also didn't know before exactly how much money you would need. How much do you plan to sell?"

"Whatever it takes," Liz said. "But he's not the only interested buyer who will be in London. Try to set up another meeting or two while I'm there. We can count that as part of the IPO road show, right?"

"Yes, will do. Anything else?" Katarina scribbled a note on her pad.

Liz glanced down at her jeans and bare feet. "Do you know what a naqib is?"

"It's a black veil."

"The kind that hides everything but the eyes?"

Katarina nodded.

"Okay, can you get one before I leave today?"

Katarina scribbled another note, her face blank. "Anything else?"

"That's it." Liz kept her tone flat. Business as usual. "I don't know what I'd do without you."

* * *

A smile spread across Katarina's face as she walked out of Liz's office. She went straight to her office and sent the encrypted text.

The target is leaving the country today.

Her partner responded in moments. *Time to take the engineer?*

Yes.

Katarina still needed Jax's password. Softer methods had

not worked. Dylan had confirmed what they'd found: Veruca was their best chance at getting access. *Drug her and get whatever information you can to access the coder's files.*

We'll get it. Then what do we do with the engineer?

Keep her hidden somewhere. Katarina paused. Better to be clear, and to get whatever leverage she could. *And keep her alive.*

Done. You'll have the password by tomorrow.

49

The black veil drew stares—more than Liz's flaxen blonde hair would—as she strolled down a main concourse in London Heathrow Airport. The cloth limited her vision. Glances to the side required a full head turn. The wrap's warmth suffocated her air, like she was wearing a mask to keep viruses at bay.

Surprisingly, she kind of liked it. She liked the anonymity, the darkness, the mystique. For a girl who was known everywhere she went, it was nice to cloak up in disguise, especially in an airport.

She found the Emirates Admiral's Club and showed her ticket to the guy at the desk. He studied the piece of paper. Then he glanced at her clothes and down to the screen on his pedestal desk. He finally met her eyes, failing to wipe the surprise from his face. "How was your flight, Ms. Trammell?"

"Not bad. Stale peanuts."

His brow raised. "I see this is your first time visiting our club. Would you like an overview?"

"No thanks. I'm meeting someone."

"Can I help you with an introduction?"

"I'll figure it out."

"Of course. Well, when you enter, if you take your first left, then the next left, you'll find the women's lounge."

Apparently women in veils don't get the main lounge. She walked in, skipping the first left, and looked around for a man in pink. The man with the tallest tower.

The main lounge held an odd mix of people. Some were Western businessmen with the finest suits and leather briefcases. But most wore head-to-toe white robes and full black beards. Aside from their attire, everything seemed as it should be for an airport lounge.

Liz approached a bar of food near the center of the room. The couscous smelled delicious, but she opted for a fruit cup.

Where is he? She'd expected the prince to spot her, grab her attention, and reveal himself. No one seemed to give her a second glance as she scanned the room.

She made her way to a soft leather seat by the window. She leaned back and pulled out her phone and began scrolling idly through photos people had posted. One had climbed Mt. Kilimanjaro. Another was bathing her two kids. A third—Dylan—shared a picture of his plate at a new restaurant overlooking the Bay.

"Elizabeth Trammell?"

The man facing her fit her expectations. His white robe failed to hide a rotund belly. His thick dark beard had speckles of gray. He looked like a man who knew wealth.

"Man with the tallest tower?" she asked.

He smiled and bowed slightly. "Please, follow me."

She followed him down a hallway to a frosted glass door. He opened it and stepped to the side.

She walked in and found a man sitting alone, wearing a gleaming pink tie. He approached her with a smile. His teeth were perfectly white, his skin perfectly tan, his face perfectly beautiful. Liz—in her black robe—felt like a lump of coal compared to this man in his immaculate suit.

"Thank you for coming so far." He held out his hand and peered through the narrow slit revealing Liz's eyes. "And for wearing the naqib. Few will know we've met."

She eyed his extended hand. It was thin and clean, as if it had never done a second of real work. It made her think of Jake Conrad and his weathered hands. "You don't wear a robe?" she said.

He laughed, a rich and confident sound. His pristine hand dropped to his side. "We're in London." He shrugged. "Neutral territory. You wear my country's style, and I wear yours."

Liz's gaze lingered on his pink tie. "Nice tie."

"I'm happy to oblige your tastes. Pink for Saturday, is it not?" He smiled knowingly. "I must say, you look ravishing in black."

Ravishing? Who says that? "It's a little somber."

"It brings out the sapphire in your eyes."

Liz crossed her arms.

"My apologies." His head bowed graciously. "It's just that, while I've seen the pictures and read the reports, they don't do you justice."

Liz's arms stayed crossed. Her knuckles whitened as she gripped her elbows. "You want to show me your tower?"

He nodded, a playful look in his eyes. "You're very forward. Come, I will show you."

He directed her to a seat at a long conference table, and he sat opposite from her. A screen lowered from the ceiling.

"Would you like anything to drink?" he asked.

She met his stare. "I'll take a bourbon."

His smile faltered, then flickered back on. "Straight?"

"One cube."

The man pressed the watch on his wrist, and his white-robed assistant showed up a moment later.

"Two pours of the oldest Macallan here. One cube each."

The man nodded. Liz had not expected the prince to try to match her. Weren't Muslims not supposed to drink?

"The thing about towers," he said, motioning to the screen, "is that only one can be tallest."

On the left side of the screen, Liz saw the image that she had released to the press. Her tower's long lines reached up into the sky to a pinnacle.

The servant brought in two tumblers of liquid like gold. He hurried out.

Liz sipped it and set the drink down. "And?"

He did not touch his glass. "And mine has long been the tallest."

On the right side of the screen, beside her tower, another tower appeared. Its top came into place below her tower.

"What's the point?" Liz asked.

His perfectly charming smile did not match the intensity of his eyes. "For now at least, I am still the man with the tallest tower."

She swirled her drink. "You have a few more weeks."

"I guess you're right, but you know…we'll never be satisfied by towers."

Liz's stomach churned. She stood, drink in hand, and walked to the window. *I will be satisfied, this time.*

He came to her side. "You need cash, yes?"

She set her drink on the floor and pulled the veil off her head. She shook out her undoubtedly matted and tangled hair. "I do not consider selling my shares lightly," she said. "I wanted to make sure that you weren't some pompous man with an inferiority complex, that you couldn't stand to see a woman outdo you, that you wouldn't want to pull out your manhood and parade it in front of me as if I'd be impressed. I'm not."

He was no longer smiling. "I expected that you would surprise me in some way. Everyone who knows you says you can be…unpredictable."

She went back to the table. The two towers still stood on the screen. She stared at him. "I know men, and you're one of them."

"You know American men."

The words made her think again of Jake. This man was all groomed and worldly. Jake was grit and overalls. But something about them was similar. "Is this about anything more than your ego?"

He laughed. "It is."

"What do you want?"

"I wanted to see if what people said about you is true."

"Well?"

He sipped his drink and winced. "You have fire. That much is true. But a piece of the puzzle is missing."

"Only one?"

"With a few day's notice, you flew all the way to London to meet a potential investor. Why would a woman who has everything do that? Just for money?"

"Curiosity, I suppose. You're the one who texted me."

"Guilty. But I think it's more than curiosity that drives you. It's the same thing that led me to ask you to come here. It's the same thing that makes a singular, tall tower remarkable."

She studied him, intrigued.

"It's lonely at the top," he said.

True enough. "You have to accept some compromises to rise

this high."

The prince smiled. "And let me guess, your compromise has been friendship, love?"

"That's no concern of yours."

"We'll see," he said. "We all compromise something. Your colleague is compromising far more."

"What do you mean?"

"She met with me again recently. She is a dangerous woman."

"Katarina?"

"Do you know she is a spy?"

Liz thought of what Hunter had told her, but would the prince reveal more? She kept her voice even. "She's passed vetting at the highest level. I wouldn't have hired her unless she passed the strictest scrutiny. Her background checks were clean. She's Russian, she's ambitious. So?"

The prince pulled a folded piece of paper out of his coat and placed it on the table. "Read."

Liz sat and studied the page. The words TOP SECRET appeared in bright red at the top. It was a short bio of Katarina Popova, aka Katarina Ivanovich. The daughter of convicted Soviet spies—a polymath, a mystery. The page told of her success in modeling, in school. No one could explain the funding that she'd received. No one could explain the regular calls she made to a secure line in Russia.

Liz looked up. "How do you know this is accurate?"

"Katarina thinks she has a deal with me, but our government has long suspected her. This company of yours gave us an opportunity to make contact. We think we can prove it soon enough. We can catch her, with your help."

Liz felt *deja vu*. Hunter Black had said the same thing. "Is your government working alone?"

"Not entirely," the prince said. "We know the Americans want to catch Ms. Popova. We know they met with you. We also know they are not telling you everything. You think it's a coincidence that their agent is building your tower?"

Liz kept her expression calm. "They're right about Katarina. She wants the data."

"Yes. And they've bugged your tower."

Liz had considered that, and hated the possibility. She needed to talk to Jax about Hunter. "What do you propose?"

"First, pretend that you know nothing."

"I'm already doing that."

"Good. The next thing you need is money, and to show Katarina that things are going according to her plan. So I'll lend you four billion dollars now, if you'll sell *half* of your shares to me once the quiet time passes after the IPO."

Liz considered the offer. She would get the cash now, plenty to finish the tower, and she'd sell her stock after the quiet time—that was six months from now. Not bad. "What price for my shares?"

"Market price."

"And what if that's not enough to pay back the loan?"

The prince smiled. "We'll call it even."

The deal sounded too good. At current price projections, Liz knew that half of her shares were worth about two billion, so either the prince expected the market price to double, or he was leaving something out. "When I show up with that much money," Liz said, "Katarina will be suspicious."

"Not if you tell her you agreed to sell *all* your shares."

It was a simple lie, but it might work. Katarina would think the prince would be acquiring complete control, but he would only own a fourth of Babel's stock. Liz would keep one fourth.

It still didn't add up. It meant the Prince was willing to pay two billion dollars to catch a single Russian spy in America. "What's in it for you?" Liz asked.

"Katarina is the tip of the iceberg. We want to catch the others working with her. This distraction will draw more of them out." The prince paused, studying Liz. "We also would like Babel to open an office in Dubai. A new headquarters for the Eastern Hemisphere."

"When?" Liz asked. She didn't like the idea, but if they could keep the Babel data servers in her tower, the risk would be limited.

"Within a year. You have a speech coming soon, for your IPO. Think about my offer, and if you agree, announce this plan about the Dubai office during the speech. The funds will transfer immediately."

It sounded too easy. And this man had already shown he was willing to lie to get what he wanted.

"What else?" Liz asked, stalling.

"That's all for now. Two easy things—tell Katarina that you will sell all your shares to me, and announce the new Dubai headquarters."

Liz could play along for now, for the tower. She held out her hand. "It's a deal."

They shook on it. His hand was much softer than Jake's.

50

The sound inside the tower was almost unbearable. Katarina and Jax wore earplugs as they climbed the stairs. Construction pressed ahead on the higher floors, making the stairwell an echo chamber as steel and concrete were forged into place. The skyscraper's facade had reached floor 250 just last week. They were adding two floors a day. Working overtime. Using machines. Conquering gravity.

Liz let the thrum of constant hammering and clanging metal sink into her and rattle her bones. It was progress. It was her tower rising.

They stepped out of the stairwell on floor 142. The sound wasn't so loud there. The bare concrete stretched out like an ocean in every direction until it met the sky. Exposed steel beams and pipe ran along the ceiling. It would be another week before the walls were finished here.

Liz loved the expectant feel of the space. She turned to Jax, the latest friend to betray her. "You still want your office on this corner?"

He pulled out his earplugs. His face was flush, breathing heavy. "Sorry?"

"Your office." Liz pointed to the southwest corner. "Still want it there?"

"Yeah," he said, "as long as the elevators are working, it's perfect. Love the view, but I'm not taking that many stairs again."

"Why did you want us to come here?" Katarina's shirt clung to her body, affixed by sweat. She wiped her forehead.

That was one reason Liz picked this place. They had to work to get here. But she answered with a different reason. "No better place for a private discussion."

"About?" Katarina asked.

"The IPO." Liz leaned against a concrete column as thick as she was tall. Five feet separated her from open air. The wind was swirling. "I received your message, Katarina."

Katarina nodded. No reaction.

Liz looked to Jax. "And I've been thinking about our code, how it's protected."

Jax's eyes grew wider. "You know it has to stay that way."

"That's the trouble," Liz said. "See, you both want different things. I understand that now. Maybe you both have good intentions. But I've found a different way."

"What?" Jax and Katarina asked at the same time. They exchanged a glance, then looked back to Liz.

Liz took her time. "I've seen this farmer a few times. You know, the one who wouldn't sell his land. I was there one morning and we found a hurt bird. Broken wing, I guess. We brought it inside, gave it shelter and rest. If that bird had been left out outside, it would have died. But if the bird heals, we'll have to set it free. We'll have done our part, nursing it back to health, but birds are meant for the open air."

"You're saying the bird is my code?" Jax asked.

"No, it's not that simple."

"The bird is you," Katarina said.

Liz met her assistant's big, dark eyes. She couldn't say too much. She just needed to put her opponent on edge. "The IPO is just a few days away. I know it's a tense time. Everyone's trying to figure out whether I'll sell my shares, and how much I'll sell."

"And?" Katarina asked.

"You both care about Babel. That's why I brought you up here together. I've decided to sell all of it. I want to finish my tower and stay here."

"Why?" Jax asked. "Keep some of your shares. You own over half the company. If you sell, who knows who will gain control?"

"Katarina knows."

Katarina didn't deny it. She kept her eyes on Liz, studying her as she spoke. "The sovereign wealth fund of Dubai has arranged to purchase Liz's shares. The only question was how much. And now we know. You're going to sell everything?"

Liz nodded. "I will receive the funds in advance. Four billion dollars."

"You can't..." Jax was shaking his head. "You could lose control over the data."

"It's a risk," Liz said. "But that's what it takes to finish this tower, and we'll still have the code."

"For now." Jax's voice was rising. "You can't do this."

"I have to."

Katarina's lips had parted, turning up into a hungry smile. "It's for the good. We can't keep the data locked up forever. It can change the world."

Which is why I can't let it happen. Liz wanted to tell Jax more, but he hardly deserved the truth after he'd hidden who Hunter was all these months.

"So the data is the bird," Katarina said.

"Maybe," Liz replied. "It's complicated." She stepped away from the column, back toward the stairwell. Katarina and Jax followed. "You know, we can't say anything publicly about this until after the IPO. SEC rules, right?"

Katarina nodded.

"To make it easier, I'm going to start staying in the tower. It's a safe place. No reporters. No investors." Liz pulled open the door to the stairs. She motioned for Katarina and Jax to go ahead. "Tonight I'll sleep on the hundredth floor. It's the highest floor with finished glass walls. Katarina, have someone send up a bed and some things."

"But..."

Liz smiled. "It's just a few days. The plumbing and the wireless are working. I'll be fine."

"What about the rest of today's meetings?" Katarina asked. "And tomorrow we're supposed to be back in San Francisco."

"I know. But you'll be CEO soon," Liz said. "You might as well handle the meetings. If there's an emergency, you'll know where to find me."

Katarina nodded. "We'll take care of it."

"Thanks."

Katarina started down the stairs. Jax followed, but turned back.

"Why?" he said softly.

Liz clasped his shoulder, looked down into his familiar eyes. Pain swelled up in her. He'd been with her so long, but she'd made a promise. She'd finish this tower no matter what—even if it meant leaving behind everything, even him. "Time will tell," she said.

Jax shook his head, confused, then turned to begin the long descent.

In the hours that followed, Liz found her way to the hundredth floor and began to settle in. An assistant brought up a table, a computer, a bed, and the other things she needed. Liz lost hours in the flow of work before a screen. No disruptions came.

It was night when Liz finally let herself unplug. She leaned back and let her neck fall over the back of her chair, staring at the ceiling. The unfinished concrete had spray-painted blue lines and figures, showing where bolts and pipes would connect. She heard the distant thrum of work on floors high above, but here it was quiet.

She looked again at the screen. The glow of it, bright pixels emanating into the empty floor, made her shudder. She was tiring of screens. The billions of configured 0s and 1s fed her snippets of delight—news about her marvelous success, about the tower, and about the ever-rising share price of Babel—but tonight the coded patterns began to feel cold, impersonal. They were no substitute for human connection.

Liz rose and walked to the wall of glass. Night was so different here than in the city. There were no lights in surrounding buildings, no sounds from the streets. The only things defending against the pitch-black moonless sky and pool of darkness where the land must be below were the stars and the lights of the construction.

And one other light, burning brightly but further away. Liz leaned closer to the glass. It was a fire near the Conrad farm. It looked like the bonfire that she had stood beside with Jake. She imagined him there now, looking beyond the fire, toward the tower and her.

She pressed her forehead to the window. The surface was perfectly smooth and lifeless. She imagined the feel of Jake's hand. Strong and warm, but surprisingly gentle. Deep emotion she scarcely recognized rose up in her, overcoming her loneliness, and extending out in longing like a pier reaching far into the ocean.

She had reached the end of the pier. Her company was thriving and the tower was nearly finished. She had set the trap to stop Katarina. Now what? Would she stay high in this tower, relishing the generalized adoration of the world and lacking the unique love of one person?

The prince had been right. There was so much loneliness here, at the top.

She longed to be with Jake.

But what was she even considering? What would it look like? Could she abandon all that she had worked so hard for just to be with a farmer? As she looked on the tiny dot of his bonfire, it swelled in her vision and her answer was shockingly clear and immediate. *Yes, I could.*

She wanted rest from the tower and the world, and she had seen where to find that rest, with him. Jake could lead her into it, his steady hand leading her.

She wanted that. But she couldn't. She stepped back from the glass and turned reluctantly to the glow of pixels. She still owed it to Daddy to see this through. To herself. To Jax, to every employee of Babel, to everyone who believed in what could be done in this Tower.

She threw her shoulders back, and lifted her weary head by force of will. Only she could do it. She had to keep going. She had to do this.

51

Rachel was slicing strawberries in the kitchen when her phone rang. It vibrated on the counter, and the name on the screen was a surprise. Jax had never called her before. She hadn't heard from Liz or any of the others since the last phone call about Jake.

She wiped her hands off on her apron, leaving faint red lines. "Hello?"

"Hey, Rachel. It's Jax."

"Hey."

"Sorry this is out of the blue, but I'd like to talk to you." He paused. "Can I come over?"

"To my house?"

"Yeah."

"When?"

"Now."

Rachel glanced around the kitchen. The kids were playing in the other room, but it would be time for naps soon. "You're in Chicago?"

"Business meetings. They finished early."

"You could have given me a little warning."

"This is important."

"So important that you waited until the last minute? I could have been gone."

"You don't travel much anymore."

His words burrowed under her skin. She couldn't deny it,

and she shouldn't have to defend it. "You can come over. You have the address?"

"Yes. See you in twenty minutes."

"See you soon."

Rachel hung up and looked in the mirror. She slipped the apron over her head. She still looked awful. Unwashed hair. Jeans and a shirt with spit-up stains. She spent the next twenty minutes cleaning like a whirlwind.

By the time Jax knocked, the kids were settling down for naps and at least the living room didn't have toys on the floor. She'd have to keep him out of the kitchen.

Rachel opened the door. Jax was there, looking small. Instinct made her glance past him, as if someone would be watching or suspicious of him entering. She saw no one.

"Hey Jax. Come on in."

"Thanks. Good to see you."

They stepped into a cramped living room. Jax sank into the well-worn cushions while Rachel poured tea. Evidence of kids was everywhere. Pictures on the walls, a basket full of pink and blue balls, and a bookshelf full of garish children's scribbles and colors.

"How's the family?" Jax asked.

Rachel sat across from him—the man whose code had taken her best friend...not that it still bothered her. "We're good." Rachel's voice came out clipped. "Just got the little ones down for a nap. Never a dull moment."

"Glad to hear it. And Paul?"

"He's fine. Working hard."

"And you?"

"Why are you here, Jax?"

"I know you and Liz aren't talking." He paused, as if

waiting for her to respond. She didn't. "Well, now she's excluding all of us in one way or another."

"Even Dylan?" Rachel asked.

Jax nodded stoically. "She's really gone manic about this tower. She found her father's design, and she's been building it."

"I've seen the news, and the show."

"Right." He paused, obviously mulling something. "Listen, what's the one thing that Liz has never done, unlike pretty much every other woman?"

Rachel couldn't remember Jax ever being so serious. "It's been a long time since she lost her confidence."

Jax smiled. "Right, she's not one to doubt herself." He glanced past Rachel, to the pictures on the wall behind her. "You and Paul chose a different life. I'm not here to question that. But think about it. Why didn't you stay with Babel? Make a fortune?"

"Paul wanted to stay in Chicago, close to our families."

"Yes. Why? And why did you stay with him?"

"Because I love him... What's your point?"

Jax studied his cup of tea as he spoke. "I've always loved Liz in my way. So has Dylan, and Owen probably did too."

They fell silent.

"He was a bright soul," Rachel said.

"We miss him." Jax's eyes were on the floor. "Liz hasn't been the same since he died. It's like she's losing it. And now she's cooped up in the tower, alone." Jax looked up and met Rachel's eyes. "Anyway, here's the point: Liz never really loved us back. Ever since her mom died, has she loved anyone?"

"Her dad."

"Anyone living?"

"She loves herself." Rachel didn't mean to sound harsh, but she felt the old anger swelling up. It didn't surprise her that Liz would hole up in the tower, claiming the murder as her own personal mark of tragedy, Owen's death like another merit badge.

"Well, I think she's starting to love someone."

Rachel set her tea on the table, hands folded in her lap. She remembered her only brief call with Liz weeks ago. *Could it be Jake?* "I'm not sure Liz knows how to love."

"Harsh."

"The truth can be that way. Liz won't give up her own independence."

"Yeah, she'd probably give us up before that."

Rachel met Jax's eyes calmly. "People lose their way when they lose their community. We weren't meant to be alone. We become like unanchored boats in the middle of the ocean." She paused. "Who's the guy?"

"He's not what you would expect. He's a farmer…"

"So it's my cousin, Jake?"

"How do you…?"

"Owen told me about him. Didn't he tell you we're cousins?"

Jax shook his head.

"He probably didn't think it was relevant, but it is. I can see why Liz likes him. They're both stubborn as it gets."

"Well she's been acting weird ever since she met him," Jax said. "Now she's agreed to sell all her shares in Babel. Soon she'll even step down as CEO."

"Good. I've been telling her to do that for years."

Jax shook his head. "Not good. Can you imagine if Babel fell into dangerous hands? I didn't write a translation code so that the world's conversations would be eavesdropped. People are after it. I think it's why someone killed Owen. And my best engineer, Veruca, disappeared for two whole days. The police think she may have been kidnapped. She wasn't hurt, but she didn't remember anything about what happened. She must have been drugged or something. She knew things that I wouldn't want others to know…"

"Why are you telling me all this?"

Jax shrugged. "I'm nervous. I don't know what to do, and I'm worried about Liz. She's not leaving the tower anymore. She's letting her hair grow longer. She's even stopped color-coordinating her shirts with the day of the week."

"Wow, she'd been doing that for over a decade."

"I'm telling you, this is a problem. She needs to get focused on the real threats. You're the only one she trusts to tell the truth, the brutal honest truth."

"She won't listen to me anymore."

"But your cousin will. He's religious, like you. Talk to him. Make him understand how Liz ticks, how she keeps coming to him just because he's a challenge. Convince him to sell his land, to get away from her."

Rachel sipped her tea, thinking.

"I think she's losing it," Jax added. "You still care about her, right?"

"Of course. I mean, we're not in each other's lives anymore, but I could talk to Jake."

"Great, that's all I'm asking. As long as he's near the tower, she can't seem to focus. She needs to get her attention back on the company and the data."

And on you, Rachel thought. She had her doubts about Jax's motives, but she agreed Liz needed help—and Jake probably did, too. She had considered visiting for her grandfather's ninetieth birthday anyway.

"Okay," she said, "I'll pay him a visit."

52

Tomorrow Dylan would be worth hundreds of millions. From the moment Babel went public, he could sell his founders' shares and rake in cash like he'd never dreamed. He could buy a mansion in Palo Alto, a new Ferrari, a year in a Spanish villa, whatever.

He didn't care. He felt terrible.

Liz had called him for another meeting. This time in the tower. This time probably worse. He watched the elevator's numbers flashing upwards—100-101-102-103... It was incredible. He didn't want to admit it, but there was something amazing about rising this high above the earth's surface.

The elevator stopped. Floor 120. When he stepped out, Liz was waiting for him. Her blonde hair was longer than he'd ever seen it. She wore a black V-neck t-shirt. Black was not a color in her weekly rotation.

"You're late," she said, hand on her hip.

"It's a long elevator ride."

She laughed and led him to two low chairs by the edge of the floor. Glass walls revealed a brilliant view. The sun was low on the horizon. The land flat as a pancake, and just as golden brown.

A small table sat between the two chairs. It held a bottle of wine, two glasses, and a tray of cheeses.

"Is this a date?" Dylan asked as he sat.

Liz shrugged, fell into the seat beside him. Her legs

crossed and her shoulders fell back. He hadn't seen her this relaxed in years. "Katarina picked the cheeses," she said.

Dylan swallowed, but kept his cool. "What kinds?"

"Who knows? Let's try them. Think they'll be poisoned?"

Dylan forced himself to play it cool. "Still think she's a Russian spy?"

"If so, I guess this is like Russian roulette. You try first."

Dylan eyed the three blocks of cheese. One had marbled blue, one was flaky white, the other yellow. "Seriously?"

She poured the red wine into his glass. "This is a cabernet from Napa. Should pair nicely. And yes, seriously."

No way any of them were poisoned. Liz had to be joking. Dylan decided to go with the yellow cheese. It was cheddar, probably American. He sliced off a piece, put it in his mouth. Tasted good.

Liz watched him calmly as he chewed, her face blank.

"Now the wine," she said.

He drank. "Not bad. A bit fruit-forward. Your turn."

Liz looked down to the cheeses. "I figure Katarina wants you dead more than me. She needs me, seeing as I'm the one who can access the data. Not sure she ever really needed you. Either way, no one poisons bleu cheese."

She pulled off a chunk and dropped it into her mouth. Then she brought the glass to her lips. "Yes, quite nice. And not—"

Her eyes went wide.

Her hands went to her throat.

Dylan rushed to her side. "Lay down," he said. "Are you okay?"

She was silent, shaking slightly.

"Liz? Liz!"

She burst out laughing and Dylan fell back onto the floor. He felt ridiculous.

"I'm sorry," she said, still laughing. "I just couldn't resist. I've never seen you so tense. So you thought Katarina would actually poison our cheese?"

"No, I mean…" He returned to his seat, trying to act calm. "That's crazy, Dylan. Unless…"

"Unless Katarina really is a Russian spy," Dylan finished.

"Right. So, is she?"

"I don't know. I really don't."

"You think this is some kind of game?" Liz asked, her eyes boring into him.

"It's never been a game. She just wants to make the data public, like I did."

"*Did?*"

"Still do," Dylan admitted. "But that's it, I swear."

"You think she killed Owen?"

"She was in San Francisco when it happened."

"So did she pay someone to do it?"

"No clue." Dylan met Liz's gaze, but couldn't hold it. He stood up and went to the wall of glass and started to pace, thinking about the cheese and Owen and Katarina. He'd realized that Katarina was trying to use him, to get info about the data and Liz. But did she really think he would betray his friend? No, he wouldn't do that, but he would try to help Liz behind her back. This was bigger than them. It was for a better world. The Babel data needed to be public.

"Earth to Dylan," Liz said. "Mr. Space Cadet clearly knows more than he's saying."

"We went kayaking."

"Oh great, that explains it."

"After Owen was shot. We were on the San Francisco Bay. I agreed to help her find a way to access the data, to make it public." Dylan told her the rest, about his meetings with Katarina, about her veiled threats.

"Sit down," Liz said, after he finished. "Drink your wine."

Dylan took another sip, a big one.

"Here's the thing." Liz was now pacing in front of him, a silhouette in the sunset. The sky was orange and red outside the windows. Not a cloud in the sky. "I knew all this," she said. "But I'm glad you finally told me, Dylan, because I never lost faith in you."

"You didn't?"

She shook her head. "Big brothers do stupid things, but they always look out for little sisters."

He smiled, feeling a turn inside, a turn that he'd been wanting and waiting for. "True."

"Katarina thought she might win an ally close to me. And she might learn more about the data from you, Dr. Galant."

"I teach about medical data. That doesn't mean I know a whole lot."

"Jax has the coding, you have the looks. Is that it?"

"It was never that simple," Dylan said. "But yes, you and Jax have your coding secrets. I never denied admiring that."

"And Katarina thought she might use you to learn them."

"I haven't given her much."

"You set up the cameras on the Conrad farm."

Dylan started to deny it, but decided against it. "That was harmless."

"Harmless until I was there, and someone knew it, and then Owen died on his way to see me."

"You don't—"

"He was shot that night, and Katarina arranged it."

"Really? How can you be sure?"

"I have my sources. She texted someone near here right before it happened. Owen warned me…"

"I had no idea."

"The point is, I want friends who stay on my side."

Dylan flinched. "I'm sorry."

"Are you?"

"I am. I really am, Liz. I never thought it would go this far, with Owen, with everything."

"You're dealing with a very dangerous woman."

"I figured that out…too late." He glanced down at the cheese, and laughed. "I guess that's why I thought it would be poisoned."

"Katarina didn't deliver the cheese." Liz smiled. "I have a new assistant for that. Katarina's too busy trying to undermine me and steal all my data to give to Russia, so they can use it against the free world. But it's not too late. I could use your help."

It was quiet then, the sun turning blood red as it fell below the horizon. Dylan's mind rehashed months of betrayal, and the money that awaited him. Babel was going public. Liz was like a little sister. He could help her. "Just tell me what I need to do."

"Tomorrow I will give a speech as part of the official IPO," Liz said. "The rest of the funds will arrive for the tower, and the data will move to the servers immediately. Katarina will try to access it. But she'll need one thing."

"What?"

Liz held out her arm and plucked out a single, almost invisible hair. She handed it Dylan. "Give her this and tell her it's the key to unlock the code. Say that you got Jax to tell you about the hair and the DNA encryption. She'll believe it."

"Why are you letting her have it? And why through me?"

"Because she trusts you," Liz said. "And this is your chance to win my trust back."

53

The D.C. attorney, Chris Planter, waited for the elevator, arms folded. He had worked with Presidents and Senators. His clients were CEOs. He wore a pinstripe suit like armor. Nothing intimidated him. But something was different—a little off—about this woman in a skyscraper in Nebraska. He felt his heart pumping faster as the elevator doors opened.

Two others entered the elevator with him. His associate and a young woman, Liz's assistant. The elevator began to rise, the numbers above the door reached 120.

"Here we are," said the assistant.

The door opened to a vast concrete space without a single wall. Before stepping out, Chris asked, "How many floors will there be?"

"250. The frame is already that high. They're filling it out as fast as they can." The assistant pointed outside the elevator, to the right. "Go ahead. She'll be over there."

Chris stepped out and saw, at the floor's edge, a slim figure holding a still pose with hands and feet planted on the ground.

"No, just him," said the assistant.

Chris turned back and saw his young associate halfway out of the elevator.

"Sorry," said the assistant. "She invited only Mr. Planter."

He nodded to his associate. "Wait in the lobby."

"I'll be watching my email if you need anything."

"Thanks." Chris turned to Liz's assistant. "You sure she's

ready to meet?"

"Go ahead," the assistant said. "She'll be ready."

Chris nodded and turned back to Liz. She hadn't moved. He walked toward her. "Ms. Trammell?"

She didn't respond, didn't budge. Music filled the space. Something with words, but not in English. It was trancelike, sounded Scandinavian.

He inched closer. "Ms. Trammell?"

This time she lowered to the floor, pressing back into a crouch, then rose up to her feet. Her face showed a smile, but also a wild sort of energy.

He glanced down, awkwardly, only for his eyes to pass over her yoga tights and settle on her bare feet. His hands went to the knot of his tie, as if loosening it might help. "Is this still a good time?"

"Yes," she said. "Have you met with the President?"

"Two days ago," Chris said. "He knew all about your building."

"And you've told him about the foreign buyer?"

"Yes."

"Good."

Chris hated one thing above all: not knowing. He had been working for her without complete information. He kept his face smooth, his coiffed hair a helmet of dignity. "What happens next?"

"When I called you a few weeks ago, I had just discovered this U.S. law, the one that could stop the deal." She was rocking on her bare feet, excited. "A foreign buyer, like the prince from Dubai, can't buy a company if it affects national security."

"Right," Chris said. "And the whole point—what I told

the President—was that you did not want this deal to go through, that you opposed the prince."

"Right, but here's the thing, the prince will be sending me four billion dollars today." Liz held out her palms in innocence. "I met with him. He told me about Katarina, who's the real danger. I agreed to play along with the prince so Katarina would reveal herself, her plan. Then we could catch her."

"Who's we?"

"Allies," Liz said. "The point is that Babel's data has to be secure. Katarina will become the acting CEO. She'll have access to the data vault, and if she uses the data it would be a disaster."

"This information would have been helpful for the President." Chris was a patient man whose patience was wearing thin. "I have a reputation with him. He trusts me."

Liz smiled, quiet for a moment. "Well, good news, I'm going to let you deliver a huge PR victory to the President."

"Go on."

"First, someone else is going to join us. Hunter Black, the chief engineer of tower construction, and as I've learned, a CIA operative."

"What?" Chris asked, trying to process why a spy would be leading the tower construction, and why Liz would tell him that.

"You'll need to work together," Liz said. "And I wanted to have my lawyer with me for this meeting. Okay?"

Chris nodded.

Liz called her assistant and asked her to bring Mr. Black up for their meeting. He arrived a few minutes later and Liz made the basic introductions. To Chris, Hunter Black looked like a typical engineer: brown hair and brown eyes, a square jaw and an easy smile. Nothing remarkable about him. Perfect for an agent, Chris figured.

"Does the President know about Katarina?" Liz asked.

The sudden and direct question did not alter Hunter's smile. "He's been briefed."

"Here's what he needs to know now," Liz said. "Today, as part of the IPO, I will announce that the data is moving to the tower. And that Katarina will be taking over as CEO. You know what that means?"

Hunter nodded. "Katarina will try to access the data."

"You'll need to be ready to bring her in. Can I trust you to do that?"

"When do you think she'll act?"

Liz shrugged. "You're the spy. I'll count on you to monitor her."

"Of course." Hunter glanced to Chris, then back to Liz. "No offense, but why is your lawyer involved?"

"Because this isn't just about the data. It's about control of my company, and Chris is going to be talking to the President again soon. He needs to know what's going on. You know about the prince in Dubai?"

"He's buying your shares," Hunter said.

"Half of them." Liz paused, holding the gazes of both men. "Mr. Planter will ensure he doesn't get a controlling stake, and Mr. Black will be handling Katarina. Are we on the same page?"

Both men nodded.

"Anything else?" Chris asked.

"No," Liz said. "It's almost done."

* * *

Four hours later Liz had put on her CEO face. No suit, of course, but she'd at least showered and changed out of her yoga pants. The news cameras zoomed onto her flawless smile with the Nebraska landscape stretching behind her and the tower looming above. Bright green grass covered the ground, and the June air was fresh.

Liz had her Babel team assembled behind her for the speech—Katarina, Jax, Dylan, and dozens of others who had joined the company in its first days. The only one missing was Owen.

"We want the world to be connected," Liz announced. "And it should also be private and safe, so we can all talk with friends and loved ones with peace of mind. Your data will be secure. Today it moves to this tower, with the most sophisticated security the world offers."

Cameras flashed. Stocks traded. The price rose.

Liz came to Babel's plans for the future. "We are a global company, and we will need a global presence." She held out her arms, motioning to the tower. "This will be our headquarters, a place for the best and the brightest. Our next regional office will be in Dubai. It will open within the year, a testament to how our translations are changing the Middle East. When people can speak freely, without borders, it brings understanding, and understanding brings peace."

Liz talked about Babel's contracts with the United Nations, with the World Bank, and with governments around the world. She talked about new frontiers of translation technology. She talked about the company's leadership. She introduced Katarina, who would become the global executive in charge of operations. She talked on, and Babel prices soared.

By the time the speech finished, Liz had four billion dollars from the prince in her bank account. She had everything she needed to finish the tower and to protect the data. She had Katarina's position. She had Dylan's loyalty.

The trap was set. Now she just needed to wait.

54

By the time Rachel, her husband, and her kids were an hour from the Conrad farm, she regretted the decision. Hours and hours in the car, with the constant chirping of two little ones in the back, had driven her crazy. They could have had a nice Saturday morning in the Chicago suburbs. Coffee, backyard toys, and a farmer's market. Instead they woke three hours before dawn to drive to a real farm. The food wouldn't be any better. But it was family. You dropped everything for family, especially when you might also help a friend who had lost her way.

It was her grandfather Pops' ninetieth birthday. He and Grandma had eight kids. The eight kids had twenty-seven of their own.

"Mommy!" shouted Tyler from the back.

She turned around and smiled, for the hundredth time. "Yes, honey?"

Her toddler pointed out the window. "Cow! Cow!"

Rachel nodded. "Yes, you're right. Cows."

They drove past another field of them. Her husband mumbled, "Smells like roses."

Rachel had barely noticed it. The air had the familiar sickly sweet tinge of manure. That meant they were close.

"What's thaaaat?" asked her five-year-old, Madison. "Look!"

Rachel saw it on the flat horizon: a needle of steel rising up in the distance. "That's a tower," she said.

"Whoa, that's big."

"I still can't believe she built it here," her husband said. "It's crazy."

"Liz was always a little crazy. You know that."

Her husband laughed. "Yeah, but it's different when you're young. Billionaires can make the crazy actually happen. I read that the total cost could top five billion. Five billion...in Nebraska!"

"Liz lost her way a long time ago."

"It's insane. I can't wait to hear what your grandfather says about it."

"Don't get him started."

As Rachel and her husband talked more about the tower, Rachel realized Liz had succeeded in at least one way. Her tower in the middle of cornfields fueled curiosity. Everyone would be mesmerized by this tech magnate's lavish project. The tower had secured Liz's spot on magazine covers for the rest of her eccentric life. She was becoming a modern Howard Hughes.

They finally saw the familiar white barn and silo in the distance, and they turned down the long, straight dirt road to the farmhouse. It was immaculately white. The only things out of place from her memory were the row of parked cars out front and the tower looming in the distance.

A troop of cousins greeted them and helped them unload. The kids flooded out into the farm, throwing stones and running on the bright green grass. It was freedom from the minivan, and they loved it.

Joyful chaos ensued, and Rachel recanted her prior regrets. It was good to be here. This place was a happy one in her memory, and it was one of the few that remained the same. Pops had always been like that—an unmoving stone within the racing river of progress.

Jake was an apple fallen from the same tree. He greeted her with a warm hug before hauling a few of their bags inside.

It wasn't until after dinner and the kids were asleep that she managed to pull him aside. They sat in rocking chairs on the front porch, watching the lightning bugs and drinking iced tea. Beyond, the lights of construction lit the upper half of the tower, high above the flat horizon.

"This place has always been so peaceful and quiet," Rachel said. "The tower must bother you."

As usual, Jake took his time before answering. "More than it should. But we're getting used to it. Nothing else has changed."

"You're older now."

Jake laughed lightly. "You, too. Things good in Chicago?"

"Paul's working hard, but he's doing well. The kids are great. Tyler will start preschool this fall. After this weekend, I bet he'll want to grow a beard."

Jake ran his hands along his thick brown hair. "He might as well start now. Took me twenty years."

Quiet fell over them. Even the conversation from the farmhouse was muted. Occasional clangs of construction and chirps of crocuses echoed faintly in the night sky. The late spring air felt alive.

"I heard you met Liz Trammell," Rachel said.

He nodded and kept his eyes on the tower.

"I've known her a long time," Rachel continued. "I've seen the effect she has on men. I'm surprised you managed to hold out. She usually gets what she wants."

"So do I."

She heard an odd resolve in his voice. The kind he typically saved for projects that improved the farm. "And what do you want?"

He turned to her. "I want God's will. He put her in my path, and He put me in hers."

At least he spoke his mind. "She's not right for you, Jake. She's unstable, vain, arrogant—"

He held up his hand. "She's spirited. That can be good, if she focuses on the right things."

Rachel laughed lightly. Maybe even Jake had fallen under Liz's spell. "She was my best friend. Don't you think I tried to change her focus over the years? I've tried by example. I've tried by words. I've tried by negotiation. The woman's path has not altered a single degree. She's still full of pride."

"Stern words," Jake said. "But you almost sound jealous."

"I'm not—" Rachel paused, forcing herself to be honest. "Only part of me is jealous. Who wouldn't want beauty, fame, and fortune?"

"I don't."

"Exactly. I just can't imagine her bending, much less breaking, the way she'd have to, to fit with you."

"We'll see. I'm going to visit her tower, and the way it stands now, one of us must break. Or at least bend." He fixed his heavy, serious gaze on her.

"It usually works that way..." Rachel realized Jake could be right. Maybe all of her prior senses of warning about this tower had been misplaced. Maybe Liz was supposed to have built it just so she could confront this immovable object in her path. Maybe God was using Jake to change her. "Why do you want to visit the tower?"

"To show her this isn't just about my farm," he said softly. "To show her I care about her."

"The latest reports say she isn't taking meetings. Apparently she's holed up in there."

"I'm still going. She'll know I tried."

Rachel remembered Jax's visit, and what he'd said to her about Jake: *Convince him to sell his land, to get away from her.* That clearly wasn't happening. She wondered if Jax was part of the problem for Liz—a constant reminder of her past and her ambition. "When you go to the tower," Rachel said, "I think you should meet Liz's friend, Jax. He'll know the most about how she's doing. But I'll warn you, he loves her."

"I can't blame him."

Rachel eyed the lights of the tower in the distance. Despite all her disagreements with Liz, she cared so much about her. She didn't want her to be hurt. So she decided to equip Jake with more background about Liz, telling him about her father's death and how she'd responded by ignoring the pain and putting every ounce of effort into starting this company with Jax. She explained that Jax had tied the Babel code to Liz, and how he couldn't stand that she was so interested in a farmer.

Jake listened intently to every word. "You're right," he said. "I should meet this Jax Wong."

55

Jake took one glance back at his land and turned down the two-lane road. He stayed on the left curb, walking at a steady pace. The sun was low on the horizon, the sky clear, and the air unusually warm—like the perfect stillness before a storm. He'd reach the tower before the spring day bloomed in full.

His mom had insisted he drive the old pickup truck. Jake had refused. A little exercise and fresh air would clear his mind this morning, and so it did. He saw the tower clearly as he approached. Its high lines made him tilt his head back even from this distance. The building seemed to have no end, especially with the cranes still hoisting beams and raising the top, higher and higher.

But never reaching a destination, Jake thought. Maybe it would be best for Liz to reach the heavens, so she'd know for certain that wasn't the way to find God. Maybe then she'd come looking along the earth, and inside herself. Jake's hope had not wavered after Rachel told him about Liz's past. He believed she'd come around.

Walking to her tower might help. She'd find out about it. She'd know then that it was no longer just pride keeping him from selling the land. It was the land that kept them tied together.

The walk took two hours. Jake drew stares as he strode down the long path to the tower's base. Parallel lines of newly planted trees ushered him in. The workers he passed wore homogenous grey outfits with rainbow patches on their shoulders. Their faces showed a hundred different nationalities. Jake couldn't name them, he just knew they were not from around here. But in a way they were the same. Humans were always the same at their core. Beautiful vessels. Broken vessels.

Jake had expected to reach a door to enter the tower. But the space beneath it was wide open for a hundred feet up. The four immense steel legs of the tower splayed out far beyond the tower's center. They planted into the earth like roots. In the center of the legs were clear glass shafts. Jake watched a dozen elevators rise and fall, carrying streams of workers in and out. Many of them huddled around this open lobby. Some had set up market stands, selling food and other things.

Jake made his way through the crowd to one of the lines to the elevators. Ten or so men and women waited in front of him. An elevator rushed down, and its huge glass doors opened. The box was twice his height. He expected to have to wait for the next one. But not only did he fit, ten more people who had lined up behind him fit as well. No one was left waiting.

He went to a corner of the elevator, ignoring the stares.

Then, like the snap of a coiled rubber band, the elevator flew up. Jake couldn't keep the gasp from escaping his lips. He'd never moved so fast, nor so high.

"First time, eh?" asked a woman beside him.

He turned to her and nodded. She wore the grey uniform and a bright smile. She reminded him of Annie.

A man standing next to the woman laughed and said something Jake couldn't understand. He didn't even recognize the language, or the man's nationality. Somewhere in Asia, he guessed.

The woman smiled at the man. "I remember, too. Feels like a roller coaster." She glanced at Jake's overalls. "What brings you here?"

"I have a meeting."

The man beside the woman said something, this time to Jake.

Jake just stared back, not understanding. The elevator soared higher into the building, now lit by lights on solid walls rather than the sun through the glass. Not much bothered Jake, but he began to feel trapped.

The man's brow furrowed. He spoke again, more emphatically.

"Forget your Babel?" the woman asked.

"Don't have one."

Their eyes opened wide. The man spoke first. He sounded confused.

"I know," the woman said to him. She turned to Jake. "Look, it's not our job to question you, but security is strict here. If you don't have a badge, much less a Babel, I doubt they're going to let you in."

Jake nodded, but didn't respond.

The elevator stopped and everyone inside began streaming out. The woman paused. "Well, nice meeting you."

Jake followed the group out and entered the biggest room he'd ever seen. It seemed the size of a football field, with ceilings almost as high as the floor was wide. The elevators were in the center. More continued up from there, and more went down.

Jake spotted a desk nearby with people sitting behind it. He approached a woman there and introduced himself.

"Welcome to the Babel Tower." She motioned to an area

with trees and benches behind her. "If you'll take a seat there, Mr. Wong should be down any moment."

Jake moved to where she'd pointed, mesmerized by the trees. They were palms planted in giant troughs. The tops rose high in the air, catching the sun that poured through the tower's glass walls. He passed the benches to one of the walls. His breath froze when he looked out. The ground seemed miles below them. The people down there were like ants.

He looked up, expecting to see the tower's top. But he didn't. The steeply sloped wall of glass rose at least as far above as it stretched down.

He turned toward the tower's east wall, hoping to catch a glimpse of his farm. But a voice stopped him.

"Jake?" A short man rushed up to him and shook his hand. "I'm Jax Wong. It's a pleasure to meet you."

"Likewise."

Jax led Jake to an elevator without a line. He pressed his thumb to a panel beside it, and the doors opened. They rode up and up, nearly as far as before, Jake guessed.

When they stepped out, Jake felt like the floor rocked beneath his feet. He stared down, not sure what was happening.

"It's the sway," Jax said. "Up here, near the top, the tower can sway a bit with the wind. But I assure you, it's very stable. Engineering's greatest feat, in fact."

Jake followed him down a short hall to a large office with window walls. Jake thought he saw a hint of mountains over the curve of the horizon.

"The Rockies," Jax said. "Hard to believe, right?" He motioned to a chair in front of the desk. "Please, have a seat. Can I get you anything to drink or eat?"

"No, thank you. I came to talk about Liz."

"Straight to business." Jax sat in the oversized chair on the other side of the table. He leaned forward on his elbows and met Jake's eyes evenly. "Rachel told me most of it. You're not the first person to fall for Liz, you know."

Jake considered disagreeing with Jax's wording, but there wasn't much point to it. *Fall for her...or called to be with her.* Both got at the same truth. Jake simply shrugged. "I know."

"And she's never fallen for anyone."

"Yet."

Jax grinned. "I must admit, you're not like most of the men who have fallen for her."

"Rachel told me I should speak with you."

"I can tell you what others have tried. That way you'll know what to avoid."

Something in the little man's voice caught Jake's attention. "What did you try?" he asked.

Jax leaned back, hands behind his head. "So I see rumors have traveled." He laughed, defensive. "Like I said, most men love Liz one way or another. She has that effect."

"Do you think you'd be happy if she loved you back?"

The question wiped away the smile on Jax's face, as if he just realized he was facing an equal. "Of course. Happier, at least."

"Why? Just because you'd have her?"

"Yes."

"I figured you were smarter than that."

"Bold words, Jake. It's been a while since someone questioned my intelligence."

"You can't solve a person like an equation."

"And you'll never get Liz."

"You know better than that." Jake felt a tilting in the air, like a tilting of his lance in a joust. "If you really love her, wouldn't you value her happiness more than your own?"

Jax stood from his chair and moved to the window. His hands clasped behind his back. He spoke softly. "Liz said you were different."

"And now she wants something different."

"Even if she does, don't get your hopes up. She's spent, what, ten hours with you?"

"Time does not limit God's plans." Jake stood, and Jax leaned back from the larger man. Jake kept his voice gentle. "I came because I want to help."

"You just want my help with Liz."

"Part of her is wrapped up in you," Jake said. "The two of you have been on this quest together, right?"

Jax's brow lifted in surprise. "Interesting theory."

"I bet she's loved you all along, you just won't let yourself see it."

"I wish you were right."

"The two of you have been partners for years. Most people today don't understand love. They think it only finds fulfillment in the body. But it's purest in the mind and soul."

Jax sighed and rubbed his eyes, as if thinking. "What do you want from me?"

"I want you to love Liz. Really love her."

Jax breathed out, weary. "I always have."

Jake put his hand on the man's shoulder. "Then give her what's best for her."

"And what exactly do you think that is?"

"Stop hiding things from her. Tell her the truth. Then bless her leaving. She's stuck in between us now—between what we represent. It's hurting her." Jake paused. "Maybe like it's hurting you."

Jax didn't respond. He shrugged off Jake's hand and walked back to the window. He stared at the blue sky. He thought of the forecasted thunderstorm. He thought of the chaos inside him, roiling and rejecting and yet relishing the prospect of freedom. He'd made Liz sign the pact so long ago, to have him alone as the one who understood the link of her DNA to Babel's data and its code. He'd believed, he'd *known*, that in time the proximity would make her love him. But it had become a weight on them both. And now he'd been hiding things from her—about Hunter Black and the information he'd given the government.

When he finally turned and met the farmer's eyes, Jax felt confident about what to do but terrified about what it might mean. "Liz is tired," he said. "She's worn herself down, especially with this tower and the IPO. She won't listen to anyone. She's cooped up alone at the top of the tower."

"You can still do something," Jake said. "You have to do something if you love her."

"I'll consider it."

Jake nodded. "I'm praying you will do whatever it takes."

56

Liz's ears popped as she climbed the stairs, past the elevators' highest reach. The pressure built with each step up. The air was thinner here, and her breathing was fast and shallow.

By the fourth flight of stairs, she sympathized with the Everest climbers. But she forced herself to press onward. Her legs began to feel the burn of anaerobic effort. Her calves tensed, her thighs screamed out. She ignored the pain. She relished the pain. She took another step.

Reg Trammell's designs had defied the world's limits, and she had his blood, his genes. She imagined him walking beside her now. No, not beside her. He'd be in front of her, setting the pace and grinning back at her.

Daddy would demand the best out of himself. He would not accept any weakness. He didn't have to expect anything out of his daughter. She saw the way he pushed himself, and that was enough. That had always been enough.

Liz pushed herself harder, taking the stairs two at a time, her chest tightening with the effort. Her head spun at the lack of oxygen.

She took the stairs three at a time.

And then she reached the top. This high in the tower, the floor was only twenty feet wide, a concrete platform with brand new glass walls. In the center was a ladder going even higher.

Liz looked down at her bare feet as she stepped forward,

enjoying the feel of virgin concrete under her toes. They'd finished the pinnacle's facade only yesterday. She kept her eyes down as she approached the ladder. She didn't want to spoil the first impression of a view sweeping over the world.

Trying to catch her breath, she pulled the carabiner out of her pocket—Jax had insisted—and snapped it to the hook on the pole holding the ladder.

She climbed a few steps and pressed her hands up against the porthole above her. It had a pressurized seal, like a door in a submarine. She spun the lock to open it. She heard the POP as the seal released. She spun it three more times around and pushed up. Her arms strained against the weight and she felt like a sewer-dweller emerging from a manhole.

The air blasted inside like an arctic gust.

She pressed her eyes closed and took another deep breath. The cold air burned her lungs, but she felt more alive than she'd ever been. She'd given up daily control of Babel, sold the company to the public, and built this tower. She'd done everything she'd planned. She was free.

She reached for the next rung of the ladder, and another. The wind whipped violently at her as she climbed. Her hair snapped over her face, her black shirt hugged her back tight and flapped like a loose sail in front of her. Her body shivered at the cold and the exhilaration.

She forced herself onward, climbing ever up. She'd made it maybe twenty feet before she stopped again. Her body refused to make another move. She squeezed her eyes, readying to open them. Ready to face the past, ready to face her inner demons, ready to face anything.

This is for you, Daddy.

Only the wind answered.

I know you're with me. But like you, I am my own, and I have made this reality.

Her eyes opened. Her knuckles were pale white, clenching the smooth steel ladder. Beyond that was the greatest emptiness she'd ever seen. The earth was so small below that it lost its color and form. It was just a blank canvas.

Tears filled her eyes. They blew away in the wind. She imagined them flipping and falling thousands of feet down until they landed like innocent, salty raindrops.

Just the wind, she lied to herself. It wasn't that she felt foolish for crying or for expecting something more. It wasn't that her father was nowhere to be seen or heard. It wasn't that her soul felt emptier and less satisfied than ever before. She clung to the ladder and cried.

LIZ.

Her sobs froze in her throat. She looked around her. Of course no one was there. She looked up into the thin atmosphere.

Then she remembered her Babel. Maybe it was malfunctioning under this pressure. She pulled it off and examined the silicon chip. It was this little chip that had built the tower. And now it was talking to her?

PRIDE LEADS TO DESTRUCTION. I GIVE GRACE TO THE HUMBLE.

Liz heard the voice from outside herself, but it resonated deep within. She thought of her father, standing atop one of his buildings the moment before he jumped. Had he heard voices? Had he lost it?

GRACE TO THE HUMBLE.

The wind wailed and the words filled her with wonder—a sense of immense, incomprehensible size, as if she and the tower were zero against infinity. As hard as she'd strived to reach this place, it was still bound by space and time. She was finite, but this voice was not.

Part of her feared and despaired this sudden sense of her own smallness, but she thought of someone who had accepted this, who seemed to know what was *enough*. She thought of Jake. She remembered their first meeting. She remembered his quiet confidence. She remembered working beside him to dig out a tree stump—work that would vanish after they were dead, just like this tower would in time. The difference between them was not their work, it was his comfort with his own place. It was his humility. She yearned for that peace, that joy, that faith. She yearned for him.

She had to get back.

The wind blasted her body, knocking her hands loose. Only the steel hook kept her from falling. As she grappled for the ladder, the wind screamed into her ears and into her mind. Had to be the altitude. The cold. The adrenalin. She glanced at the Babel in her hand, then threw it down. She unhooked the rope so she could begin climbing down. Unsteady. Woozy.

She forced herself to focus. Tried to grip the ladder harder. The wind was picking up. Storm clouds were approaching. She had to get down. One foot at a time.

Step. Another step.

She was five rungs from the roof when a gust slammed into her. Her foot slipped and she fell off the ladder. Something in her ankle popped. Her body whipped down, head thudding against concrete.

Her eyes were closed, her consciousness gone. But the rope still held.

She had made it to the top. There she lay, alone.

57

Jake walked back home from the tower, down the line of its shadow. As the sun fell, the shadow lengthened. He felt like he'd never reach the end of it. But he didn't have to, because all at once the shadow was gone, swallowed.

He turned back to see thunderheads growing from the west. They were dark grey, almost black at their base. He'd checked the weather this morning. A storm was supposed to come tonight. It was coming early.

Jake picked up his pace. He still had a few miles to go. He did the quick math. Clouds on the horizon, swallowing the sun at 3 o'clock. He'd be home by 5, but clouds move fast. Big ones like this, racing with a storm, can travel 40 or 50 miles per hour. They'd already passed the Rockies. They had less than 200 miles to go. He should beat them home, but it would be close.

He thought about the short man in the tower, and about Liz.

Why do I love her?

She was of the world and the tower. He belonged on the farm. He belonged to God.

But so does she. He knew it was true. He wrestled the doubts. This wasn't a whim. It wasn't a fairytale, either. Challenges would come, but he would face them.

She could change. He could change. A year on the farm together and they could move closer to each other. They were so different, but so much alike at their core.

Would I want to change?

Jake strode faster. It wasn't about what he wanted. He didn't go trying to find this girl. She showed up on his farm. She built her tower next door. It wasn't choice that led to their encounter, their sparks. He would find a way to show her. He would change, too, if he had to. The little things, anyway. He'd talk more. He'd take a trip away from the farm. He'd shave.

No, no shaving.

They'd find a way. A compromise.

God, please show us a way.

He prayed more. He thought more, around and around in circles. He tried counting his steps for a distraction, but it was no good. He kept glancing back at the clouds, feeling the darkness there, sweeping toward him.

The wind was picking up. The sky felt hollow, like the air was sucked out.

He checked his watch. 4:23.

He could see the farmhouse better now, but he still had half an hour.

The first drop of rain tapped the back of his left ear. Then another on his neck. He turned again. The clouds still seemed a good ways off. Certainly not overhead. How could he feel rain already?

Had to be the wind. It was starting to gust.

He began to run. The rain fell harder, covering the road and making it slick. His boots slipped. He ran faster.

A final half-mile stood between him and home. He paused to catch his breath, and turned to check the storm.

Black and grey and boiling clouds filled the sky, stretching from heaven to hell, ripping a seam in existence. The funnel had no point at the bottom, only chaos.

Jake's mouth fell open as a huge twister ripped into the ground. Black at the top, brown at the bottom. Dirt and debris speckled the sky.

And right in front of it, square in its path: the tower.

Dear Lord, protect her.

Jax had said she was alone at the top. Surely a tornado couldn't knock down a building. It had steel rooting it deep into the earth. It had concrete frames, built to last. No storm, not even *this*, could topple it. *Right?*

Jake shook his head, forcing himself to focus on the things under his control right now. His body, his home, his family. He turned and sprinted. Adrenalin firing, muscles pounding, storm chasing.

The farmhouse was close. White walls, red tin roof, and still-blue skies beyond. The wind was wailing now. It hammered at his body, tugged at his shirt. Each racing step was a battle against the wind, trying to stay upright. Hail the size of peanuts started to fall.

He had a couple hundred yards to go when he saw Pops, far to his right, far away from the house. He stood still, gazing at the approaching storm.

"Pops!" Jake shouted.

It was no use. The wind muffled the sound, yanked up a thousand feet. Lightning struck. Thunder an instant later.

He needed to get his grandfather. Bring him into the house. He needed to make sure the rest of his family was in the storm cellar.

It was a split second decision. Confirm the family was secure, then go for Pops. He charged into the house. It was oddly quiet. He went to the kitchen, lifted the heavy door over the stairs leading down.

"Jake?" His mom's voice.

He bounded down the stairs to the cellar. His mom, Annie, and grandmother were gathered around a small table. Candles were lit.

"You made it!" his mom said. "Where have you been? We've been worried sick."

"Pops is still out there," Jake said. "I have to get him."

Grandma shook her head. "Your grandfather knows what he's doing. He'll take care of himself. It's no use putting yourself in more danger."

Jake couldn't believe it. He didn't know what to say.

"He could die out there!" Annie cried.

Jake sprinted back up the stairs and out the front door. He had to shove his whole weight into the door to make it through. The wind had whipped into a howling gale.

He paused at the edge of the front porch. His gaze rose like a kid's watching a balloon fly away. The storm had engulfed the tower in the distance. The biggest tornado he'd ever seen.

He glanced to where Pops had been, but no one was in sight. There was nowhere to hide that direction. No cellar. No shelter.

As he stepped forward, he glimpsed something huge out of the corner of his eye. He ducked just as a tree limb soared over his head. Wood and metal and everything else were in the air. The tornado fought gravity. It fought order.

Jake turned back into the house, rushed to the cellar where the others were huddled. He sealed the door behind him.

He sat at the little table, praying and watching the candle in the center. Its flame shook. The walls and the floor groaned at the pressure against them. It sounded like a threshing machine rolling over the house.

Then light flooded the cellar. Shards of wood flew into the room. The door had been ripped off.

Jake jumped to his feet and rushed the three women to the far corner. He wrapped his arms around them, his back to the gaping door and the cyclone. They held onto each other as the storm battered everything they knew.

58

Liz regained consciousness before her eyes opened. The first thing she felt was her heartbeat, steady. Then her shallow breathing, in and out, in and out. Next came pain. The worst of it was in her shoulder. It felt like someone had sliced it off. Her ankle and her head hurt, too. But all these things were okay. The heart, the breath, the pain, and life going on. It meant the tower stood.

She slowly lifted her eyelids. She blinked once, twice. But the object was still there, beside her on the top floor of the tower. Half of an old, battered wood table. Glass shards were everywhere around her feet. *But there had been no windows here.*

Her mind slowly put the pieces together, but the steady breeze made the answer clear. The tornado. It had shattered glass and sent it flying. It had thrown this table at her.

It wasn't much longer before the shouting came. "Liz! Liz!"

Multiple voices.

She turned her head and saw them hovering over her. The familiar faces looked worried, but relieved, too.

"Hunter, go, get help!"

He nodded and disappeared from view. But Jax remained. He will always stay, Liz thought, and it was a comfortable thought. The tower stood, and Jax was here. Things might be okay.

"How…how bad is it?" she asked, surprised at how her

voice croaked out.

"I don't know." Jax held her face in his hands. He smiled. "You're alive. I can't believe it. The tornado hit us pretty hard."

"Any damage to the tower?"

"It's standing strong. Lots of windows broken, but seems like no structural damage."

"Thank God," she said, trying to lift up on her arms, but failing. "Help me up."

"I'm not sure that's a good idea." He touched her temple, then her shoulder. "You're bleeding."

"I want to get up."

"Alright." He crouched closer and slid her good arm over his shoulder. "On three, let's stand together."

She nodded.

"One. Two. Three."

Her ankle screamed at her as she rose, but it held. Jax wavered a little under her weight until they found their balance. "Okay?" he asked.

She nodded to the edge of the room. "Over there. I want to have a look."

He glanced down. "You don't have shoes."

"So?"

"The glass. It's everywhere."

"Just clear a little path. It's not far."

Jax did it, swiping his feet in front of them, making a path just wide enough for her to walk through. The glass was shatterproof, so the shards clung together. No fragments pierced her skin as they shuffled to the side of the room.

Liz peered over the edge, taking in the scene below. Everything was small, distant, as before. But something

301

seemed out of place.

"How bad is the damage?" she asked.

"Hunter said the sensors weren't showing any problems. It's a miracle, really. He said it's the largest tornado on record in Nebraska. Nothing around us is still standing. The worker camps, the trees—all flattened. We don't have estimates yet of how many were hurt."

She nodded, studying the land again. Then her breath froze. The sun was behind them. Which meant they were looking east. The Conrad farm was to the east. But it wasn't. There wasn't a white farmhouse to be seen. The land was empty. The peaceful happy place, where she'd read Daddy's note, where she'd met Jake…it was gone. Tears began to fill her eyes.

By the time Dylan and others showed up, Liz was kneeling on the concrete floor, crying. Someone helped her lay back, then lifted her body to a stretcher, connected an IV, and wheeled her to the elevator.

* * *

Jax watched them cart Liz away. He knew what really tore at her, and the truth of it ripped at him, too. He had been with her when she learned that her dad died. He had seen her hurt before. But he had never seen her like this.

Well after the others were gone, Jax sat alone at the tower's top. His legs dangled off the edge, hanging over Nebraska and the world.

Dangerous thoughts swirled in his mind, stoked into chaos like the storm. He'd lied to Liz, and to himself. The lies were coming back, wrapping around him.

She will never cry for you like that. So why not slide off? You'll never have her. You've failed.

"No," he muttered to himself. He still had time…maybe the farmer was dead.

Stop kidding yourself. A six-foot goddess and a five-foot runt? You were made for different worlds. Maybe it's easier to leave. To jump.

He nudged forward an inch. Maybe it's easier.

59

Dylan was tending the laceration on Liz's shoulder when he got the text from Katarina.

It's time. Servers.

There wasn't much else he could do for Liz here. The medical staff had arrived. They had more experience than he did. Katarina must be thinking Liz would be distracted now. She'd told him it was almost time to put the plan into action.

Before leaving, Dylan plucked a single, fine hair from Liz's arm. A backup. He smiled down at her beautiful face. *This is for you.*

He rode the elevator down to ground level, then he descended the stairs deep underground. He found himself constantly looking back, but no one was around. He stopped in front of the open metal door. The vault was unlocked. It was his last chance to turn back.

Does Katarina know that it's a trap?

He stepped inside, and a gust of cold, metallic wind greeted him. The forever-long rows of servers hummed quietly. He didn't see Katarina, so he walked down the center aisle. The humming surrounded him, settling into a rhythm, pulsing with his footsteps. Every twenty feet or so there was a thin gap, with the perpendicular rows of servers going to the far walls.

The road of our future, Dylan thought. The servers stored enough conversations to know the heart of humanity. He could study that heart, he could learn it like he'd learned the body, and he could find the cures. But he couldn't betray his friend, not any more.

"Took you long enough," said a woman's soft voice.

Katarina appeared. The blinking green lights of the servers gave her skin a sickly glow.

"Is everything clear?" Dylan asked.

Her full, pouty lips curved up in a smile. "It's just us. And it's time. Ready to give the data to the world?"

"You picked an awful time for this. Liz is hurt."

"I heard. You have the key?"

A rustle in the air made Dylan shudder. *Just the cooling system*, he thought. But he knew others should be coming soon. He needed to delay.

He met Katarina's eyes. "This whole thing has to be fair. The world gets the data. And nothing bad happens to Liz."

"Just the data." Katarina shrugged, playful and far from innocent. "I'm starting to think Liz will thank us. She just wants the farmer, anyway."

Dylan glared at her. He didn't trust himself to say much else. The sound of humming metal seemed to ring louder around him. His pulse pounded harder.

"The hair?" Katarina asked.

Dylan nodded, patting his coat pocket. "You think this is all you'll need?"

She held out a slender piece of paper. "Yes, I already have Jax's password."

"So now we just combine the two?"

"Exactly." Katarina pulled out a slim device. She inserted it into the wall of servers and studied the small control screen. "Place the hair here."

"Then what?"

She tapped her foot, impatient. "The data is released."

Dylan's throat tightened. "Immediately?"

"That's what you wanted."

"Yeah..." *But I thought someone would be here to arrest you by now.* Once the data was released, there would be no going back. Someone could save it somewhere else. He hadn't thought they'd have to go this far. "I just didn't know it would happen so quick."

"No one will know where to find it unless we tell them."

True, but who have you told? This was the final decision. Let the data go to catch the spy? Or save the data and try to stop the Russian himself? He'd wanted the data free all along. But he couldn't do that to Liz.

"Okay..." He pulled the almost invisible hair from the case in his packet.

"Yes." Katarina sounded primal and ecstatic.

Dylan kept his face blank as he handed the hair over. Katarina took it and turned toward the control screen.

There was no time. No help.

In moments the data would be released. Dylan's base instinct told him he had to do something now. He had to stop her. So he did the only thing left to do.

He tackled her. His body slammed against hers, sending both of them crashing to the ground.

But she reacted fast. A knee crushed into his groin.

As he crumpled, she twisted away.

Then he felt a gun at his temple.

"Don't move." She stood slowly, keeping the gun aimed at his head. She held out her other hand, smiling. "I have what I need. But nice try..."

As Katarina turned to the control panel, keeping Dylan in the corner of her eyes, helplessness flooded over him. He had tried. He had failed. And now he had given Katarina what she needed to steal what Liz had always protected. Any attempt to fight her now would be suicide.

"Kat," he said, trying to think of some way to slow her down, some way to distract her.

But she didn't answer.

"Just tell me," he said, "were you using me the whole time?"

No answer.

Dylan's voice came out weakly. "Was there really nothing between us?"

This time her gaze turned to him, contempt filling her glare. "Nothing, Dylan. Idealists like you are always pawns. The world's players are—"

A blur of motion passed between them. Something struck Katarina's arm, knocking her gun to the ground. Suddenly she was down, pinned under a larger man.

It was Hunter Black.

"I'm placing you under arrest." He clasped cuffs around her wrists.

Dylan staggered to his feet, letting out a heavy breath. His part was done.

But then Hunter rose and turned to him and was putting handcuffs on Dylan before he could even react.

"Both of you," Hunter said, "have questions to answer."

60

Liz awoke and bolted upright, panting. It was just a dream. Jax and Jake fighting on top of the tower, with her tied up and forced to watch. Jax had taunted and lunged. Jake had dodged and, with a storm in his eyes, knocked Jax out. Then he'd come to her, put his hands to her cheeks, lips drawing closer.

Liz shook her head, forcing herself to focus. She rubbed her wrists and her swollen ankle. Then she touched her lips, remembering the dream again.

She noticed someone was asleep in the chair by her bed. It was barely light outside, leaving only a soft grey light over her old friend, Rachel. It was hard to believe she was here, in the tower. She seemed to be sleeping.

Liz swung her legs over the side of the bed and stepped down gingerly. Her sprained ankle protested but held. Pain pierced her shoulder, but it seemed to be working fine. She managed to take a step, then another one.

"You're awake," Rachel mumbled.

"Morning, Rach. I really didn't expect…"

"I know. I came as soon as I heard about the storm. A lot of people I care about were in its path."

"Thanks for coming," Liz said. "Are the Conrads okay?"

Rachel stood slowly and came to Liz's side. "The damage was bad."

"How bad?"

"Pops and Annie were both hurt. They're recovering."

"And Jake?"

"A few bumps and bruises, but okay."

"I want to see him."

"Now?"

Liz expected some kind of protest. Rachel never just went along. But when Liz nodded, Rachel did too.

"I'll take you," Rachel said. "You're in pretty rough shape."

"Thank you."

The two of them made their way to the elevator, with Rachel warding off questions from those they passed. Not many people were around.

"Where is everyone?" Liz asked as they rode down the tower.

"A lot happened while you were out." Rachel told her about Dylan and Katarina's arrest, and about how they'd plotted to take over Babel.

Liz's trap had worked. "Is Dylan in jail?"

"Yeah, conspiracy charges."

"And Katarina?"

"She'll be locked up for a long time. The FBI wants to talk to you. Not to mention the press."

Liz smiled. "Maybe tomorrow."

They found Liz's car in the tower's underground garage and Rachel drove out to the farm, filling in Liz on more of the details. The tornado had taken the lives of fourteen workers, and injured hundreds. Crews were working non-stop to clean up the damage. Support had been streaming in from around the world—the tower had been getting more attention than ever, and many were worried about how the great Elizabeth Trammell was doing.

Liz stared out the window as she listened, awestruck. The soft morning light cast a dreamy haze over cornfields with gaping holes ripped through them. Wood and debris covered everything. A few cars sat on their backs, tires facing the blue sky, like overturned beetles. It looked like a war zone.

By the time Rachel turned down the road to the Conrad farmhouse, Liz was having trouble breathing. The emptiness pressed into her chest. There was no farmhouse, no barn, no silo. The fields of crops were torn up like some giant had grabbed fistfuls of the earth and flung them away.

But as they approached the place where the farmhouse had been, a smile spread across Liz's face and she began to laugh softly with joy and disbelief.

Jake was back at work. He was hauling a load of wood on his shoulder. He laid the planks on a waist-high stack—the remnants of his world. He turned to the car as Rachel stopped.

Rachel came around and helped Liz out. Liz limped heavily, but declined Rachel's offer of support. She wanted to face Jake on her own two feet.

"Hey Jake," Rachel said, embracing him. "You look tired. You've got to rest sometime. How's Annie?"

"About the same." He met Liz's eyes. He looked like he hadn't slept in days. "You're hurt, too."

"I was on the top of the tower when the storm hit," Liz said. "It's a miracle I survived."

"A miracle, or a gift?" he asked.

Liz felt the same bareness under his stare. "Both, I guess. It made me realize how small I am, how weak, even on top of the tower."

It was hard to see through his beard, but Liz thought she saw the corners of his lips turn up.

"God is infinite," he said. "Anyone who gets that understands how small we are."

Liz nodded, but wasn't sure how to respond. She glanced past him to the hole in the ground—the hole where the house had stood just days before. "What happened to Annie?"

Jake looked down. "I couldn't protect her... She's been in and out of consciousness."

"How did any of you survive?"

"We had a bunker under the house," Jake said. "It held pretty well, but the top ripped off just as the tornado passed. Debris flew in, hit Annie hard in the head. And Pops was outside...he still hasn't explained how he did it, but somehow the old soldier survived with only a gash on his shoulder, about like yours."

Liz thought of the girl smiling down at the hurt bird, and of the old man handing her the package with Daddy's book. It wasn't fair. The Conrad farm had turned into a wasteland overnight, while her tower had only a few broken windows. For some reason she felt guilty.

"It's not my fault," she said quietly.

Jake and Rachel both stared at her. "Of course not," Rachel said.

"But what if...?"

Jake shook his head. "No one can blame you."

Liz kept her eyes on Rachel. "I built the tower in spite of your warnings. You told me it was like the Tower of Babel, that it was pride to do it. I built it like a middle finger to God. Maybe he gave me this storm as answer. The storm that almost killed Annie and Pops, and that destroyed your home. Meanwhile, I got only scrapes and bruises. Is that justice? Is that God's idea of making things right?"

311

They were quiet a few moments, then Jake answered in a low and steady voice, "Job's friends told him to think the same thing. But God said: *Where were you when I laid the earth's foundation? Tell me, if you understand.*"

Liz stared at him, the hair of her arms on end. She felt energy flowing from his words, something that shook her, like what she'd heard on top of the tower.

Jake looked to Rachel, and Liz sensed that something passed between them.

"What does that mean?" Liz asked.

"Who are we to question God?" Rachel said.

"Only he knows the fullness of time. Even this—" Jake nodded to the destruction behind him—"can be worked for good."

"I don't believe that." Liz remembered the beautiful and peaceful white farmhouse with the green tin roof. "How can this be good?"

"It's not good, but it can bring good. Sometimes we need changes to help us see the truth." Jake's gaze was fixed on Liz, as if expecting something from her.

She opened her mouth to object, but hesitated. She remembered her dream about Jake and Jax fighting, and she thought maybe it represented some battle between her own desires. Was she going to follow her old world-savior mold that she'd shared with Jax, or the new mold of Jake, of simplicity and humility? She'd wanted Jake to win in the dream, and he had.

"It can bring good," Liz agreed. "I see that now."

His expression softened. "You've changed."

Liz didn't know how to explain it, but he was right. "Maybe we could help you rebuild. Would that be okay?"

Jake glanced down at the bandage wrapped around her leg. "You sure?"

Liz smiled. "You may have noticed we have a few workers around, even some construction materials."

"We don't need—"

"Jake," Rachel interrupted. "You do need help."

He studied her, then nodded. "Okay."

"But first," Rachel said, turning to Liz. "We have to get you back for some rest. There's medical staff waiting for you in the tower. And Babel needs you."

Liz kept her eyes on Jake. "I will come back soon."

He smiled. "I'll be waiting."

61

Jax leaned back in the leather chair, feet propped on the desk. He'd backed off the ledge and slept. He felt a little steadier, and now he was reading the news about the mother-of-all tornadoes and the survival of the tower. Babel stock had fallen hard with the revelation of Katarina's corporate espionage, but analysts predicted a rebound. The company still had the best translation software the world had ever seen. Jax couldn't help but grin about that.

He didn't budge when Liz entered the office. She looked different, and wasn't just the limp and her arm in a sling. She seemed more grounded.

She sat in the chair opposite his desk. They smiled at each other, both quiet for a moment, in the familiar way of old friends. She now knew everything that he'd hidden about Hunter Black. She also knew he'd been trying to protect her.

Liz broke the silence. "You look good there."

The grin froze on his face. "You're leaving, aren't you?"

"That was the plan all along," she said. "Now that Katarina's gone, Babel needs a new CEO…only one person comes to mind."

"The deal hasn't changed. I'm the coder, the brains. You're the face."

"I *was* the face. It wasn't all it cracked up to be."

"What about the tower?"

Liz glanced to the windows and the sweeping view

beyond. "It survived the best God could throw at it."

"You sound like the farmer." Jax didn't try to hide the contempt in his voice.

"Yeah, I guess so." Liz looked down at her hands in her lap. "Some of our workers are helping him rebuild his farmhouse. With our resources it'll be done in a couple weeks."

"Just being a good neighbor?" Jax asked.

"Yes, but…it's more than that."

"I know."

"I'm sorry," she said, meeting his eyes.

"Don't be."

"I'll always love you, Jax. You know that."

Her words sank into him. Maybe he'd known she loved him, in a way, but he'd never heard it before. Hearing it was different—the words dancing through his mind and lifting an invisible burden that had weighed on him for years.

"We make a good team," he said, his voice tight.

"The best." Liz paused, smiling. "That's why I want you to lead Babel. I'm sure the board will be delighted."

Jax stepped to the window. Years before, he had programed the code to require Liz's DNA. He could have used any source with a unique configuration. But he'd chosen her. Something about the translation existed only in connection with Liz. She had been the bridge for him. She had been the translation of the future into the present. Now that bridge was gone, and for the first time, he felt like he could survive without it.

I'll always love you, she'd said.

But what to do with the code, and the company? He was okay with it all ending. He didn't need the money. He'd never been like Dylan, wanting to create utopia in the world. If Liz didn't want Babel, why should he? And yet, looking out over the earth below, he realized he *did* want to keep this tower, this vantage. Maybe Liz had given birth to it, but he could adopt it. He thought of the scientists competing to conquer death. He thought of his own ideas, his unformed inventions—a space tether to the tower's top, or travel to Mars. He thought of his team of engineers. He thought of Veruca, with her fire-red hair.

He turned back to Liz. "Okay, I'll do it, at least for a little while."

"Thank you, Jax." She stood, facing him. "I have just one request."

"It better not have anything to do with the farmer."

She laughed. "No, it's about the data."

"What about it?"

"We're going to destroy the servers and eliminate all data collection."

Jax winced, like he'd taken a punch to the gut. "But the algorithm needs…"

Liz held up her hand. "I know, it needs the data to keep improving. But Babel is good enough. The data is too powerful." She paused. "You know the Lord of the Rings?"

"Seriously? I thought we were friends."

Liz smiled. "The data is like the one ring. The evil ones will never stop pursuing it. Can you imagine what Katarina would have done with the data? If we hadn't prevented the transfer just before she accessed the system, many secret words would have been uncovered. Privacy is a basis for trust, for love—and it should be protected. We have to destroy the data."

"I do like secrets, but…you think the board and the

shareholders will go along with this?"

"I'm not asking for permission. We're going to do it now, and I need your help."

Jax considered arguing against it, but she had a point. As long as the code still translated languages, the company would be fine for a long time. His algorithm had already learned enough from people's conversations. It would be safer to stop storing the data. It would be better to focus on the next frontiers.

He agreed to help her.

The two of them made the long descent into the bowels of the tower. There they had their final rendezvous. Jax holding her arm, taking the hair. Liz leaning close, her presence warming him. But this time it wasn't unmet passionate love that linked them, it was the comfort of old friends. Deep and settled and capable of great things.

With a few minutes of coding, and with Liz's life code, Jax unraveled the whole data storage system. He destroyed the one ring.

62

Katarina tried to ignore the whispering. The low, constant sound repeated in the same rhythm, each word like a drip from a faucet. She'd be a moment from sleep when the sound would come again.

Help me, Jesus...help me, Jesus...help...

Finally Katarina sat up. "He's not helping."

The woman in the other bed turned to her with a smile.

"What are you grinning about?" Katarina asked. "I'm trying to sleep."

"He is helping," she said, before she started again with her stupid praying whisper chant.

Katarina could have dealt with a murderer, another spy, or at least someone with an evil intention. But no, they'd given her Samantha as a cellmate. A Catholic girl turned bank robber turned wannabe nun. Katarina hated her.

Katarina hated everything about this place. Her convictions were of the white-collar variety, landing her with a twenty-year sentence in a low-security prison. It was unbecoming of a spy of her caliber. These petty little charges were beneath her dignity. But at least the place was sterile and routine. She could use the time to read, to get healthy, and to plan. Her revenge list was long.

She eventually managed to fall asleep. The mattress served well enough. One could get used to a lot after a few weeks.

The next morning brought a surprise. The guard came

after breakfast, and after another thousand *help me Jesus* prayers from her cellmate, to tell her there was a visitor.

Finally. They've come to get me out.

She walked as tall and proud as she could in her orange jumpsuit. A guard opened the door to a small visitation room with a plain table and two chairs.

It wasn't a Russian waiting for her. It was someone she never would have expected: Hunter Black.

"What are you doing here?" she asked.

"Nice to see you too." He was not smiling.

"Did Liz send you?"

He motioned to the chair beside Katarina. "Why don't you have a seat? Would you like coffee?"

"No." She did want coffee, but she wouldn't give him the satisfaction of providing it. She remained standing.

Hunter looked to the guard behind Katarina. "You can go now. I'll knock when we're ready."

"Warden said you get as long as you want. I'll be here." The guard closed the door, leaving them alone.

Katarina began to worry a little. It was unusual for a guard to leave a prisoner alone, and Hunter seemed awfully comfortable in a jail cell. She stayed composed and sat down slowly. "Where's my attorney?" she asked.

"Not invited." Hunter sat across from her.

"What's this about?"

Hunter folded his hands on the table. The smile on his face showed confidence. "Yoga on Friday mornings," he said. "You were a regular."

Katarina forced herself to stay calm. That was her only routine contact with her Russian counterparts. "Yeah, so?"

"Another man was a regular there, too. Your friend?"

319

"I have several friends from yoga. Acquaintances, really."

"I'd like to know his name."

"Charlie Timball. Is that who you have in mind?"

The smile slid away from Hunter's lips. "His real name."

"I don't follow," Katarina said. "His name is Charlie. Charles, I guess."

"Okay, let's call him Charlie then, if that makes you feel better." Hunter leaned back, crossed his hands behind his head. "He's an interesting guy. A low-level software engineer, right?"

"I think so," Katarina said. "I didn't know him all that well."

The smile returned to Hunter's face. "Charlie earns about $100k per year. But a few months ago, he transferred $10 million to an account in Russia. Interesting, right?"

Katarina's mind raced through the possibilities. Could she be sure that Hunter was a U.S. agent? Could this be a test of loyalty sent by her colleagues? "I don't know anything about that," she said.

"You talked to him every Friday, with your Babel off."

"We talked about yoga, the weather, stuff like that."

"What's odd is that the $10 million transfer happened on a Friday after he talked with you, and a couple days later someone shot Owen Strand in a field in Nebraska."

"We were all crushed when we lost Owen."

"I'm sure you were." Hunter leaned forward again. "But it did make things easier for you, for your plans. And then when you were in the data room under the tower, you tried to make a transfer."

"I'm not talking about that without my lawyer."

"Good thing Dylan and I stopped you, because guess who

had an IP address connected to your attempt? None other than Charlie Timball. What's his real name, Katarina?"

Katarina put her hands in her lap, to hide the shaking. She was furious, devastated. All the work, a twenty-year sentence, and the data hadn't budged. She studied Hunter's composed gaze. "Who are you?"

"I'm your ticket out of here, Ms. Ivanovich."

Katarina's heart was racing. No one in America should know that name. No one except her agency, and even there it was only a handful. She'd left it behind so long ago.

"Who are you working for?" she asked, failing to keep her voice calm.

Hunter sipped coffee from his styrofoam cup. "Your colleagues have five of my friends. I want them back, but I also want to find your friend Charlie."

CIA, Katarina thought. He has to be CIA. Five of their agents had been locked away in Moscow for over a year. The implications flooded over her. Hunter Black, the man who had managed the tower construction, who had access to every worker's feed and the cameras everywhere. He knew too much, but he still needed Charlie's name. "How can you get me out?"

"Your charges are pretty routine. Corporate theft, conspiracy." He paused. "We let Dylan off without charges because he talked to us."

"What did he tell you?"

"Everything I needed to know. He's back in San Francisco. They even let him have his teaching job back." Hunter paused. "You could be back in Moscow this week. But I need a name."

Katarina shook her head. If Dylan had talked, and the data

hadn't transferred, then what awaited her in Moscow would be even worse than her constantly chanting cellmate. "I don't know," she said, her voice quiet.

Hunter shrugged. "That's too bad. We'll have to find it the old fashioned way."

Katarina looked down at her hands. "I don't want to go back."

"Sorry, Ms. Ivanovich," Hunter said. "But you aren't going to have much say in it. They want you, and we want our colleagues. It's only a matter of time."

63

Liz awoke with the sun in her eyes. She stretched in bed, enjoying the smell of coffee. She rose and made her way to the kitchen.

Grandma was there, frying eggs. She had a mug in one hand and a spatula in the other. Her wheelchair sat empty just behind her, and her bony elbows shook with the weakness of age, but Liz figured no one could have looked as comfortable in that pose. She'd been frying eggs for fifty years.

"Good morning," Liz said. "Need any help?"

The old woman gave her a smile and pointed to the brand new countertop with her spatula. "Get the flour, won't you?"

Liz picked up the heavy container and stood beside Grandma, waiting for more instructions. None came.

Grandma flipped an egg. "My little ones will be here soon."

"Where did everyone go?" Liz asked.

"Workin'. Starts at dawn here. Better get used to that."

Liz nodded. "What should I do with the flour?"

"Ever made gravy?"

"No."

"Well you better learn." The old matriarch laughed and began to give her instructions. A pan already had the sausage grease. Pour the flour in, bit by bit. Stir in the milk. "And keep on stirring."

She gazed out the window as she stirred. A bird landed on

the branch of a small tree near the house. The tree had the first buds of fruit. Apples. For some reason it made her think of Babel. This single tree had so much complexity and beauty. "That apple tree is a survivor," Liz said.

Grandma shrugged. "I can't see that far anymore, but I'm glad to hear it."

"You don't have glasses?"

"I can see what matters, the things close to me," the woman said. "I reckon maybe God lets our eyesight get blurry because that's a wiser way to see the world. I'm not so bothered by what's far away from me."

They were quiet after that, making breakfast. By the time Jake and his mom entered the kitchen, Liz had a pan full of gravy. A few lumps here and there, but she was proud of it. They sat and ate, with the gravy poured over the biscuits Grandma had made. Eggs, sausage, biscuits, gravy, and coffee. All by 9 am. Liz could get used to this.

The door burst open before they finished. "You started without me!" Annie rushed in and took her spot at the table. The scars from her stitches were healing fast.

"You'll take any excuse to sleep in." Jake's mom smiled. "Some things never change."

"Maybe the little things." Annie twirled a curl of bright red hair around her finger. She turned to Liz. "But big things do change."

"Like your new house?" Liz asked.

"And our new guest." Annie's freckled cheeks showed a touch of color. "Will you tell me more about Dubai today?"

"Of course."

"And will you join me for a walk after breakfast?" Jake asked.

Liz nodded. "Best part of the day."

They finished eating and headed out. Liz glanced back at the rebuilt Conrad home. It had the same classic style, but larger and with nice new touches. The Babel construction team did good work.

They reached the bank of the river by the apple orchard. Half of the trees still stood, the other half taken by the twister. Jake sat on the bank and Liz sat beside him.

His hand moved to hers.

Liz smiled. "I'm starting to get used to this."

Jake squeezed her hand gently. "Me too."

As he gazed over the river, the morning light made his sharp features soft. This invincible and implacable man made warmth swell up inside her. She never would have believed it a year ago, but she wanted to stay here, with him.

A gentle breeze rustled the branches above and lifted her eyes to the sky, where the tower gleamed in the distance. She thought of when she'd climbed to its top with a tornado on the horizon, and of what she'd heard there. She took a deep breath. She needed to tell Jake.

"When I was up there, on top of the tower..." Liz shook her head. "I know this will sound crazy, but as the wind was wailing, I felt like I heard a voice."

Liz paused, as if expecting Jake to laugh.

He didn't. "What did it say?"

"I felt like I heard: *Pride leads to destruction. I give grace to the humble.*"

Jake studied her, waiting for more.

She formed her words carefully. "I thought I was building this tower for my dad, and for the world, but it was actually for my own pride. And I was going to destroy myself...just like my dad did. Then came the storm, and the words."

"Maybe God got your attention."

"Yes." She looked at her injured arm. "He made me feel as small and weak as I really am."

"We're still the created, not the creator. We can't be God, no matter what we build."

"Rachel tried to tell me something like that when I first had the idea about the tower. I didn't want to hear it. My other friends just went along with whatever I said. Nobody tried to stand in my way, except you."

He nodded, but didn't answer at first. He ran his hand along Liz's cheek. His touch and the sound of the river and the sun warming her skin made her body relax and her eyes close. She felt her pained memories and strains evaporating.

"Do you regret it?" he asked.

She glanced to the Babel tower, studying its lines of steel stretching to the sky. "I regret the way I tried to do it and some of my reasons for it, but...we are creators, too. My dad had the vision, and now the tower is standing. The company translates languages and helps people communicate. These can still be forces for good." She paused, then turned back to Jake. "After all, they led me to you."

He smiled and leaned closer, his hand finding the back of her neck. The space between them shrank as the tower faded from her mind.

THE END

ALSO BY J.B. SIMMONS

The Omega Trilogy
Unbound
Clothed With The Sun
Great White Throne

The Gloaming Books
Light in the Gloaming
Breaking the Gloaming

Non-Fiction
The Awakening of Washington's Church

J.B. Simmons lives and writes outside Washington, D.C. He is the author of seven books and countless legal briefs. His acclaimed *Unbound* trilogy tells the story of a rich kid from Manhattan with nightmares of a dragon and the world ending in 2066. Learn more about the author and his work by visiting www.jbsimmons.com.

Made in the USA
Coppell, TX
05 February 2021